# SWEET BEA

## SARAH EDWARDS

Cover: Deranged Doctor Design
First Electronic Edition: October 2019
ISBN: 978-1-990731-01-3
ISBN: 978-1-990731-00-6

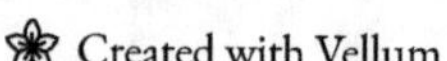 Created with Vellum

Garrett clung to his mother's hand. He was tired and hungry, but he dared not make a sound. He wanted to cry and ask his mother to tell him all would be well, but he knew better.

Four nights past, a great army had appeared beneath Alethorpe castle and laid siege to them. The army had stretched as far as Garrett could see from the very highest tower of the keep. At their head rode a huge, dark-haired knight. He rode beneath the banner of a sable dragon rampant upon argent.

Garrett had heard his name whispered in fearful conversations throughout the keep. Sir Arthur of Anglesea. King John's man, some had said. Others had told terrifying tales of his battle prowess, his lack of mercy, how he had never been defeated.

Alethorpe had not defeated him either.

This morning, Garrett's father, Sir Wulfric, had ridden out to meet Sir Arthur.

All morning the clash of steel, men's shouts, screams, and horses shrieks had sounded from all about them until Garrett had run and hidden with his hands over his ears.

Then, an awful silence had descended, and the Alethorpe folk had drifted onto the battlements. The carnage was sickening. Bodies lay everywhere, the earth churned and running red.

At midday, Sir Arthur had raised Sir Wulfric's severed head on a pike. He had driven it into the soil beside the gate and demanded they surrender.

Not a soul had cried for Sir Wulfric. Not his horse-faced wife, not Garrett's beautiful mother, and certainly not Garrett.

Garrett had not known his father well. In truth, he feared the large, angry man who came some nights for his mother. On those nights, Garrett had been told to sleep by the kitchen hearth. In the morning, he would return to his mother and find her still abed. He hated those mornings when his mother would be pale and listless. Some mornings she still bore the marks of Sir Wulfric's rough treatment on her lovely face. Garrett had dreamed of the day when he would be grown enough to take her from Alethorpe and keep her safe. He had not foreseen their departure would come as it did.

Sir Arthur had sacked the keep and driven all the occupants out. They were allowed to take nothing.

They stood in small groups and watched all they had known burn.

His mother stared at the vivid orange light that spread across the horizon. By morning there would be naught left of Alethorpe but charred stone and timbers.

To their right stood a huddle of folk about Sir Wulfric's widow. She turned and stared at Garrett and then his mother. "Whore." She spat the word.

His mother stiffened and tightened her hold on his hand.

"Leave," Sir Wulfric's widow's face turned even uglier in her hate. "And take your bastard with you."

Turning about, his mother tugged his hand. "Come, Garrett. We must leave this place."

"And go where?" Alethorpe was his home. Had been his home.

"I know not." Mother sighed and pushed her hair back from her face. "But we will find our way."

Garrett turned as they walked away for one last look at his former home. He saw only one thing against the raging fires engulfing the castle; a sable dragon rampant upon argent.

# *Chapter One*

Beatrice had a secret. A secret of the most delicious sort.

She was being wooed. Wooed with honeyed words and sweeter touches. Tingles spread to Beatrice's fingertips, rushed back again, and pooled in her stomach.

Ducking her head, she kept her pace to a saunter. There was nothing amiss with her. No reason for anyone to pause their day and watch her.

Spring filled the air with scents of new grass and wildflowers. The sun beamed from a cloudless arc of blue above her. Birdsong serenaded her as cornflowers merrily bobbed beside the path. Even the insects buzzed encouragement. She was young, she was in love, and the world could not be more perfect.

Garrett. Just his name made her shiver.

If she tarried much longer, someone from the keep would come looking for her. Beatrice shifted her basket to the other arm and investigated a patch of what might be vervain. From the keep, anyone would see her picking wildflowers. Just as she intended. But there was only so long a girl could pick flowers.

A footpath disappeared between the dense green beech thicket. It crossed a small stream before meandering through the trees and down to the village below. Was he still down in the village? She tried to picture what he'd be doing. Working at the forge, perhaps?

She gave up on the plant and straightened. She wouldn't know vervain from, well, anything. Opposite the village, a path shot straight as an arrow through the meadow toward the castle. For certain, Garrett wouldn't come from that direction. Perhaps he wasn't coming at all. He'd made her no promises. There was no understanding between them. But, she dearly hoped all the same.

Hoping, however, didn't make him appear.

He might not come at all, and her joy vanished.

The sun blazed down harshly on her face, and she'd freckle.

*"Wish, wish, planted a feather and wished a bird would grow,"* Nurse's voice sang in her head. It was nonsense, pure and simple. Nonsense like lingering alone on a path, pretending to pick wildflowers, while waiting for a man she barely knew to appear. A man with dark and mysterious eyes that whispered of secret places and forbidden pleasures. She was a goose. When she pictured the scene in her mind, it went thus. A beautiful maiden, garbed in her finest blue samite, engrossed in the gentle occupation of picking flowers by the roadside. The sun gleamed off her flaxen hair and brought roses to her alabaster cheek. Her slender form, bent like a reed to her feminine labors...

Roses be damned; she was sweating beneath her silk. It would leave stains on the fabric. She'd never hear the end of it from Nurse.

A soft whistle jolted her.

Her heart leapt.

There he stood, by the thicket.

Smiling to warm her from the inside, one shoulder propped against a tree, arms folded across his broad chest.

An answering grin tugged at her mouth. She fought it back. A girl mustn't appear too eager. Inside her mind, the lady in the blue samite capered. *He is here, he is here, he is here.* Beatrice breathed deeply to steady her heart. Her damp palms slipped on the basket handle.

Looking for all the world as if he owned the ground beneath them, he jerked his head, motioning her to join him.

*How presumptuous.* Beatrice clicked her tongue, but moved toward him anyway. She'd tell him so as soon as she caught her breath again.

"Were you waiting for someone?" The breeze ruffled his hair. It was too long, but so thick and lustrous, like purest sable.

"Nay." Her cheeks heated at the lie. His mocking laughter irked her, but not enough to stop her willful feet from moving beneath the canopy of trees.

"What a pity." Dark and rich as treacle, his eyes filled with deliciously wicked intent. He took her basket and dropped it to the ground. "I hoped you might be waiting for me."

"And why would I do such a thing?" Her voice sounded breathy and eager. It would never do. He was already too sure of her. But how to dissemble when just being in his company was enough to make her limp as a pudding.

Garrett drew her out of sight of the path and the castle.

Excitement tripped along her spine.

"I could not say. I could only hope." A bump marred the straight blade of his nose, as if it had been broken.

Her legs trembled. She longed to know the secret behind that tiny imperfection. All his secrets.

"I hoped you enjoyed my kisses and wanted more." He traced the line of her cheek. He was so terribly, delightfully, and wonderfully bad when he spoke thus to her.

"Nay." She shivered. Gentle maids didn't allow such things to be said to them.

"Nay? Mayhap I am not doing it right then?" Jaw firm, mouth full, he had a strong, beautiful face. He brushed her mouth with his thumb.

Her lips tingled. *Oh, please, please, please kiss me.* Her mind shouted what would be too brazen to utter.

"Shall I try again?" His voice sounded rough, like the coarse fabric of his tunic beneath her fingers.

Wordlessly imploring him to fulfill his teasing promise, she tilted her chin upward.

His lips brushed hers. Leather, fire, and earth, a scent uniquely his, would cling to her clothing long after he'd returned to the village.

Beatrice rose onto her toes, crushed her mouth against his. *Heavenly.* There was no other word for his kiss.

His tongue sought entry at her lips.

With the slide of Garrett's tongue over hers, heat settled in an ache between her thighs. She pressed closer to his hard, strong body.

He groaned encouragement.

Her blood pulsed faster and wilder.

He cupped her bottom in his large hands and drew her to him.

His male flesh firm against her belly shocked her and summoned a wanton inside her. He hadn't dared to go so far before. Yet, each time Beatrice encountered him, he took her further and further along a path that some tiny part of her mind warned her against.

When she was alone, reliving these stolen moments, her cheeks heated at her own daring. But when she was with him, male musk overwhelming her, she was powerless against the onslaught of his mouth and his hands. Need drove her.

Beatrice dared to rub her belly against his hardness.

His hands tightened, roughly urging her on as his tongue plundered her mouth.

The taste of him raged through her senses. So male. She wanted more.

One hand slid across her hip and upward. His touch burned right through her silk gown and the fine linen beneath it. He took and she gave, willingly. His hand curved around her breast.

She relished the swell of her bosom against his palm. It made the place between her thighs tingle. Thrilling. Too thrilling. She tore her mouth from his. "Nay."

Immediately, his hand dropped away. His fingers dug into her hip, and he rested his forehead against hers as he took deep, calming breaths. "Forgive me, you have no idea what you do to me. I lose all reason."

"We must not." She wasn't sure on whom she was trying to impress this.

"You must know how I feel about you, Beatrice." He planted a soft kiss against her temple.

"It is wrong."

"Do not say so, sweeting. Do not say it is wrong. Nothing can be wrong for us." His lips burned the sensitive skin beneath her ear.

Already, her traitorous senses were responding. The chaste maiden retreated to the back of her mind and grumbled. This was not so shocking. Harmless kisses. She tilted her chin so the sweet torment could continue, if only for a bit longer. "I should not."

"Let yourself feel," he said. "Just for this moment. You and I, here and alone, let yourself feel what is betwixt us."

"It is a sin."

"Nay." He nipped at her bottom lip. "Sin would not feel this wondrous." Garrett moved his hand toward her breast.

Beatrice's knees weakened. Her head grew light. She could have stopped him. She should have stopped him, but she wanted more of his touch. A chaste girl would protest. Beatrice didn't want to be that girl. She wanted to feel this wondrous always. Especially when his long, hard fingers brushed against the stiff peak and her nipple tightened.

He took possession of her mouth. Hot and hungry, he demanded a response.

It seemed the most natural thing in the world to arch her back and push her breast deeper into his hand. His rumble of approval reverberated through her bones. She made a soft protest as he withdrew his hand and lifted his mouth from hers.

"Beatrice," he murmured.

She sucked air into her starved lungs, breast still tingling from his touch.

"I ache for you." He placed her hand on his braies. "See what you do to me?"

His hard flesh pulsed in her palm. She let him curl her fingers around the shaft. It was so carnal and base, so incredibly exciting. Her thighs clenched together. She wanted him to join his body to hers, to ease the damp ache at her core. The chaste maiden whispered in the back of her mind. She tugged her hand away.

He let her go without protest.

Beatrice staggered back.

A flush stained his cheeks. Garrett straightened his shoulders and his hands clenched over his rope belt.

"We must stop." She wet her parched lips.

Heavy with desire, his dark gaze tracked the motion. "Why?"

She couldn't think of a good answer. Each time it grew more difficult to walk away. *Disaster*, hissed the maiden. It didn't feel like disaster, though, or sin. It consumed her, glorious and so very, very tempting.

"I will be missed." She gestured toward the castle. "I need to get back."

He dropped his head as she retreated. The grip on his belt tightened, the skin going white around his knuckles.

Beatrice hesitated. She wanted his touch again, but that way led to trouble. "On the morrow?"

"I do not know."

"Nay." The word burst from her. He was the best part of her day.

He stepped away from her, raking his fingers across his scalp. "We cannot continue like this."

She shivered and wrapped her arms around herself to ward off the sudden chill. "You do not want to see me?"

"Beatrice." He frowned. "You know I cannot tarry here. I would have been gone long since if it were not for you."

"What are you saying?" He couldn't be telling her he was leaving. It caught inside her like a barb, and she struggled to draw her next breath.

"I cannot stay." He grasped her shoulders.

"You are leaving?" She could barely form the words past the constriction in her throat. Pain raked inside her chest. He could not leave.

"You know I must." He shook his head. Regret lined his beautiful face. "I cannot stay here, like this, and not have you."

"But you do have me, Garrett, you do." Beatrice grasped the front of his tunic. She had to keep him here.

"Not in the way I need you." His words hung in the air. He wanted to lie with her.

She wanted to, but doubt gnawed at her. Beatrice stepped back. Her thoughts were cloudy when she was close to him. He'd never said the words, but he touched her like he loved her.

Her virtue, however, must be prized and guarded. It had been impressed on her since she became old enough to understand the notion. Still, what could be better than to give such a cherished gift to the man she loved? And, yet, that maiden shrieked caution.

"Where will you go?" The thought of him leaving opened a yawning pit beneath her. This must be love. It could be nothing else. Since he had come at summer's beginning, the loneliness hadn't existed. With him, she was whole. She belonged. If he left, he would take that away. Her life would be gray again. Gray and boring and the same, day after cursed day.

"It does not matter." He shrugged. "I have been many places and will be many more before I am done. But here, Beatrice—" He opened his arms wide. "Here I have come home."

It so nearly echoed her thoughts tears flooded her eyes. She blinked to stop them from spilling over.

"Do not cry, sweeting." He cupped her cheek and caught her tears with his thumb. "I am not worth your tears."

"But you are." Fresh tears spilled down her cheeks. "You are worth it to me."

"My sweet, sweet girl." He tugged her to him.

Beatrice burrowed into his chest, willing the world to fall away and let her rest here forever.

"We knew it could not be this way always. Sooner or later, we will get caught. Then, it will go badly for both of us."

Beatrice shivered. Her family would kill Garrett if they knew.

"Your father will die before he gives you to one such as me." He leaned his head back and looked at her. "I am a churl, Beatrice, a penniless traveler with naught to my name."

She shook her head. It didn't matter to her.

"And you are a princess." He rested his chin on the top of her head. "A beautiful, fiery princess, living in her castle on the hill, too good for any man to claim as his own. For you, there must be a brave paladin on his pure white charger to carry you away to his kingdom in the sky."

"I do not want a paladin. I want you." With everything in her, she wanted Garrett.

"But you have me, Beatrice. All that I am, I give to you." He pressed a kiss to her crown. "I have only my love and my body, and both are yours. Held between your delicate hands. You could drop my heart beneath your dainty slippers and step on it. I would not care."

His words sank about her like golden honey. He did love her. She knew it.

Gently, he set her aside. His eyes glowed down at her and warmed the aching hollow in her chest. "You must go back before you are missed."

"Do not leave." She grabbed his tunic. She must have his promise before he left, or she might not see him again.

"Beatrice." He raised her fingers to his lips. "If only you knew how you torture me with your words."

"I do not mean to torture you." Her heart twisted. She wanted to take her words back and wipe the sadness from his brown eyes.

"I know that," he said. "But you tempt me beyond bearing, when I know what I must do." He looked deep into her eyes, as if he could see right down to the secrets of her soul. His sigh whispered through the air. "Very well." He kissed her hands again. "I cannot leave you, not today, but soon."

"But not today?" She would find a way for them to be together. She didn't know how, but she would. She only needed more time.

"Nay, sweeting, not today."

# Chapter Two

Beatrice entered the castle through the postern gate to avoid being noticed by the guards. The main gates were kept tighter than Henry's braies. With their father and older brothers away, Henry treated his responsibility for Anglesea with his usual, infuriating zeal.

She slid along the curtain wall to the entrance of the inner bailey. Guards on the outer wall had their backs to her, their eyes trained outward. There were far too many people about for this time of day. Bodies swarmed everywhere beyond the open inner gate. She jerked back into the gatehouse shadows.

"Damn." She couldn't stay here either. Someone was sure to pass through the gate and notice her. Holding her breath, she inched around the gate tower.

Beatrice ventured a few steps into the bailey then darted behind three horses a boy was leading to the stables. She stuck to the castle wall shadows, gliding from one to the other until she made it to the keep entrance.

A guard stepped in front of her.

Beatrice froze, her heart in her throat.

"My lady." He bowed his head and turned away, scanning the busy bailey.

Her knees sagged in relief. She hurried into the keep, avoiding the hall. Fisting her skirts in her hand, she dashed up the stairs. Once she made her chamber, she would be safe from prying eyes. They were lucky at Anglesea to have the top floor so divided. If she were in an older keep, she might have to make a dash for safety across a wide-open space.

She threw open the door and slipped into her chamber.

"There you are." Nurse pounced.

Beatrice screamed and clapped her hand over her mouth.

Hands on her ample hips, Nurse glared from below her wimple. As usual, Nurse's wimple rested just above her eyebrows and pressed her face inward. "Where have you been?"

Beatrice needed a story, something to explain her absence. Her mind emptied.

"Saints," Nurse shrieked. "Is that your new silk?" Nurse's sharp eyes narrowed on the hemline. "And is that dust on your new silk?"

"What is all the bustle?" Beatrice tried for distraction.

"You should well ask." Nurse charged toward her. "Your uncle has sent word he arrives in time for the evening meal."

"Godfrey?" That would explain all the people about. "Do you think he brings word from London?"

"How would I know such a thing?" Nurse folded to her knees with a sigh. She grabbed Beatrice's hem and examined it minutely. "Why have you got grass stains on your gown?"

"Leave it." Beatrice wrested the material from Nurse. She wanted to hear more about Godfrey and what was happening in London.

"I will not." Nurse held firm. "I cannot abide to see a fine fabric ruined. Stand still and I will brush these out. What are you doing wearing your best gown, anyway?"

"I merely wanted to wear it." Beatrice waved an airy hand. She looked toward the embroidered flowers clambering the silk of her bed curtains. Anywhere but at nurse and those bright, beady eyes.

Nurse yanked on her skirt, forcing her closer. "Where have

you been that demands your best gown and you leaving the keep?"

"I went for a walk. That is no sin, is it?" The lies were piling up in her throat, faster than flies on bad meat, waiting to gush out of her mouth.

"You went for a walk?"

"Aye."

"Where?"

"To the beech thicket." Heat crept up her face, and she cursed mentally.

Nurse sank back on her heels and studied her. "And what was there in the beech thicket that had you all dressed up like a dog's dinner?"

"Nothing." Beatrice threw her arms up. "I wanted to wear the dress. Then I got bored and went for a walk."

"Hmmm." Nurse pursed her lips. "You are keeping secrets, my girl. I can see them on your face."

"Why do you think Godfrey comes? He must know how father fares in London."

"Saints have mercy." Nurse shook her head. "Here we are chattering away and you could be called to the hall at any moment." She gave the skirt a hearty shake.

Air rushed up Beatrice's shift and cooled her. Nurse mustn't find out about Garrett. Nurse would tell her mother for sure. Then, her mother would tell her father and—Beatrice shied away from the direction her thoughts were taking.

"Your uncle brings a party with him." Nurse waved a pudgy finger at her. "There could be a young knight amongst them. A young knight desperately needing a wife."

"He would have to be desperate, indeed, to come courting here." Men looking for a wife stayed clear of Anglesea and the Lady Beatrice. Three failed betrothals took care of that.

"You will never be wed if you think like that." Nurse never gave up. "Your sister, bless her sweet heart, stood always ready to receive her suitor."

Beatrice rolled her eyes. It wouldn't do any good to interrupt. Nurse would have her say. The sun was still high, forming patterns on the gleaming stone floor.

"And Lady Faye was ready, looking pretty as can be, when ill weather blew the Earl of Calder into the keep. And what happened?"

"He fell in love with her," Beatrice recited.

"I know not of love." Nurse stopped fussing with the hem and swayed to her feet on a lusty groan.

Beatrice held out a hand and steadied her rise.

"But what I do know is Lady Faye was ready, looking every inch a nobleman's wife."

"Faye was born looking that way." Beatrice couldn't quite control the surly note to her voice.

Her sister had been married for seven years and still Nurse carped on about her perfection. The entire kingdom knew of the beauteous Lady Faye. No less than eight ballads were written in her honor. Eight. Beatrice snorted. What was any sensible girl to do with eight ballads caroling her beauty?

"Faye never snorted like some vulgar trollop." Nurse snatched up her brush from the oak chest in the corner. "And Faye did not go traipsing around the countryside wearing her best gown, sneaking back home with her pretty eyes full of secrets."

"Faye was a saint." Beatrice glared back at Nurse.

"And she still is." Nurse nodded. "She is the image of her mother."

"She is my mother, too." Beatrice winced as Nurse dragged the brush through the snarl the breeze had made of her fine, straight hair.

"That she is." Nurse tugged at a stubborn knot. "And you should make it a point to be just like your mother."

Beatrice tried, she honestly tried, to be demure and mild-mannered and tranquil. But there was an awful lot of sitting about to being a lady. Sooner or later, the itch would start somewhere within and end in her breaking for freedom as fast as her legs could carry her.

She yelped as Nurse hit another tangle and pulled. It was hard to be the family disappointment. Of the five living children Sir Arthur and Lady Mary had sired, it stood to reason all five could not be exceptional. Her only outstanding characteristic appeared to be a propensity for finding mischief. She didn't have to try. Every time there was mischief about, it landed at her feet.

Blessedly, Nurse found no more snarls and brushed Beatrice's hair in long, soothing strokes.

Garrett loved her hair. He thought her beautiful and passionate and clever.

He was leaving.

Beatrice's heart sank.

"What is that face?"

Beatrice smoothed her expression, but not fast enough to stop the interrogation.

"You are having a mope again, are you not?"

"I am not moping." Beatrice ducked her chin to hide her face. "I do not like to be constantly reminded I am not Faye."

It worked like a magic potion. Nurse's expression softened. "There, there, pet." Nurse grasped her chin. "You will find your own way." She gave Beatrice's cheek a pat as she released her. "You will find what makes you special."

She already had, Beatrice wanted to yell. Garrett made her special. She shrugged and let Nurse draw whatever conclusions she wanted. Anything was better than letting Nurse get a hint of the true reason for her sudden glum mood. "How is Mother today?"

"Too old to be having another babe." Nurse's gaze flew to Beatrice's and away again. "She will be fine. She has brought five healthy babes into this world and only two stillborn. She is a strong woman, your mother, and she will bear this one fine."

Nurse sounded too hearty. The old besom was hiding something. "Will she meet Sir Godfrey?"

"Nay. Lady Mary is not having a good day, and I have tucked her up in bed. Henry will have to do what is needed."

"Shall I go and see her?"

"Nay." Nurse squeezed her hand. "She is resting. It is the best medicine for her."

"She has been resting a lot of late," Beatrice said.

"Aye." Nurse turned her back and smoothed the bed linens. There was naught wrong with the bed linens.

Beatrice stepped closer to see Nurse's face better. "Mother will be all right, will she not?"

"Aye, aye." Nurse moved to smoothing the furs. She chewed on her bottom lip like she did when something troubled her. Nurse caught her looking and stopped. "Wipe your face." Nurse swiped the cloth over her cheeks.

"Nurse." She grabbed the cloth and pulled it away from her face. "Tell me true. Mother will be all right, will she not?"

Nurse opened her mouth and shut it again.

"Tell me."

Nurse sighed. "I do not know."

She snatched back the cloth and tucked it into her pocket.

Beatrice's belly dropped. How could Nurse not know? Her mother was a constant in her life, always there and always capable and beautiful. She searched Nurse's face for comfort.

"Nurse, you are not scared mother will..." That horrible word lodged in her throat.

"I am not saying anything, pet." Nurse cradled her face between her palms. "I am a foolish old woman, and why would you mind me now, when you never have before."

Suddenly, Beatrice wanted to run to Garrett. To have him hold her and tell her all would be well. Nay. She was a selfish, wicked girl to be thinking of a man of whom her mother would, surely, not approve. She should've been by her mother's side today. She would do better, be a better daughter in every way.

"There is no sense fretting," Nurse said. "God's will shall prevail."

God wouldn't take Lady Mary from this earth. Would he? Lady Mary was good and kind and beautiful.

Nurse adjusted Beatrice's girdle, then stood back and surveyed her handiwork. "There, now you are ready."

## *Chapter Three*

She was almost his. The sweet-faced Lady Beatrice of Anglesea with her blue-green eyes and sinful mouth. A tasty armful of sumptuous curves he liked to stroke. Garrett strode down the path toward the village. A few more hints about him leaving and she would be ripe for the plucking. The subsiding stiffness in his braies returned with a rush of blood. Soon now, he would rest between Lady Beatrice's ladylike, white thighs.

His guilt over using Beatrice was an unexpected and inconvenient reality, but it had no place in the ugly business of vengeance. Nobody had shown his mother any mercy. Nobody had cared, and for her he must stick to his path. He touched the small pouch he always kept about his neck. A connection with his mother, a reminder he must stay strong and not give in to sentiment.

The village had settled into its morning stillness. Most of the women were working the fields, their men eking a living from the sea. Not that he'd made many friends in the village. He stuck to himself for the most part. It was an attractive village. A tidy group of cottages overlooking the sea with their gray stone walls and mellow brown thatch. Not too large, but prosperous and thriving. The sort of place he might have settled, if he were of that mind.

The strike of steel on anvil rang from the forge. Lyman was within, plying his trade. This being Garrett's half-day, Lyman expected him later, where he would spend the remainder of his day pounding out farm implements. He reversed his path and slipped behind a row of cottages so he wouldn't pass the open smithy door. Lyman liked company, and if he caught sight of him, the smith would want to visit. Garrett needed to gather himself.

Not wanting to announce his presence, he carefully skirted a bustling cluster of hens. He'd found work with the local blacksmith when he'd first arrived in the village beneath Anglesea keep. The forge was hotter than hell and the work hard, but it fed him and put a roof over his head while he drew Lady Beatrice into his trap. His timing was perfect. Sir Arthur was away from Anglesea. No keen eyes to watch his youngest daughter or question the new smith's apprentice.

As soon as Lady Beatrice ceded him the ripe prize of her virginity, he'd be off again, stopping only long enough to ensure Sir Arthur knew what Garrett had taken from his youngest daughter. Sodding Sir Arthur of Anglesea would pay dearly for what he'd done to Garrett's mother. Behind the forge, large wooden shutters were open to allow heat to escape. Garrett ducked beneath the sill and crept toward the small hut Lyman had given him.

Lady Beatrice had been hot for him today. His rod throbbed in agreement. It was a good thing he lusted for Beatrice, or it might've made his plan a bit more difficult. Truth was, he wanted her and it fit neatly with his aim. Had she been any other girl, he might have pursued the same goal regardless.

It wasn't her doing her father was Sir Arthur of Anglesea. She disarmed him at times, even charmed him, but he chose not to dwell on that. He wouldn't be drawn from his quest for vengeance. The innocent must suffer alongside the guilty. Had his mother not suffered through no fault of her own.

The inside of the hut was dim after the bright sunlight. Lilly stirred on his small pallet. Garrett bit back a curse. He had only a few minutes and he wanted to spend them savoring his victory. Planning his next step. Lilly and her visits were an annoyance. She no longer demanded payment, but Lilly had her own mouths to feed. He gave her what he could spare.

Her gaze dropped to the front of his braies. "It looks as if you were expecting me."

"What are you doing here, Lilly?" As if he didn't know. The ache in his rod was persistent enough to stop him from sending her about her business immediately.

She rose and padded on the packed earth floor toward him. Lilly was pretty, buxom, and rosy-cheeked. Her hand slipped past his belt and curled around him. She murmured appreciatively as she stroked.

Garrett closed his eyes. Instead of Lilly, he saw Beatrice, flaxen hair streaming over his arm, her mouth full and soft, her lush body pressed to his. He groaned.

"You are a big lad, Garrett." Lilly giggled against his ear.

The giggling irked him. He concentrated on the skilled motion of her hand.

"I am glad I could get away for a bit," Lilly said. "It is not easy when Gil is up and about."

Garrett caught her wrist. She looked up at him with a murmur of protest.

"Speaking of your son?"

Lilly rolled her eyes and stuck out her bottom lip. "Jesu, Garrett, but you fret more about my boy than his own da."

"Where is your boy, Lilly?"

"He is with his auntie," Lilly said.

"Did he eat today?"

"Aye, Garrett, the boy ate today."

"And you bought him shoes with the money I gave you?"

"Aye, Garrett, I bought shoes. He will only outgrow them, you know."

"Good." Garrett didn't release her wrist.

He liked Lilly; they were friends of a sort, but he wouldn't tolerate her ignoring her young son. Not for the first time, he thought Lilly might be seeing him as a replacement father. He couldn't be that for her or any woman, and he would break one heart already before he left Anglesea.

Gently he nudged her hand away. "Go back to your son, Lilly."

"But..."

He shook his head. A swift cut was the best course. "There is nothing for you here."

Chapter Four

Despite Nurse's preparations, nobody called for Beatrice, so she visited her mother. She couldn't believe her mother wouldn't recover. Sir Arthur would have stayed if he knew his lady was in mortal peril. He adored his Lady Mary. Women older than her mother had babies all the time. Still, she couldn't rid herself of the worry curled viper-like around the dark recesses of her mind.

Her mother had looked tired and a trifle wan, but seemed in good spirits. For once, she and her mother had been in perfect accord.

Winding down the staircase, Beatrice wanted to do something to cheer her mother up. Mayhap she could gather her some fresh flowers from the meadow. Or finish her embroidery without the entire thing becoming an unrecognizable snarl. There wasn't much chance of that happening, and flowers were too commonplace.

She wanted to do something to take her mother's breath away. Something big that would stand out in the family history. Perhaps a quest to the Holy Lands to bring back a sacred relic or a pilgrimage to Bath to return in triumph with the healing waters. Except she had no way of traveling to the Holy Land, or Bath for that matter. Garrett's face flickered across her mind. Such a thing would certainly warrant mention in the family history, unfortunately, for all the wrong reasons.

Voices drifted up the stairwell. Henry, her brother, spoke.

Her uncle replied.

Not able to hear them clearly, Beatrice quickened her step. Visitors were always welcome, and her uncle, doubly so.

"You should not have come here," Henry said.

Beatrice stopped. She couldn't have heard right. Henry was as fond of Godfrey as she.

"This is madness," Henry continued.

"Calm your fire, Henry," Godfrey replied. "And keep your voice down. Anyone might be listening."

The screens shielding the hall from the heat and bustle of the kitchens were empty. Nobody was in the dim corridor leading to the kitchens. The people of the keep were preparing for the evening meal.

"She shouldn't have come." Henry's voice came softer now as he heeded their uncle's warning.

"I had no choice," a woman said.

*Faye?* Beatrice's heart gave a happy leap. Her sister was here, too. She took a quick step forward.

"You have placed us all in terrible danger." Henry's words stopped her a second time.

"Where else would I go?" Faye replied.

Beatrice's pulse quickened. She should announce herself. If she did, however, the conversation would stop, as it always did when she approached. Her family kept her swaddled from anything they considered unpleasant, and they considered a great many things unpleasant. Beatrice hesitated. Her mother would disapprove of listening to a conversation that didn't include her. Perhaps, because her mother didn't need to listen in secret. Nobody ever kept things from Lady Mary.

Beatrice stole closer and peered through the decorative carving at the top of the screens.

Henry and Godfrey stood at the opposite end of the hall, their heads together.

Faye stood nearby, dressed for traveling with her hood thrown back. Her pale blond hair had escaped its braid, and mud splattered Faye's cloak to the knees.

Beatrice had never seen her sister as disarrayed.

Her nephews were here, too. She adored her little nephews.

Beatrice almost gave up her hiding place.

Sir Gregory, the knight who always accompanied Faye, stood patiently to the side with the children. Little Arthur curled up in the large man's arms. His sweet face was pressed against the knight's tunic, his mouth open in sleep. Young Simon gripped Sir Gregory's thigh with one arm. The knight dropped his hand and touched the top of Simon's golden head, his large, rough hand so gentle on the child. Gregory took no part in the quiet conversation between Godfrey, Faye, and Henry.

Damn. She couldn't hear them much better from here. Of course, if somebody were to remain concealed beyond the group, behind the great tapestry portraying one of her father's numerous victories, then that person would hear everything said. And one could reach the tapestry through the chapel.

Beatrice crept out of the screens and raced back up the stairs. She slowed as she crossed before her mother's chamber, but pelted the rest of the way toward the secondary staircase. From here, it was easy to slip through the back of the chapel and find the entrance concealed by the tapestry. She was breathing heavily by the time she reached the small alcove beside the entrance. She took a moment to calm her breathing before she snuck closer.

"Do you have the money?" Godfrey asked.

"Nay." Henry sighed and muttered something Beatrice couldn't quite catch, but she did hear the word scutage. The king had levied the tax once again, shortly before her father decided to join the other barons in their Army of God.

"Is there any truth to these allegations?" Godfrey asked as parchment crackled.

If she dared peer around the edge of the tapestry, she'd be directly in Henry's line of sight. She contented herself with merely listening.

"Of course, there is no truth," Faye said. One of the children murmured, and Faye lowered her voice. "My father would never abuse his position as sheriff in such an unconscionable manner."

"Of course, he would not," Godfrey replied in his smooth, deep voice, good for stories and soothing. "But the king does not have to provide evidence to damn your father. The rumor alone will cause dissent amongst the rebel barons. The burden lies with your father to prove the king wrong."

"If he were here," Henry continued stiffly, "he would answer these ridiculous charges in an instant. The king only charges him now because he is not here. It is despicable." Something thumped the table and made Beatrice jump. Must be Henry. He was a table pounder.

The baby's startled wail cut the air.

Hurried footsteps, and Faye shushed him.

"It is called politics, dear boy," Godfrey spoke quietly. "And it is a battleground on which you had best tread warily."

"I cannot send for my father," Henry said.

"But you must." Faye's voice shook.

Beatrice desperately wanted to see what was happening.

"It is impossible," Henry snapped.

If it were a simple matter of answering charges, her father should be here to do so. She wished she knew how it all worked, but her knowledge was somewhat vague. Her oldest brother, Roger, might explain it to her. Henry would rather have his toenails drawn than explain things to a simple girl.

"Indeed," Godfrey replied. "Not with the way matters are poised in London. I am not long back from there, and tensions are high. Arthur must remain in London, for the sake of the kingdom."

Her father shouldn't stay in London. He was needed right here, by his family.

"We have to do something," Faye spoke. "As soon as Calder realizes I am gone, he will look here for me."

*Why would Faye's husband not know she is here?* Faye never did anything without approval. She'd been Sir Arthur's flawless older daughter, married brilliantly, and spent her days being Calder's perfect wife and mother to his heirs.

"You might have thought of that before you rushed heedlessly for Anglesea."

Boots rapped against the floor.

Beatrice wanted to smack Henry for speaking thus to Faye. She held her breath to hear Faye's response.

"I needed to warn you of what Calder plans."

"I understand, Faye, but by being here you have placed us all in danger. Calder will come for you."

"He will not come for me."

"He will come for his boys then." Henry could be such pompous oaf at times.

"*Whist*, children," Godfrey chided. "We have enough trouble without fighting amongst ourselves."

Beatrice wanted to cheer her uncle.

"Can you pay the sum your father is being accused of stealing?"

Fabric rustled in the silence. Henry spoke. "Nay. I would not do it, regardless. It goes against everything in me to pay money to that thieving scoundrel."

"That thieving scoundrel," said Godfrey, "is your king. I would have a care how you speak of him. Especially if you do so where people can hear."

"Nobody is listening now," Henry grumbled, his voice growing softer as footsteps moved away.

*I am.* Only part of the conversation made sense to her. The king had accused her father of stealing money. It was preposterous. Anyone who knew Sir Arthur would recognize the idea as ludicrous. The king knew her father. He'd been a great favorite with King John. Then something had happened. She didn't rightly recall because she had been a few years younger, but she did remember her father's anger and lots of visitors coming to the castle to speak with him.

Mostly what she remembered of that time was her betrothal. The first of the three. And how it had ended. It was one of the first times her father had ever raised his voice to her. She shouldn't have punched Ralph in the nose, but he had pulled her hair.

"What of Calder?" Godfrey asked.

She would've asked about that before now.

"Calder is King John's man," Faye replied. "He plans to stand with the king against father."

"Calder has joined sides with the king?" Godfrey asked. "This is a surprise."

It was indeed.

The footsteps approached again, tapping quickly as their owner paced, probably Henry.

"Aye," Faye said. "He despises the French. He would lief see the king keep his throne than see it given to a Frenchman."

"We all despise the bloody French." Godfrey chuckled. "But they are a necessary evil. After seeing how he ousted John at Bouvines, King Philip may have the might to tip this in our favor."

"Still." Henry made a noise in the back of his throat expressive of his displeasure. He normally saved those for when she was in sight. "I had not thought to see the day we would offer our throne to a Frenchman."

"Like many, I do not see the alternative," Godfrey said. A chair creaked. "John's reign is a disaster. Richard was bad enough with his incessant wars. He nearly made beggars of the lot of us. The timing is diabolically clever," Godfrey continued. "You are shorthanded here. Your father left you only enough men to hold the keep. Calder has the perfect excuse to lay siege here."

"I had to come," Faye said. "Calder is changed. He is not the man I married."

"But he is still your husband." Henry's voice grew louder as he paced nearer.

Beatrice stepped back from the tapestry.

"And Sir Arthur is still my father," Faye said. "You know what the king's court is like. Calder has become one of them. He has threatened to put me aside and take my children from me."

Beatrice gasped, then clapped her hand over her mouth to muffle the sound. It was unthinkable, putting aside Faye and taking her boys.

"The boys are his children too, Faye."

Beatrice wanted to rush from her hiding place and hit Henry. How could he say such a thing to Faye? Her sister adored her children.

"You would countenance a mother being separated from her children?" Faye's voice shook, but like their mother, she never shouted. "You would stand by while my children are taken from me?"

"Mama," Simon wailed.

Beatrice's heart went out to him.

"Hush, sweeting," Faye said. "Sir Gregory?"

"Aye, my lady," he murmured.

Simon stilled.

"I did not say that." Henry sounded chastised. And rightly so. "I am merely trying to point out how precarious our position is now that you are here."

More pacing.

"I know, Henry. And you must believe I would not have come here unless it were my last resort," Faye said wearily.

"We understand." Godfrey spread oil over troubled waters. "And nobody will allow your children to be taken from you. Least of all your father."

"But Father is not here," Faye said with a small catch in her voice.

He should be. If her father were here, he would deal with all of this. He was Sir Arthur of Anglesea, legendary knight of the realm. Not many would stand against such might.

"And our mother cannot know," Henry said.

"How is she?" Faye asked.

"She is not faring well," Henry spoke heavily. "This will not help."

For once, she agreed with Henry. If there was trouble, their mother mustn't be burdened with it.

"Then, she must not know," Faye said. "I will make up an excuse for my presence here."

"And what if the king forces these charges? What if he distrains our property?" Henry's voice carried a hard edge. A boot scraped against the floor. Henry could never sit still. "We could lose everything. Father could return from London to find his land forfeit and his castle razed. Mother's health could not withstand such a burden."

Beatrice stopped her careful inching away from the tapestry.

"Surely, it is not that bad?" Godfrey said.

Fabric rustled, and then Henry spoke. "Nurse is very concerned."

Faye made a soft noise of distress. Light footsteps were followed by the grate of a bench on stone.

"We will all pray for the safe delivery of her babe," Godfrey replied. "In the meantime, we need to keep your presence here as quiet as possible. I would counsel you to do nothing. Arthur is needed in London. Men look to him for leadership. I am sure a solution will come to us."

"What of Beatrice?" Faye asked. "We will have to tell her something."

"We will tell Beatrice only what we want her to know," Henry said. "She understands nothing of these matters. God knows what she would do if we trusted her with something like this."

The tapestry moved suddenly.

Beatrice leaped back a step, but not quick enough.

Sir Gregory loomed over her.

Good Lord, he was huge. And his shoulders? They blocked out the light from the hall. Beatrice managed a wan smile.

"My lady?" He bowed over the sleeping Arthur still cradled against his chest.

As one, the others turned and stared at her.

"Beatrice." Henry took a threatening step toward her. It was hard to see how handsome he was when Henry scowled all the time. "What are you doing?"

She could think of nothing to explain her presence. Sheepishly she waved at her glaring relatives.

"She does not know how to keep her mouth shut." Henry ran his fingers through his hair, golden like her and Faye's.

Beatrice wanted to yell that she knew how to keep a secret.

"Nay, she will not tell," Godfrey said. He had the look of their father, but his face was more finely sculpted. His hazel eyes were copies of Sir Arthur's.

Beatrice gave him a grateful glance.

"She is a flighty piece, but she knows when to keep her own counsel. Don't you, Beatrice?" His teeth flashed white in his darker beard.

"Of course I do." Beatrice raised her chin. She didn't like being called a flighty piece, but she had bigger concerns. "I have some questions."

Henry glared at her, clasping his hands behind his back like a confessor.

Faye stepped around him and held her arms out. "Sweet Bea."

Beatrice drew a big breath as she hugged her sister. Even travel-stained, Faye smelled sweet as a lady should. "It is good to see you." Faye drew back and looked at Beatrice.

"What is all of this about?" It seemed pointless to pretend she hadn't heard the entire conversation.

Faye glanced at Henry.

Henry clamped his lips tightly together.

"What?" Beatrice glanced from one to the other. Why would

they not tell her? This is why she was reduced to skulking behind tapestries.

"We will have a cozy chat later, Bea." With a tired smile, Faye grasped her hands. "For now, could you please see to young Simon and little Arthur? The boys are quite worn out with travel, and I did not bring their nurse with me."

"I heard everything." Beatrice held her ground.

Blank stares greeted her.

"Take the boys, Beatrice." Henry straightened his tunic. "We will speak of your appalling habit later."

Beatrice's hated when Henry used that tone on her. "You are not Father." Henry was only a year her senior. He needn't think he had the right to check her behavior.

"Father placed me in charge."

"Aye, but that does not give you the right to lord it over the rest of us."

"Please take care of them, Bea." Faye touched her arm. There were lines of tension around Faye's mouth that hadn't been there before. Shadows lined the skin beneath her blue eyes. Beatrice wanted to soothe them away from the perfect oval of her sister's face.

"Of course." Beatrice had not the heart to keep arguing.

Godfrey gave her a nod.

"I must speak with Henry and Godfrey." Faye pressed her smooth cheek against Beatrice's.

Beatrice kept her voice low. "Will you not tell me?"

"Not now, Sweet Bea." Faye smoothed Beatrice's hair behind her ear.

Beatrice swallowed the questions frothing in her mind. They never told her anything. It was as if she wasn't even a part of this keep. She wouldn't even know this much if she'd not listened.

Little Arthur still slept in Sir Gregory's arms. Simon watched her approach with big brown eyes. His arm tightened around the knight's thigh.

"See now, young Simon. Here is your aunt, the Lady Beatrice, to find you a bed for the night." He had a deep, rough voice, as if he didn't use it much.

She fancied she could feel his dark eyes watching her every move, weighing her up. "Hello, Simon." Beatrice crouched eye level with her nephew. "Have you no greeting for me?"

Simon shrank closer to Sir Gregory and fear flitted across his pale face.

Her heart twisted as she looked to Sir Gregory.

"It has been a difficult night," he said. "If you lead the way, I will bring them."

Beatrice gave a stiff nod and rose. "I can carry Arthur, if you like."

"My thanks, my lady, but he is fast asleep, and I hate to wake him." Sir Gregory smiled, and his severe expression dissolved into the most startlingly handsome lines.

Beatrice grew breathless under the impact of such a smile. "I will see your tunic cleaned then. I see he has drooled all over it."

"It matters not," he murmured. "Come along, Simon."

Simon grasped a handful of the knight's tunic as they walked.

Sir Gregory climbed the stairs behind her.

There was a lot more to this than met the eye.

She led Sir Gregory and the boys to a small chamber beside her own. It had been used as a sewing room. Now, it would serve as a good place for them. "I assume you know all about the difficulty with Calder and King John?"

Sir Gregory gave her an inscrutable look. "It is not my place to say."

Beatrice wanted to scream, but she doubted it would do any good with Sir Gregory.

"Can you tell me anything?" She tried to modify her tone, but it still sounded petulant.

Sir Gregory gently disentangled Simon's fingers from his tunic.

Beatrice hoped he would answer.

He cradled Arthur against his shoulder, his hand spanning the babe's back. "I can tell you the danger is real. Calder conspires with the king against your father," Sir Gregory said. "Your father should be here."

"That is what I say." Relief surged through her. At last, someone had some good sense.

"But it does not matter what you or I say." Sir Gregory calmly dashed her hopes. He shrugged. "Neither of us will make the decision."

Beatrice clamped her lips together.

Sir Gregory inclined his head toward the sleeping infant. "Let us see to the boys."

Settling her nephews, Beatrice kept her patience, but all the while, she wondered what was happening with Faye and Henry. She had the serfs find two pallets and make them up. Beatrice also arranged for some warm water. With Sir Gregory's help, she washed the boys' faces and stripped their outer tunics, boots, and chausses. When the children were comfortable, he helped Beatrice get them onto their pallets.

Beatrice went down to the kitchen and warmed milk for the boys. Returning, she heard the deep rumble of Sir Gregory's voice before she entered the room.

Sitting on the floor beside the pallet, the knight spun an unlikely tale to delight any boy's heart. Dragons, lions, and lots of thwacking with swords made up the largest part of the adventure.

Simon's eyes drifted shut and stayed closed. His little face slackened in sleep. Such a tiny boy to be so afeared.

"I will see you settled." Beatrice walked through the door.

"I will stay here." Sir Gregory shifted on the stones.

"On the floor?"

Back against the wall, long legs stretched before him, he rewarded her with another smile, as startling as the first. "It is not so hard. And I do not want them to wake and be frightened."

Beatrice's heart melted. "I will send some blankets to make you more comfortable."

"As you will, my lady."

Beatrice closed the door behind her. She'd been longer settling the boys than she would have liked. The keep was silent as she walked to her chamber.

"Blast." Her father and brothers didn't discuss politics before her, but she knew her father was at odds with the king. The king had sent her brother, William, home from court. It was an insult and a sign to all Sir Arthur had lost favor.

She perched on the edge of her bed. Long shadows stretched from the clothe's tree and inched along the ground. Dust motes glittered in the air like faeries. She'd been too caught up in her secret romance to give any thought to the world all about her. Her father had committed treason, openly and decisively. The king would act.

The gravity of the situation settled like a dull weight in her middle. Her father had left enough men to defend the castle. What if the king were to bring an army to bear? He had an army, because he was always asking for taxes to pay for it. If her father had thought it fitting to speak of politics more in her presence, she would've understood more.

She dug her fingers into the silk of her bed covering. Her mother might have explained, but she couldn't ask her.

Henry would only give her a superior look down his perfect nose and tell her women should not involve themselves in men's affairs.

Beatrice didn't see how women could avoid being involved in men's affairs, since every decision some man made affected some poor woman, somewhere.

Beatrice got to her feet. Beyond her casement, the beautiful day drew to an end with the sinking sun gilding the river. The breeze carried the ocean's tang, and the plaintive cries of roosting gulls echoed her mood.

Just this morning she'd been free as one of those birds. She'd been selfish.

Intent on Garrett, she'd ignored the signs that all was not well within Anglesea.

On the river, a fisherman poled his boat back to the village for the night. The same village Garrett called home. For now.

She had no business thinking of Garrett when her family was threatened from all sides.

Below her, Tom crossed the bailey toward the stables.

She hadn't seen as much of Tom since Garrett had appeared in her life. They'd been friends since both of them could toddle off without their mothers. Tom was Nurse's son and he had his mother's pragmatic nature, without her bite. He'd grown much taller of late, towering a full head above her. His shoulders cast a broad shadow before him.

Soon, Tom would be courting. Suddenly, she ached to be with her old friend. Tom had a way of looking at the world that made sense to her. He didn't judge her or laugh at her. Tom listened and then put matters to rights in her head.

*Chapter Five*

Garrett woke with a start. His head thudded like someone kept putting the boot to it. His arms screamed the agony of stretched sinews. He tried to move them. They were held fast, wrenched from the socket and suspended above his head like a crucifixion. Searing pain spread down his arms from the bindings constricting his wrists.

Alarm shot through his blood. He forced his eyes open. Everything swam, and he closed them again. Wanting to spew his guts, he swallowed hard. It took a long moment for his head to stop the cursed whirling.

He needed to remember. His belly heaved. Breath sawed through his nose as he clenched his jaws shut. It came to him in fits. Finishing in the forge, sweaty but too tired to bother with washing. Thinking of Beatrice. Falling asleep. Then, waking up with the dread someone was in the hut.

They'd clobbered him. He forced his eyes open. Instinct to fight surged through his muscles. Icy water hit his face and he gasped. Nothing would be gained by striking out blindly.

"Welcome back," a man drawled. In the dimly lit forge, he sat atop a water barrel, looking strangely out of place with his fine tunic and clean boots.

The pressure on his arms was unbearable. Icy water dripped down his chin onto his bare chest. Sweet Christ, he was naked, stark-bollock naked. He got his feet beneath him and tried to stand. His legs were weak as wet linen, but he forced them to take some of his weight. The relief on his arms made his eyes water. It must be late. The great fires were banked to the coals. Lyman would be asleep.

"I thought we might speak." The stranger sounded like a bloody lord.

Who was the cur? Darkness concealed most of his face, clean lines with a patch of a neatly trimmed beard. A man of fashion, then.

"Who are you?" Garrett licked his lips and tasted the bitter iron of dried blood. His stomach roiled.

"It is better for you not to know." The stranger wiped his hands on a kerchief and tossed it into the hearth. Flames leapt around it and subsided.

Sod that. He tried to think, but his head was fuzzy. Did he owe the dog money? A wife. Had he tupped this one's wife?

"We are not acquainted." The stranger rose and gave a curt wave.

Three men materialized out of the shadows.

Garrett went cold. He hadn't seen them before, and he should have. Growing up rough left few gaps for mistakes.

The men moved to the door and out.

Alone with the overdressed cur meant no aid, but also no witnesses. It was either a very good thing or a very, very bad thing.

He tested the ropes. The knots pulled tight.

"There is no need to be concerned." The stranger dusted the seat of his tunic.

Garrett nearly laughed in his face. He was strung up like a slaughtered pig with his wedding tackle dangling. There was every bloody reason for concern.

The man had light hair with eyes either brown or green.

He took keen note of the face. If he got out of this situation, it was a face he'd be sure not to see again. And if he did, he would grind those pretty features beneath his boot and laugh while the whoreson squirmed.

"I have been watching you for a time now." The stranger stepped carefully, avoiding the filth on the floor. "And I thought it was time we had a talk."

"So talk." Garrett's head pounded in time with his pulse. He hoped like hell he wasn't going to spew in front of this cur. "You have my attention."

The man's eyes widened. "Wit?" He cocked his head and contemplated Garrett. "At a time like this? Do you think it apt?"

"You tell me."

The man came closer and studied Garrett from head to toe. He might be one of those who liked other men.

Jesu, if the sod put his hands on him, Garrett would tear the roof down about their heads.

"Oh, cease." The man waved at him. "I am only here to have a mannerly conversation."

It surprised a laugh out of Garrett. Jesu. If this was mannerly, he was a pig's ass.

"At first, I was confused by your obvious interest in the Lady Beatrice." The man leaned down and peered at a lump of steel.

Garret went still. Was this Beatrice's brother, the one not in London? The stranger looked too old, somewhere in his middle years. Garrett waited.

"No hot denials?" He sauntered about the forge, lifting Lyman's apron and peering into the pouch.

"Would there be any purpose?" Garrett's legs firmed, and he stood. The man was shorter than he and slighter. If it weren't for the three feet of steel at the whoreson's side, Garrett was sure he could take him. Experience had taught him not to underestimate the speed or accuracy of that steel. It was all useless speculation while he hung here.

"I was intrigued by you." The stranger ran his hand over Lyman's hammer. "Intrigued enough to do a bit of checking on you, young master Garrett. When I discovered you were, in fact, Wulfric's bastard, the entire thing began to make sense. Let me take a guess as to your intent." He hefted the weight of the hammer.

Garrett's neck prickled.

"You are going to seduce Lady Beatrice as a sort of revenge on her father. Am I right?" He flicked his fingers. "I know I am right. Your mother became a whore, and you make Beatrice one. It is a disappointingly unimaginative plan, but effective in its simplicity."

"What do you want from me?" Garrett snarled. The man was clever. He'd give him that much.

"Nothing too onerous." The stranger tucked his hands behind his back. "My purpose here is twofold. Firstly, I wanted you to know I see you, Garrett, son of a traitor and a whore. And secondly, to inform you we share a purpose. Neither of us holds any love for Sir Arthur. We could be of benefit to each other."

"Sod off."

The man's eyes widened. "You really are your father's son, are you not? You have the same innate charm." He chuckled at his own joke. "I met your father, you know? It was not an experience I chose to repeat. And yet, here I am."

"I am not my father." Hate boiled in his gut for the rutting pig who'd sired him.

"You favor him. But you also have your mother's features. You should thank God for that. She was a beautiful woman." He waved. "Before the pox and the scars got to her, that is."

Hot rage seared through Garrett. He wanted to get his hands around this cur's neck and squeeze. He heaved against the restraints. The man talked of his mother as if she were nothing. Garrett remembered every excruciating moment of his mother's illness.

"I see I have hit a raw spot." The man strolled over to him.

Garrett strained to get free. The ropes cut into his wrists. He wanted to kill this sod.

"You should keep your vengeance and your anger apart. The one makes the other much harder to achieve. Anger will not aid you. Neither will pulling on those restraints. I tied them myself."

Garrett lunged for him. Jesu, he needed to reach the sod and break him. Break every bone inside that prissy clothing. The dog would choke on his own words with Garrett's hands at this throat. No blade, but bare hands tightening the life from the sod.

The man stepped back.

Aye, the rutting whoreson should be afeared. When Garret got free, he would show him anger. Vengeance. Christ, the cur didn't know vengeance.

"Do not make me call my men in. They are not the brightest, and I am loath to start our partnership on such a painful note. Painful for you, that is." A small smile played around his mouth. He was laughing at him.

The smile near drove Garrett from his mind. He forced himself to still. He was doing naught but scraping his wrists raw and tearing his muscles. One day, he'd take great pleasure in wiping the smirk off the dog's face. He could wait. Sir Arthur had taught him as much.

"Good." The stranger nodded. "You are mine now, Garrett. Because if not—" He took a step closer, within striking distance.

Garrett breathed deeply.

"I will bring the wrath of the goodly Sir Arthur on your head, once again. You barely survived the first time. You will not live through Arthur's response to your filthy hands on his little girl."

Garrett clenched his teeth together. He would squeeze until his pretty face turned black and his eyes started from his head.

"Now, we have that unpleasantness aside, I have a small task for you."

He would ram this one's small task down his wrung throat.

"Aye, I can guess what you would like to say, but this task will benefit both of us. You see, boy, I care nothing about your plans for Lady Beatrice. I will help you achieve your vengeance, and you will help me regain what is mine." He tucked his hand behind his back.

He didn't trust the man, but Garrett listened.

"In a day or two, the Lady Beatrice will come to you for help. You will aid her." He shrugged. "You see, no big matter. All you need do is come to the aid of a lady. It will set you in excellent standing with Lady Beatrice. I am not an unreasonable man. I am giving you what you need to push your victim right into your ready arms."

"And if I choose to refuse your gift?"

"You will not." The man nodded and spun on his heel. "You would be stupid to do so." He swung open the door.

Cool night air rushed in. Garrett sucked it into his lungs.

"Send someone to cut him down," he said to his men. "But not yet. Let him hang there for a time. It might take some of the fire out of him."

# Chapter Six

**B**eatrice would go to London.

The idea struck her midway across the bailey, and she stopped dead in her tracks. She only narrowly missed being run over by a huge laundry basket.

"I beg your pardon," she said to the irate laundress.

She headed for the stables to find Tom.

It was a wild and improbable notion, but it stuck like a burr. Henry was wrong not to send for their father. Father would want to be here.

She rode better and lighter in the saddle than any of Henry's men. It wouldn't take her as long as three days to reach London. If she pressed, she could make it in two. She knew London lay roughly to the north and a bit to the side. Roger had shown it to her once on one of their father's maps.

She would leave in secret. If her family, or Nurse, caught wind of what she planned, it would be the end of it.

She must go.

The more she thought about it, the clearer it became. Her mother would be well again when she saw her beloved husband. Calder wouldn't dare to challenge her father, and Faye and the boys would be safe. Sir Arthur would deal decisively with those ridiculous charges against him.

It would be a thrilling adventure. Her, bent over the head of her mount, riding recklessly for London—a gleam of determination kindling in her eye, a slim figure, astride her chestnut mare, stopping for naught and letting nobody stand in her way.

Excitement simmered beneath her skin.

This must be how her father felt when he was on the cusp of one of his great battles. He must feel the call to greatness gathering like a tempest within him. Beatrice raised her chin and thrust her shoulders back. Beatrice of Anglesea, daughter of the mighty Sir Arthur, heard the call and would answer.

She dodged a pile of horse dung as she entered the stables. The light was dim inside, and she blinked to clear her vision. The air was heavy with the mixed smells of hay and horse. Tom worked toward the far end.

All her family had received their call and answered it. Now it was her turn. Nurse had been right all along. She would find her way. Her path spread before her, glimmering and beckoning at her to place her feet on it and run.

She nodded to a young stableboy. The folk at Anglesea would tell her tale around the hearth for winters to come. How, when all else had failed and the family teetered on the precipice of complete and utter doom, Beatrice strode forward. She'd be called Beatrice the Bold, and minstrels would take up her tale. Or, mayhap, Beatrice the Brave. It had an excellent ring to it. She liked it. Beatrice the Brave.

"You do not know where London is." Tom drove his pitchfork into the loose pile of feed. Streamers of hay glittered in his wake as he crossed to a feed trough and filled it.

Life or death hung on her quest, and Tom didn't even stop his work long enough to look. He was exactly like his mother sometimes.

Beatrice wanted to box his ears. "I will ask someone. London is huge. I can't miss it."

Tom leaned on his pitchfork and eyed her askance from beneath his shock of wheaten hair.

It wasn't Tom's fault. His only ambition lay in owning land to grow things. He didn't have the blood of warriors thundering through his veins. He didn't hear the call.

"You cannot merely ask someone." Tom leant the fork up against the stall and grabbed a water bucket. "These are dangerous times. You will be lucky if you reach Bath."

"Is Bath on the way to London?" Beatrice leapt out of his way as he strode past her.

"Do not ask me. I do not know where London is either. What do you think is going to happen to a young girl, all alone, asking for directions to London?" He plunged his bucket into the water trough. His rough tunic pulled tight across his broad back.

He had a point.

Tom gave the horse water. He leaned his shoulder into the horse's and spoke softly to the animal as it moved for him.

The horse whickered and nudged him with its nose.

Tom had a way with animals. His hands were gentle as he stroked its neck.

"I shall disguise myself as a boy." She'd heard a story to that effect. It would make her tale all the better for the telling. Beatrice the Brave, eschewing her womanly garb to see justice brought to her people. It would also make riding astride much easier.

"You are going to cut your hair?" Tom peered at her over the horse's back. He was so tall now he stood shoulder to shoulder with one of her father's destriers.

Beatrice touched the smooth fall of her hair. Her hair was her secret conceit, one of her few claims to beauty. Even Faye didn't have hair quite as thick or silky as hers.

Tom's smug expression said he knew her thoughts. He'd spoken of her hair on purpose. He grabbed his pitchfork and moved to the next stall.

"I shall dress as a boy and tuck my hair in a cap." Beatrice followed him, raising her gown over the hay scattered on the floor.

"You are daft. And I have a good mind to tell my mother."

"Nay." Beatrice's stomach dropped. Everything would be ruined.

"Forget this barmy idea." Tom shook his head and speared the loose hay.

"It is not barmy. My family is in trouble, and I am going to save them."

"You are merely a girl."

The blood rushed to her head in a throbbing, red haze. If she were less of a lady, she would kick Tom for saying that. "I may be a girl, but I am girl enough to know when I must rise to the rescue."

Tom ruined her speech with a snort. He filled the second trough and went for more water.

If he would just stop long enough to hear her out.

The horse snorted and sidled as Tom let himself into the stall. He disappeared behind the animal.

Beatrice stamped her foot. "If you tell your mother, I shall tell her about you going down to the village to visit Lilly."

"Eh?" Tom's head reappeared over the horse, his blue eyes almost starting right out of his head.

She'd only been guessing. Many of the castle lads spoke of visiting Lilly. She tried to imagine Tom going there, but the idea made her head spin.

"What do you know of Lilly?" Tom ducked beneath the animal's neck and took a threatening step toward her.

"Fornication." Beatrice held her ground.

Tom stalked over, close enough to tower above her. "I never went there."

"You did, too."

"You cannot prove anything."

"I would not have to." She arranged her features into an innocent expression. "Nurse? Why are Tom and Lilly such good friends?"

Tom actually growled at her. He wouldn't strike her, but he

mightn't hesitate to toss her in a rain barrel. His arms were brawny enough to do it, too.

Beatrice hopped back.

"You cannot go haring off to London on your own. You could get murdered or worse." Tom's expression was stony. "You can tell my mother whatever you want, but nothing you say would be worse than me letting you go to London on your own like this." Tom let himself into the next stall and barred it behind him.

The air rushed out of Beatrice's lungs. Alone and not knowing the way was too dangerous. Unless? Hope flared again. "Then I will not go alone."

"What do you mean?" He spun back to her.

"I will take someone with me, someone who is able to protect me and knows the way to London."

"I do not know the way to London, and if I did—"

"I am not speaking of you."

"Who then?" Tom planted his elbows on the top of the stall.

"Someone you do not know." She did, indeed, know the perfect someone. The thrilling new development made her heart gallop.

"You do not know any such person," Tom fetched his fork.

"That is how much you know." Beatrice snapped her fingers at him. "I do, too, know someone who would be happy to take me to London."

The more she thought about it, the more she liked the idea. Garrett would take her to London. It would be perfect. Nobody would try to accost her with Garrett by her side. Garrett was big and strong. And, more importantly, he'd traveled just about everywhere. She wasn't precisely sure if he'd been to London, but it stood to reason someone who'd been as many places as Garret had to have been to London. Garrett and her, alone, on the way to London. She shivered with delight.

"Who is this person?" Tom loomed nearer, his pitchfork held

like a spear. He had a look on his face that made Beatrice tread warily. There was only so far she could push Tom.

"Nobody you know."

"That is it. I am telling my mother. Let her deal with you." The fork clattered to the ground as Tom strode toward the door.

"Nay." Beatrice jumped over the implement and caught his arm. "You must not. Please, Tom." She tugged on his sleeve until he stopped. "You must let me do this." Her voice wobbled as she saw all her newly hatched dreams crumbling at her feet. "You know how ill my mother is. And Faye. Faye's husband could come and take her children from her by force. Only my father can stop that. He must come. Henry does not see it, but he must come home."

"I understand." Tom's expression softened. "But it is not you who must go. It is too dangerous."

"There is nobody else. I am the only one who is ready to take action."

Tom took her hand from his sleeve. He held it in his large, roughened palm. "Bea, you are hatching crazy notions in that head of yours."

Beatrice bit her lip to keep from crying. He didn't see any of it. "If I do not do this, I will never be one of them. Here is my chance to make my family proud. I can make up for all those broken engagements and all the embarrassments and everything." She stopped because she ran out of breath.

Tom rolled his eyes and gave her hand a squeeze. "There were only three broken engagements."

"Exactly." Beatrice blinked against the sting at the back of her eyes. The humiliation was a bitter taste in her mouth. "This is my chance to prove to my family I am one of them."

"Of course you are one of them. You do not need to prove yourself to them, Bea. Your family loves you."

"I know that." Beatrice dashed her cheeks impatiently. Treacherous tears wouldn't stop leaking onto her cheeks. "I know they love me, but they do not take me seriously. It is always *oh, Beatrice is up to her tricks again,* or *you know Beatrice.*"

And everything else she'd said or thought dropped away. Beatrice knew this was the real reason. "I need to do this. For my mother, for all of them."

"Ah, Bea, it is all in your head." He released her hand and rubbed the back of his neck. "You think you need to measure up to your family because your father is this big legend and your mother was known everywhere. Beneath all that though, they are merely people, like you and me."

Beatrice wasn't going to argue the point with him. There were two sorts of people. Some were made in the image of God, and others were nearly Him. "I am going to do this, Tom," she said. "All you have to decide is whether you are going to stand in my way or help me."

Broad face impassive, Tom stilled and searched her eyes.

Beatrice held her breath.

"I must be mad." Tom looked past her at the twilight spilling into the stable and sighed. "My mother, for sure, is going to flay me alive for this. And I would not blame her." He threw up his hands. "Of course I am going to help you, Bea."

"Oh, Tom." Beatrice finally breathed. Victory. She flung her arms around his neck. There was nowhere a better man than Tom and he was her best friend.

He wheezed as she tightened her grip.

"But—" He unwrapped her from his neck. "You are not going alone, because I will go with you."

Beatrice didn't want Tom along. She wanted Garrett. She chewed the inside of her cheek. Tom wouldn't approve of Garrett and he might be difficult. Then again, it was better than Tom putting a stop to the entire scheme. If he came with her, he would have no opportunity to tell tales on her. "I love you, Tom."

Tom bent and grabbed his pitchfork. "Remember you do when my mother gets hold of me."

# Chapter Seven

Beatrice opened the door to her mother's chamber. Lady Mary sat in her bed, propped against a mountain of pillows. Her braid trailed over her shoulder and pooled in her lap. It had once been bright as new gold, but was dulled with age now. Her face, as unlined as a woman half her age, lit in a smile as warm as the sunlight pouring in.

The chamber smelled of roses. All around were those little touches that spoke of Lady Mary. The huge bowl of flowers by her bed. An embroidered fire screen before the hearth, stitched by her mother's hand. And fine silks draped over the chest at the foot of the bed.

Beatrice's belly churned with the lies she was about to utter.

"Sweet Bea." Her mother patted the silver fur bed throw beside her. "Come and tell me what you are planning for today."

She couldn't do that. Beatrice climbed on the bed and tucked her feet into the silky pelt like she had every morning since Lady Mary had been confined to her bed. She would miss her mother. There would be no more morning visits until she got back from London. Her heart gave a sharp twist. "The weather is fine today."

"I see so." Lady Mary gestured toward the open casement. "You should take Simon and little Arthur to collect seashells."

"What?" Her mouth dried, and she eyed the cup of tea beside her mother.

"I said you should take Simon and Arthur to the beach."

"I would if they were here."

"And they are not here?" Mother raised an eyebrow. Lady Mary's eyes were the same piercing blue as Faye's. They could strip you to your chainse.

Beatrice adjusted her skirts over her legs and played for time. She pointed to the cup. "May I?"

Lady Mary pulled a face. "Please. It is one of nurse's tisanes."

Beatrice put the cup back on the gleaming oak table. Her mouth wasn't that dry.

"I thought I heard Simon this morning." Mother folded her arms over her large belly.

"Nay. Perhaps it was a child from the village?"

Lady Mary pursed her lips. "It sounded just like Simon."

"It may have." Beatrice's throat tightened. She hated lying to her mother. "But Simon is at Calder Castle with his mother and his father, so you could not have heard him."

Lady Mary studied her.

Beatrice dug her nails into her palms to stop herself from fidgeting. Please, just this once, let Mother not see through her. Her heart pounded so loudly her mother must be able to hear it.

"Did Godfrey arrive?"

Beatrice unclenched her hands. She wiped damp palms on her knee. "He did. The Army of God still holds London, but he has not seen father or the boys."

"I pray they are well." Lady Mary sighed and looked out the casement. Her mouth was drawn down at the corners and she looked tired and sad.

Renewed determination surged through Beatrice. This was why she had Tom preparing supplies right this minute. When Sir Arthur and her brothers were back, her mother would smile again. She touched her palm to her mother's belly. "How is the babe?"

"Restless." Her mother covered her hand with her long, delicate fingers. "He is a strong lad."

"Lad?"

"What girl would cause her mother such discomfort?"

Guilt took a swipe at Beatrice. She had caused her mother all manner of discomfort and was about to add to her tally. When she returned from London, there would be no more upheavals and trouble. She would settle down and become a good daughter, just like Faye.

"Look at me, Bea." Lady Mary squeezed her hand. "You do not cause me discomfort."

Of course, her mother would say so, because she was her mother. Her mother was uncanny the way she could read her face so easily. Bea forced a smile to her lips. "Not at this minute, I am not."

"There." Her mother smiled. "We are in perfect agreement. Now, tell me what you plan for the rest of this lovely day."

Beatrice chatted with her mother until Nurse came in with instructions for Lady Mary to rest.

"See you on the morrow, Sweet Bea," her mother said.

It was time to say goodbye. Beatrice's throat closed around a huge lump. She ducked her head to hide her face from Nurse's view.

"Actually." Her voice came out in a rasp, and she cleared her throat.

Her mother raised her brows.

The prepared excuse lodged behind Beatrice's breastbone. She forced the words out in a rush of breath. "I thought I might go to the sisters at St. Thomas in the morning."

"Did you?" Nurse glared from beneath her wimple.

It was easier to look at Nurse than her mother. "I thought I might light a candle for father and William and Roger."

"And our chapel will not suffice? Father Bernard has run short of candles?"

Beatrice raised her chin and met Nurse's penetrating stare.

Nurse jammed her hands on her hips.

"I think it is a fine idea." Lady Mary's soft voice broke the joined battle.

Beatrice let her breath out slowly. Her mother was a saint and she was a liar and a worm.

"Light one for the babe and your mother while you are there."

Beatrice pressed a kiss to her mother's cheek. She inhaled the comforting rose scent clinging to her mother. "I love you."

"And you, Sweet Bea."

* * *

In the moonlight, Beatrice slipped out the postern gate. It clanged shut behind her and she jumped. The rest of the keep was at Vespers.

Tom waited for her just as they had arranged. He had three horses and all the provisions for their journey. "Did you leave the message for Faye?"

Beatrice rolled her eyes and mounted. Just because Tom had agreed to help her, didn't mean he would come quietly. "I left her a message," Beatrice whispered. "I think it is a vastly stupid idea, by the by. What is to say Henry will not come charging after us the moment Faye tells him where we have gone?"

"You said Faye would not tell him." Tom stood beside his horse, arms crossed over his chest.

"I said Faye was not likely to say anything." She wasn't at all sure Faye would keep the information to herself, which was why she'd made a point to leave the message where it wouldn't be delivered before the morning. Faye wouldn't wait up for her, and Nurse believed she slept beside Faye. By the time the keep rose to break its fast, however, and she was still nowhere to be found, questions would be asked. Her story about the convent would buy her a little more time. By then she planned to be well on her way. If Tom would just get on his horse.

He had picked the calmest horse in the stable. Old Parsley would trudge along happily as long as you fed him and didn't ask him to do anything too onerous. Besides, Parsley was in love with her mare, Breeze. Where Breeze put her dainty hooves, Parsley was sure to come crashing after.

"You left the message I told you to leave?"

"I said what you told me to say." Mostly. "As we discussed."

Finally, Tom mounted. He took up the reins to the third horse. Badger jerked his head and blew hard. Tom clucked, and the gelding reluctantly shambled forward.

Beatrice nudged Breeze into a walk. Tom's constant carping threatened to snuff her spark of adventure. Still, that was Tom for you. He had his uses like procuring food, human and animal, and other bits and pieces necessary for the journey. His thought to bring sleeping blankets was inspired.

They crossed the meadow and wended through the towering beech trees toward the village. The moist ground muffled the horse's hoof falls in the still night.

Faye mightn't tell Henry. And if Faye did tell him, Beatrice doubted Henry would do anything about her absence.

An owl hooted. Badger shied, and Tom soothed him.

If it were Roger, no threat on earth would've moved her to leave a note. Roger would've been on his destrier in hot pursuit before he'd reached the end of the message. It was fortunate Roger remained in London. Or mayhap, not. Roger would not be dithering like Henry, in the family's darkest hour.

She missed her oldest brother. He was her favorite, with his quick temper and quicker sense of humor. Roger came closest to understanding her within the family. Not all the time, but enough to keep her feeling like less of a cuckoo in the nest.

All that would change after she reached her father in London. Her family might be angry with her for taking such a risk. Roger would definitely thunder and rant, but all would be forgiven when her purpose became clear.

Breeze cleared the trees and took the gentle descent to the village. Fishing nets, strung between stakes to dry like giant spiderwebs, glittered in the moonlight. Warm yellow light spilled from casements onto the green.

She pulled Breeze to a stop. "I will have to go alone."

Tom reined Parsley in beside her. Badger pulled at the bit before he settled. "Why?"

"Because, we do not want everyone to know what we are doing, or someone will tell Henry for sure. Then where will we be?" Must she explain everything?

"Tucked up safe in our beds, where we should be." Tom hunched in his saddle. "I am beginning to think we should stop this before we travel any farther."

"We cannot, Tom." Beatrice's heart missed a beat. "You said you would help me."

"Aye." Tom rubbed the back of his neck. "But that was foolish on my part."

"Are you going to keep whining the same old tune all the way to London?" Tom was so blasted stubborn.

"I am not whining. Bea, will you listen to sense before you get us both mired in something we'll regret." Badger stamped, and Tom tightened his lead rein.

"Well, I shall not regret it." If Tom didn't want to help her, he could go cringing back to Anglesea. "Go back, if you like, but I am going to get the man we need." Tom would make a raw spot if he kept rubbing at his neck. "Come now, Tom. Think of this as a grand adventure. We used to talk of them all the time when we were younger."

"You spoke of grand adventure." Tom jabbed his thumb into his chest. "I wanted a farm. I still want a farm."

"Of course you do." Beatrice leaned across and patted his knee. "And think how grateful my father will be you helped save the family from certain ruin."

"Sir Arthur will skin my hide for letting you do this."

"Nay, he will not. He may skin my hide, but you will receive his gratitude. Not only did you help save the family, but you remained steadfastly by my side to protect me." She stroked Breeze's neck. "And if it comes to that, I shall take full blame. My father will have no trouble believing as much."

Tom grunted. He tapped his fingers against his thigh.

"Besides," Beatrice said, "if we go back now, there will be a huge furor. My mother will hear of it, for certain, and you know she is not to be worried."

"Have you not thought this start of yours may well scare her half to death?"

Beatrice's stomach tightened. She'd steadfastly avoided thinking what would happen if Lady Mary discovered where she'd gone. Beatrice shoved the concern aside. When she brought her father home, her mother would improve. "Nobody will tell her. I stressed that in my message to Faye. Mother is not to be caused any undue worry."

She trotted forward.

Tom stayed.

Beatrice halted Breeze and turned. "Come along."

He was at his neck again. "Beatrice, we should turn back."

Why had she ever thought to involve him? He was ruining everything.

"I am not turning back, Tom. I will find Garrett and he will lead me to London. You"—she glared over her shoulder—"can do as you please. But if you betray me, I will never, ever, ever forgive you. Now, run along, Tom." She flung one hand toward Anglesea. "Run back to your mother and carry tales with you. Perhaps she will let you hide beneath her skirts."

"That is not fair."

Beatrice kept her eyes on the bright moonlight showing the path. Her decision was made. Beatrice the Brave wouldn't be craven and hide when duty called.

"And that is another thing bothering me about this," Tom

called after her. "Who is this Garrett? I know no one by that name."

Beatrice let Breeze pick her way down the path. The soil beneath the horse's hooves was sandy and their pace slowed. She was done with Tom and his questions. She would find Garrett. Her heart gave a happy thump. He would be surprised to see her. Her own boldness thrilled her. How would Garrett react? Would he try to steal a kiss?

Tom's cursing interrupted her fantasy as he lumbered along in her wake.

There would be no kissing with Tom lurking about and muttering his disapproval.

# *Chapter Eight*

"Garrett."

Her voice woke him instantly.

"Garrett," Beatrice called louder this time.

Beside him on the floor, Gil stirred. Lilly was entertaining tonight, and Gil had crept into his hut shortly after dark. Garrett put his hand on Gil's shoulder to hush him.

Gil stilled.

Beatrice called again, growing more insistent.

"Jesu." Beatrice stood right outside his hut. He shook Gil hard enough to wake him.

Gil opened his eyes and grinned at Garrett. "Are we going to eat?"

"Nay, Gil. You need to go home." Garrett tugged the boy to his feet.

Gil blinked at him. "But there will be men there, and—"

"They will be gone by now," he said, praying he was right. He let the boy stay with him because he remembered well lying in the dark, listening, while men had rutted on his mother. No boy should have to hear that.

"Garrett, are you in there?" Beatrice rattled the latch.

Garrett tugged Gil's discarded tunic over his head and hunted for his boots. "Do not come in. I am not decent."

The latch rattling stopped.

"Oh?" Beatrice squeaked from the other side of the door.

He imagined her cheeks going pink.

Gil stood there, hair tousled, staring at him.

"You must go, Gil." Garrett located the boots and handed them to Gil.

"Why? And who is at the door?" Gil rubbed his eyes and peered at the door.

"Never you mind." Garrett gave him a gentle push. "Go now and mind your step in the dark."

Gil sighed and tugged on one boot. "I do not like the men."

"I know, lad." Garrett kneeled and put Gil's other boot on.

Hope kindled on Gil's face. "Then I must stay."

"Nay, lad." Garrett had no idea what Beatrice was doing outside his door in the middle of the night, but if anybody discovered her his entire plan might be over. "Another night."

Gil's face dropped, and he hung his head. "I shall hide, and your visitor will not see me. I am good at hiding."

Garrett's ached for the lad. "I'm sorry, Gil. Come another time, and we will go fishing."

"Really?"

"I swear it." And Garrett would make good on his promise. He steered Gil to the rear of his hut.

One of the wallboards was loose, and it came away instantly in his hands. He'd fix it in the morning. "Go straight home." He grabbed a blanket and wrapped it about Gil's shoulders. "And keep that about you. There is still a chill from the ocean."

"What about you?" Gil tried to hand the blanket back. "You will get cold if I take your blanket."

"I do not feel the cold." Garrett smiled to reassure him. "The heat from Lyman's forge sits in my bones."

Gil giggled and clasped the blanket.

"Garrett? Is there someone with you in there?" Beatrice sounded impatient.

"Who would be here?" he called back.

Stopping halfway through the boards, Gil cocked his head. "I know that voice."

"Nay, you do not." He nudged Gil toward the gap in the boards.

Nodding, Gil said, "Aye, I do. I have heard it afore."

Garrett drew a careful breath. Gil was but a lad, and one with a loose tongue. What Gil knew, Lilly knew, and she would waste no time in spreading it about the village that Lady Beatrice had visited Garrett in the depth of the night. News from the village would travel to the castle, and then all his efforts would be wasted.

"Garrett," Beatrice called. "I must speak with you. It is a matter of utmost urgency."

"It sounds like Lady—"

"It sounds like nobody." Garrett put his hand on the top of Gil's head and guided him through the opening. "Straight home."

"Let me find my clothes, sweeting," he called to Beatrice. "Unless you would prefer—"

"Nay." Beatrice giggled.

He picked up his tunic. Then dropped it. Let Lady Beatrice get an eyeful of what she came here for. His rod twitched at the thought. He wouldn't have thought her this bold, but the threat of him leaving must have played on her mind. Exactly as he intended.

"Oh, hello, Gil," Beatrice said.

Garrett's heart gave a great jump. He bolted the two steps to the door and wrenched it open.

Beatrice spun around. Her hair was bound in a long braid. Moonlight played lovingly over the delicate lines of her face. Her gaze dropped almost immediately to his bare chest and widened.

Behind her, Gil stared open-mouthed.

Garrett made a shooing motion at the boy.

"Good evening, Lady Beatrice." Gil attempted a clumsy bow,

ruined by his attempt to gaze at her adoringly. "The boys shall not believe it when I tell them I saw you."

Beatrice started and her shoulders tensed. "Do not do that." Movement played along her long throat as she swallowed. "Gil, is it?"

Gil lit up like a taper as he breathed. "Aye."

"There is no need to mention that you saw me here. I came to...um...ask Garrett something?" She fidgeted with the edges of her cloak.

Gil drooped. "I should not mention seeing you?"

"Nay." Beatrice cleared her throat and made a show of looking about her. "Indeed, it will be our secret, young master Gil."

"Our secret?" Gil breathed, his eyes shining. "I am good at keeping secrets."

Garrett wagered the lad was at that.

"Then, will you keep mine?"

At Gil's age, he would have been struck as dumb with worship at the idea of a secret betwixt himself and Lady Beatrice.

Gil puffed his chest. "I will keep your secret, my lady."

"I am honored, Gil." She touched the boy's cheek, her face gentle and lovely.

Garrett cleared his throat. "Run along, lad."

"Aye." Gil took a moment to stare at Beatrice before turning back to Garrett. "And you will not forget about the fishing."

"Did I not swear it?" Not so struck in worship that he forgot Garrett's promise to him.

"You did." Gil turned to go, and then stopped and came back. "I mean no offence, my lady, but you should not be out alone so late. Sir Henry would not like it."

"But we will not tell him." Beatrice put a finger to her lips. "It is our secret, remember?" She squared her shoulders. "Besides, it was Sir Henry who sent me to speak with Garrett."

Garrett winced and prayed her last lie did not open a barrage of questions.

"But—"

"Home, Gil." Garrett put some heft in his tone. "And do not forget you are sworn to keep a lady's secret."

Nodding, Gil turned and vanished into the night.

Garrett breathed. That had been too damned close. When he turned to Beatrice though, his smile was firmly in place. "Hello, sweeting. Somehow, I do not think your brother sent you to speak to me."

* * *

Beatrice's knees nearly buckled, and she grabbed at the door frame for support. Her palm touched warm skin. She jerked her hand back, but the imprint of his chest still tingled along her arm.

"I thought I would die when I saw the boy here." Her heart was still running like a startled rabbit. "I thought nobody was about."

"Which brings us to what you are doing here?" Garrett's hair was rumpled and his chin shadowed with growth. She'd only seen him clean-shaven, not sporting a beard like many other men. He was near naked, save for a small pouch about his neck, alone with her in the midst of the night. Mere steps from where he slept.

Her mouth went dry and she licked her lips.

"Beatrice?" A small smile played across his mouth. His eyes gleamed down at her in a way that made her stomach clench. Wicked, wonderful smile.

"I need you."

Garrett's mouth softened, and the heat in his eyes reached out as sure as a touch.

She knew that look. Her blood warmed in response.

"Sweeting." He slid his hands beneath her cloak and caged her hips. Firmly, he tugged her toward him.

Beatrice wanted him to pull her into the dim hut behind them. Fortunately, she remembered Tom waiting for her outside the village. She didn't think Tom could see, but she didn't want to take a chance. She pulled away from Garrett. "I need your help."

Garrett stopped but kept his hands on her, warming her right through her clothing. "Anything for you." A small frown creased his brows. He slipped his hands beneath the hem of her tunic.

Beatrice had trouble remembering why she'd come.

"My family." Her breath grew short. If she rose onto her toes, she could reach his mouth. She could forget everything under the enchantment of his kiss.

"Your family?" His lips twitched as if he read her every thought. He traced the top of her braies, brushing the bare skin of her waist.

"Aye." Beatrice reached for her scattered thoughts and rounded them up. The future of her family depended on her. Beatrice the Brave would remain steadfast in her quest, even if she wanted to trace the sulky fullness of his bottom lip with her tongue. "There is trouble. I need help."

His frown deepened. He roamed further, slipped his hands from beneath her tunic and tugged apart the sides of her cloak. He dropped his hands.

Beatrice shivered in the sudden chill.

"What are you about, Beatrice? And dressed like that." His jaw hardened.

Beatrice struggled to put the words in the right order. "I need to go to London. Tonight. I need to get my father. You could take me."

"Stop." He propped his elbow against the lintel. Dark hair tangled beneath his arm. It seemed such an intimate detail.

A hot shiver spread over her.

"Start again." Muscle rippled across his chest and belly. A trail of hair disappeared beneath the low-slung band of his chausses.

Beatrice drew a shuddering breath. She was making a mess of this, but it was hard to think when he stood there virtually unclothed. "My sister came to the castle yesterday."

"Your sister?"

The door creaked, and she jumped. Anybody could be about. "Aye, Faye, she is escaping from her husband."

Garrett raised a brow.

"Calder is conspiring with the king to bring charges against my father. They say he has stolen money, but it is not true." Beatrice reached for him, to impress on him the truth of her words. Her hands touched bare chest.

His muscle jumped beneath her palm.

She lost track of her purpose for a fascinated moment.

"Beatrice?"

"Aye." Her story. She had come to get Garrett's help. "My father would never steal from the king. I know he would not. But my father is in London." His skin was warm and firm, like iron sheathed in silk. Part of her wanted to linger there and let her fingers explore.

"And?"

"And Faye's husband will attack Anglesea because Henry does not have enough men."

"What does this have to do with you being here?" His long fingers fastened about the strange, little pouch at his neck.

"My mother is ill, and she must not be worried by any of this. Godfrey says the country needs my father. But we need him too, Garret. Henry will do nothing. So I need to get to my father and tell him what has happened, before it is too late."

"Beatrice, this is not making any sense." Garrett clasped her hands and frowned. "I do not understand it all."

She hadn't prepared for Garrett's refusal. He'd always said he'd do anything for her. However, if Garrett refused to take her, it would all be for naught. From the far side of the forge, a voice rose in question, another answered. She best make haste before some well-meaning soul, besides Gil, discovered her and sent her home. "I heard my uncle and my brother, Henry, talking with my sister. She has come to Anglesea with her boys because her husband is in league with the king. They are accusing my father of having used his position as sheriff to steal money from the king.

"Did he?" His finger tightened on the pouch.

"Of course not. He would never do such a thing."

"Of course he wouldn't." Was that anger in Garrett's voice? Beatrice peered into his face.

Garrett straightened and shoved his hands into his rope belt. "So, Calder?"

"Aye." She must have imagined it. "Calder used to be a good husband, but Faye says he has changed. He threatened to take her children away from her. So she came to Anglesea. To warn us and to keep her boys safe. But now that she is there, Henry says Calder has the perfect excuse to lay siege. The king will support Calder, because he fears my father."

"The king fears your father?" His lip curled.

There was the anger again, in the sharpness of his tone and the cold, dark of his eyes. "Garrett?"

"Beatrice, the king."

"Indeed." The wind carried the stench of burnt metal from the forge. The trees rustled, startling her. "My father has become too powerful, and the other barons listen to him. Unless we pay or my father answers the charges, we could lose everything. Everything, Garrett." She leaned forward to stress her point. "And my mother is ill. We do not want her bothered with any of this. Henry will not go to London because my father is needed there, but I think he is needed here more. So, that is why I must go. Only, I do not know the way to London. But you do, which is when I thought of you."

"Does your family know what you plan?"

"Nay." Beatrice shook her head so hard her braid knocked against her back. "If anyone knew, they would try to stop me."

* * *

Garrett almost laughed aloud. He couldn't have dreamed up such an ideal situation had he tried. The sod from last night had known this would happen. Garrett had made up his mind no force on earth would get him to conspire with the whoreson. But this. He had her.

Sir Arthur could rot for all he cared. And he would. The justice of it flowed hot and sweet through him. Arthur rendered nothing, with no castle and no fortune. Betrayed by the king whom he'd served so well. His family ruined. Let noble, bloody Sir Arthur see how quickly the other barons turned their backs on one in trouble. He fingered the pouch about his neck. He would see his mother avenged.

Beatrice stared at him, her eyes large and imploring.

Garrett wanted to throw back his head and crow his triumph to the moon. His blood surged. It was pitifully easy. "Beatrice." He knew better than to mistake her innocence for stupidity. "London is a long way away. And it is a dangerous journey. You cannot ask me to knowingly put you in harm's way. I would die first."

"I know." She fidgeted, shifting her weight. "But you are the only one who can help us...me."

"What if your brother comes after you?" He pretended to give the matter grave thought. "He would run me through for being within a hair of you."

"We can travel fast," she assured him. "No one will discover I am gone until after the keep breaks its fast. By that time, we can have put a lot of distance between them and us."

He let the silence draw out long and tense between them.

A dog barked, and she jumped. "I am not sure Henry will stop me even if he knew. My father left him with only enough men for defense. Henry cannot risk being short of swords if Calder should come, and he is sure Calder will come."

He heaved a sigh and let her ferment.

"Please, Garrett." She moved closer to him. "There is nobody else to whom I can turn."

"You ask much, sweeting."

"I know." She pressed her hands against his chest.

*Lower. Move your hands lower.* His skin prickled beneath her hand.

"What would you have of me in return?" she whispered.

"Nothing," he declared valiantly. He almost made his gut churn with his performance. "You need only ask."

"Oh, Garrett." Moisture glistened in the depths of her huge eyes.

A heaping of gratitude was all he needed to serve her up to him. "Beatrice"—he stroked her cheek—"you know I can deny you nothing."

"You will do it?"

"I will do it."

She released a long breath. Her smile near blinded him. "Thank you, Garrett. You will not regret this."

Nay. Garrett turned to dress. He would not regret having her to himself with no family to intervene one jot.

"Make haste," Beatrice said. "I will meet you at the edge of the village."

Garrett grabbed what he would need and hurried to meet Beatrice. Lyman would be short-handed on the morrow, but he would find someone else to fill Garrett's place. By the time the journey to London was done, Garrett would have no need to return to Anglesea.

A tall form emerged from the dark.

Garrett stilled. The cur was back. He balanced on the balls of his feet. He wouldn't find it as easy to take Garrett this time. People had mocked him when he wanted to train as a knight, but there were other ways of fighting. Garrett had made it his business to be good at those.

"At last." Beatrice waved Garrett forward. "I want to be far away from Anglesea before first light."

The big brute with Beatrice was not from last night. "Who is he?"

"Tom." Beatrice dropped her head. "He is helping me. As you are."

She'd lied to him. Garrett balled his fists by his sides. Tom was tall, but Garrett liked his chances against him. Garrett felt the weight of the other man's stare. He lifted a brow in challenge.

Tom tensed.

"What are you two doing?" Beatrice hurried between them. "Did you not hear me? We need to cover a large distance before it is discovered we are gone."

"You forgot to mention your friend."

"Did I?"

"You know you did."

"Aye, well—" She dragged in a quick breath, ready to come up with more lies and half-truths.

"If he goes, I go," Tom spoke to Beatrice, but glared at Garrett.

"Fine," Garrett said. "Go without me."

"Nay." Beatrice whirled toward him. "We cannot go without you. Tom does not know the way."

"What is he doing here, then?"

"Protecting Beatrice." Tom locked eyes with him. Not as stupid as he looked.

"I can protect Beatrice."

Tom stepped toward him, his chest squared, arms braced. "Who will protect her from—"

"There is no time for this." Beatrice shoved at Tom's chest. "You can both protect me. I will be doubly safe."

Garrett weighed his options. A heaven-sent opportunity on the one hand, a zealous boy on the other. The boy would be trouble. Garrett would lay his life on it. But at the first sign of an approaching army, Beatrice would be locked up in Anglesea and out of his reach. He motioned Beatrice to precede him. "After you, my lady."

"Right." Beatrice clapped her hands. "Let us go before we are found here in the morning, still arguing amongst ourselves. Come along."

Garrett grit his teeth. He would rid her of her habit of leading him around like a trained bear.

Beatrice approached a leggy, chestnut mare with a white blaze on her nose. "Mount up."

Garrett froze. A hulking brute stood beside two other horses.

One leg was cocked and its head hung, as if it might expire from boredom at any moment.

Beatrice lithely pulled herself onto her mount.

"Ah, Beatrice." He grabbed hold of his belt and twisted. "I think it would be better if we went by foot."

Her soft laughter floated toward him. "Why should we walk, when we can ride?"

"Do you not ride?" Tom looked down on him from atop a large horse, more plow beast than anything else.

"I ride." He would be damned before he admitted his weakness before these two. "Only, I have not had much opportunity to do so."

"Oh." Beatrice sounded genuinely distressed. "I did not think." She swung her leg over the saddle, and slipped to the ground.

Garrett's chest burned as she walked toward him. He should know how to ride. He should have his own horse. It was his birthright. His mother had said so since he was old enough to understand. But serfs couldn't afford horses, could they?

He owed Sir Arthur for this, as well. When he'd approached his local baron for sponsorship, the man had seemed amenable. Garrett was, bastard or not, the son of a knight. Until Sir Arthur poured his poison in the man's ear. Then, he'd become a joke to them.

"I beg your pardon, Garrett." Beatrice touched his arm.

A fine tremor racked him as he fought the urge to shake her off.

"I have been most thoughtless," she said. "Tom, you must ride Badger. You are more accustomed to riding, and you know him. Let Garrett take Parsley."

Parsley? It shook Garrett out of his bitterness. *Parsley?*

Tom snorted. The smug dog crossed his arms over his saddle and smirked down at Garrett.

Garrett bunched his fists. He wanted to smash Tom's face. "Nay." Garrett would rot in hell before he had them take pity on him and put him on a horse called Parsley. "This one will suit me well."

Beatrice's teeth flashed as she smiled at him. "His name is Badger." She stroked her hand down the horse's forelock. "And he is a sweet boy. Aren't you?"

Garrett didn't mind horses. He'd shooed his fair share of them, but he'd never ridden in his life.

Beatrice remounted.

Garrett studied how it was done. He would hack off his arm before he let either of them know he couldn't ride. He approached the horse.

It stared down its long nose at him.

"Hello, Badger." He put one foot in the stirrup.

Badger shifted away.

Garrett was forced to hop after it.

Badger shook his head and whickered softly, as if the bloody thing was chuckling at him.

Beatrice and the boy were looking at him. They were laughing at him.

Humiliation crawled up his neck and lifted his hackles. He hopped closer to the sodding horse.

Badger shifted again. Slightly farther away this time.

Garrett yanked his foot from the stirrup to keep from falling on his face.

"Badger is a bit tricky," Beatrice said. "Let Tom take him." The sympathy in her voice exacerbated his shame.

"Here, take Parsley." Tom dismounted.

"Nay." Garrett stomped after Badger.

The overgrown donkey shook his head and trotted away.

Right toward Tom, who grabbed Badger's reins.

The horse turned obediently toward him.

"I will ride Badger."

Garrett's words fell on deaf ears as Tom swung his leg over Badger's back. The hell horse stood still as a post for the other man to mount.

"Ride Parsley." Tom's eyes glittered down at Garrett. "We do not have all night."

Garrett stalked toward Parsley. Tom would pay for the insult. And as for Badger? He glared at the horse. The first, the very first opportunity he got, the bloody horse was dog meat.

*Chapter Nine*

Garrett's ass ached, and his balls were bruised black and blue. All through the night and, barring a short rest to break their fast and water the horses, all day, he'd sat on this bloody horse. Beatrice stayed slightly in front of him as they went east.

The road stayed empty as it followed the sheer drop of the cliffs to the ocean below.

He envied Beatrice's absolute ease in the saddle. He also admired the way her shoulders tapered to a waist so tiny he could span it with his hands, before flaring to the sweet curve of her hips and ass. It was all that kept him from obsessing about the pain in his own saddle.

Soon, he'd be able to explore with more than his eyes. The prickle of sensation at his nape warned him Tom had his eyes on him again. He was a leery one, Tom. Like a bad-tempered weasel, he watched Garrett constantly. Whatever he said, Tom listened keenly, narrowing his eyes as if assessing every word.

"Look." Beatrice turned her head to appeal to him. Her cheeks were flushed with enjoyment. "Do you see that tree? I swear I have never seen one quite that size. Have you?"

It looked much like any of the countless trees they'd passed since the sun had risen. "The tree is large."

"See how the branches are perfect for climbing?" Beatrice clasped a hand to her throat, enraptured by a blasted tree.

Garrett wanted to shake his head.

Beatrice talked, almost constantly. He'd not noticed that about her before. Mayhap because he'd kept her mouth busy when she was with him. Everything she saw required commentary. Every new sight became a thing of wonder that needed to be chattered about at great length. Were the hills not the most wondrous green? Had he or Tom ever seen a sky so blue or as endless? What was that bird? Was that a rare blossom?

Tom had the knack of knowing which of her pronouncements required a reply and when Beatrice was happy to burble on to herself. Garrett hadn't mastered Tom's trick yet. Every time she turned to him, her face alight with her new discovery, he couldn't stop his response. His replies would earn him a beaming smile before she was off again.

They kept a tough pace, and Garrett struggled to keep up. It was getting harder to hide his ineptitude as the miles wore on.

Beatrice, however, thrived. Her big blue eyes sparkled like gems, her cheeks rosy with excitement. It caused an odd twinge in his chest. Or the twinge could be a result of not chewing his bread properly when they'd stopped to eat. Except it wasn't an unpleasant sensation. It was like the sun on your back, warm and comforting.

She turned to talk to Tom.

Those two were thick as pease pottage. There was the sort of ease between them that came of years of knowing each other. It irked him. The couple didn't mean to exclude him, but there were times when neither of them would complete a thought before the other took it up. Not that Tom said much. He left the speaking to Beatrice, which suited the lady perfectly.

He'd stopped sulking around the time he noticed Tom was no

more adept in the saddle than he. From the pained grimace on the boy's face, Garrett guessed Tom ached almost as badly as him. It cheered him immeasurably. It also proved impossible to hold onto his anger in the face of Beatrice's relentless enthusiasm.

She turned and smiled at him.

He forgot the pain. His mouth tilted up in answer. She had one of those smiles. It invited you to join in. The moment was over in a blink, and she turned away. It was the strangest thing. He hadn't thought her beautiful when he first engineered their meeting. Not plain, by any means, but her face was too strong and the lines too definite for typical beauty. As the days had passed and their meetings grew more numerous, however, he started to notice other things. Her smile, for instance. Beatrice smiled with her entire being. It lit her from within. Her eyes, too, drew him in. They changed constantly. It was like watching the swiftly flowing current through a stream. Her eyes reflected the ceaseless ebb and flow of her thoughts.

He wanted to catch up to her and Tom, but the evil-tempered thing he rode didn't respond to his urgings. It had taken him hours to recover from his humiliation over the horse. It wasn't sensible, his anger. He understood, but it mattered not a whit.

*You should have been fostered and trained as a knight.* His anger always sounded like his mother. As a lad, he'd stood and watched the knights ride by. Like all boys, his heart had swelled with dreams. Impossible dreams, as he'd discovered. His mother was unable to let it lie, either. Always, she insisted he was robbed of what was his by birth.

Garrett grunted. His by birth? What a jest. His father was a traitor, his mother a whore. All that was his by birth was betrayal and swiving.

"Did you say something?" Beatrice turned around once more.

Tom snorted.

"Nay." He forced a charming smile. "I was merely enjoying the view."

"Oh." Beatrice took a moment to catch his meaning. She flushed bright pink. "Oh." She grinned.

Tom muttered and shook his head.

Garrett met the boy's hostile stare. He held their locked gaze until Tom looked away. He truly hoped he wasn't going to have to do something about the overgrown clod. Even he paused at the notion of having to make Tom vanish.

"Should we stop for the night?" he called.

"In a short while." Beatrice waved her arm through the air. "It is a fine day for riding, and we are making excellent time. We should press on until dark. Do you not agree?"

"As long as you are not too fatigued." Garrett swallowed some very nasty words. Words he would wager neither Beatrice nor Tom had heard in their lives.

"You are sweet to be concerned for me." A small dimple danced in her right cheek. It appeared only when she smiled. "But I am much heartier than you would think."

Garrett gave her a slow smile and filled it with sensual promise.

It brought instant color to her cheeks. The dimple appeared again.

*Jesu*, it was an effort to be charming all the time. At least with women such as Lilly, one didn't have to exert oneself. But the seduction of a gently reared virgin was an exercise of an entirely different kind. Only the end result was the same. Garrett's eyes strayed over Beatrice's luscious lines.

"I thought London was more to the North?" Tom interrupted his viewing.

"It is," Garrett replied. Tom was boy enough not to toss a knave, like himself, into the nearest hedgerow and yet, man enough to recognize he should. "But if you can make the road bend in that direction, we would all be grateful."

And that should've been the end of it.

Except Beatrice cocked her head, a certain sign she was thinking. She stopped suddenly, and Garrett's horse almost plowed into the back of hers.

"Perhaps we should go across country?" She indicated the landscape to their left. This close to the sea it was still a series of gently undulated dips and rises; farther on it would get more wooded and rugged.

His seat throbbed in sympathy.

"I do not think we should." Tom rescued him.

Beatrice thrust her chin out. "It will save all sorts of time."

"Aye," Tom said. "If we do not get lost, and if we do not run across brigands or worse."

"Brigands or worse, Tom?" Beatrice laughed.

Garrett liked the husky sound.

"What could be worse than brigands?" she asked.

"Cutthroats." Tom reddened. "Murderers, desperate characters, villains…"

"I get your point, Tom. And we will stay upon this road until it leads us where we want to go. Only"—she frowned at him and Tom—"could we not go a bit farther. I need to get to my father."

"We will need to rest." Tom reined in. "And we should not push the horses. They need to carry us a long way."

Beatrice stroked her horse's neck.

Garrett admired the lines of the horse Beatrice rode. Sleek and powerful, the mare seemed to read her rider's mind. Garrett still couldn't see how Beatrice controlled the horse's movements.

Parsley stumbled over a small stone in the road, jarring his aching bits. The stupid animal needed a more permanent sort of rest.

"We will stop soon." Beatrice moved off down the road.

Garrett cursed and trundled along behind.

Shortly after sunset, they stumbled upon a large encampment of some twenty people. The group was meanly dressed with heavily laden carts.

Tom grumbled suspiciously.

For once, Garrett was inclined to agree with him.

Beatrice would not be dissuaded. She agreed to let Tom hold her purse for the night, but there was safety in numbers, she insisted.

She had a point and Garrett gave in, but he would stand watch through the night. These were not the times to be too trustful of strangers.

*Chapter Ten*

The smell of roasting meat made Beatrice's stomach rumble appreciatively. Voices murmuring over the fire were reassuring. Around their camp, the forest pressed closer. Tree limbs, twisted into ghostly shapes by the shadows, rose against the night sky. The moon hovered above it all, flirting in and out of fickle clouds. It was the first time she'd spent a night outside of the keep. The night pressed against the borders of their tiny camp.

Garrett sat with his back against a tree, apart from the group. The starkly handsome lines of his face were set severely. She'd never seen him look so serious. Despite everything they'd shared, they were nearly strangers. She wanted to unravel the mystery of him, strand by precious strand. Like why he could look so grave one minute and the next, like his mind was full of naughty thoughts. And the pouch about his neck, the one he touched often. What was in it, and what did it mean to him?

Tom didn't like him. He didn't say anything, but Tom was easy to read. He watched Garrett as if he expected the other man to bite.

Garrett rose to the challenge, every time.

It made her uneasy, the tension between them. That aside, she was enjoying her adventure. Garrett said they would reach London before week's end. There would be time for her father to ride hard for home. Being beyond the castle walls was also liberating. There was no lurking voice of experience to click their tongue at her and correct her behavior.

Garrett didn't care if she behaved like a lady. As if sensing her gaze, he looked up to where she sat with some of the women on the far side of the fire. Their eyes met. Awareness tingled along her skin.

A slow, hot smile spread from his eyes to his full mouth.

A hot flush crept over her cheeks.

"Is he your man?" one of the women asked. Thank the Lord for the faint light cast by the cook fire. Her cheeks must be red.

"Nay." Was Garrett her man? She wasn't sure. He touched her like he might be.

Cackling, a woman elbowed her. The woman's face was thin and streaked with dirt, as if they'd been traveling for some time. Her age was hard to gauge. Her features were drawn, but she moved as if she were younger. "I would watch myself." The nudger went again with her pointy elbows. "Or one of us might take that sort of trouble off your hands."

The other women chuckled with her, and Beatrice grit her teeth. Not bloody likely.

Several women eyed Garrett. A couple pairs of eyes lingered over Tom. It was Tom, for the love of God. She didn't see the reason for their interest.

"How did you manage to get two lads at your side?" another woman asked. "Most of us are struggling to find half a one."

It was true. The males in the group of travelers were older or children. No men of the ages between.

"Where are your men?"

A woman with graying hair checked the rabbits spitted over the fire.

The travelers didn't have much food. Garrett had been lucky

setting his traps. Tom had added some of their supplies to a communal meal.

"Dead," said the woman. "Dead or gone to war, which is as good as dead."

There was no war that she knew of. Sir Arthur had spoken of a battle somewhere in France called Bouvines, but Beatrice hadn't paid much attention. She wished she had. It had certainly made her father furious. Godfrey had also spoken of it the night she'd overheard their conversation. "Is the war not over?"

"Bloody kings and their wars." An older woman folded twig thin arms across her rough wool tunic. "There is no end to the wars. Richard and his crusades marching off to fight the bloody infidel when he should have stayed home and taken care of his own people. Might have lived longer and we would not have this whoreson on the throne."

Beatrice's mouth dropped open in shock. The woman spoke of their king. Not at his angriest would her father speak thus. "But Richard carried the word of our Lord to the heathen."

Hard faces with weary eyes stared at her, and she shut her mouth. She must have erred in some way.

"Try feeding that to a starving child," the thin woman said.

It was treason to speak thus. Yet nobody around this fire thought it strange. At home, folk would express their anger, but it was done quietly, as if it shouldn't be heard.

"Quiet down now, Mother." A younger woman handed the older woman a heel of bread. "Does no good to be getting yourself bent out of shape. For all he is a bad one, King John, you will only knot your stomach, and there is no reason when we have bread today."

Beatrice swallowed her questions. She didn't want to appear stupid or ignorant. She wanted to know, though. Tom wouldn't have the answers. Garrett. He would know. Garrett knew everything about the world.

She excused herself and got to her feet. Stepping carefully, she wove through the clusters of people.

Garrett watched her approach. His gaze heated, lingering on her face and drifting over her body.

When he looked at her thus, it went to her head, like the time she'd drank too much wine at Christmas. Only, this headiness didn't make her want to laugh at everything.

"Good evening, my lady." He sketched her a mock bow.

Beatrice looked down at her boy's chausses and laughed. My lady, she was not.

With a gentle tug, he brought her to sit beside him. A nightjar rattled from the forest, clear in the still night. Light from the fires cast deep shadows over his face.

She basked in his fixed regard, like she was the only woman in his world. She prayed it was true, because he was the only man in hers.

"What troubles you?" He traced the skin between her eyes with his finger. "When you are worrying something in your mind, you always frown so."

He knew her well enough to read her expressions. It warmed every part of her.

"May I ask you something?" Beatrice shivered beneath the light touch.

"You may ask me anything, sweeting." He curled his fingers around hers.

She hoped he meant that. "Why does everyone hate King John?"

He straightened, his chin dropping to his chest. "What?" All traces of the lover left his face.

The rapid change made her uneasy, adrift. Like she sat beside a total stranger.

A heartbeat later, a sensuous smile transformed his face.

It warmed the slight chill inside her.

"Sweeting." He raised her fingers to his lips, his mouth hot against her knuckles. "Let us not talk of King John on a night like this."

Pleasure slid across her skin as she took her hand back.

The nightjar fell silent, and the soft pop of the wood fire drifted over. The night wrapped around them.

"This is a night for more important things." He edged closer, his thigh solid and strong against hers.

"What things?" She held her breath, waiting. Would he kiss her? She desperately wanted to be kissed.

A woman laughed.

She started. They weren't alone. Best to return to her purpose in seeking him out. Tom mightn't be able to see them, but from the cook fire, the women would have a clear view of her and Garrett.

Beatrice eased her leg away. "I want to know why the women here are angry with the king. I always thought the people loved their king. He is ordained by God, after all."

Garrett's lip twisted. "That is what the king wants you to believe." He took her hand. "Let us talk of something else. Or not talk at all."

It was difficult to stick to her purpose when he played lightly with her fingers. He raised them one by one to his mouth.

She disengaged her fingers. "I know, in part, why my father has gone to war with him. But why do they hate King John?"

"Do not concern yourself." He flicked her chin with a finger. "In the morning, this lot will be gone and you will not have to think of them again."

Roger might do something like that. She didn't like it when her brother did it either. "Will you not tell me?"

"Why do you ask?"

Always answering a question with a question. Could she not just get a straight answer? From anyone. She wasn't a child. "Because nobody ever tells me anything. These women are bitter and angry. I want to know why. I want to understand why they are so thin." She had hundreds of questions. Each one birthed another. "Why do they travel? Should they not be settled in a village or farming? Why do—"

"Enough." He placed a finger across her lips.

"I thought, at least, I could trust you to tell me the truth," Beatrice said.

He leaned farther away and frowned.

"Forgive me." She'd spoken too hotly and made him angry. "I did not mean to vex you. I only wanted to understand. I ask too many questions anyway." She caught his hand. "We will talk of something else."

"Nay." Garrett glanced at where their hands joined and placed them on his thigh. "I shall tell you." He shook his head slowly and smiled.

"What?" She blushed, shy under his fixed regard.

The look vanished as if it had never been there. "Their men have all gone to war or been chased off their land as outlaws." His jaw hardened. "Those who remain are forced to pay taxes they cannot afford. There is no food and no money to buy more. People do not understand much other than their children are starving, and the king demands more taxes from them every day." He gestured to the cook fire. "These women are looking for a better place. Somewhere to settle where the land is rich enough to support them and the liege lord merciful."

"Will they find it?"

"Nay."

The older one, the angry one, handed out food. She started with the youngsters before moving to the adults. She took a meager portion for herself. Beatrice wished she had more to give them. "What will they do?"

Garrett gave a short bark of laughter. "They will do, my lady Beatrice," he drawled her title, making a mockery of it, and Beatrice flinched, "as the poor have always done. They will fight to survive. Some of them will lose that fight. Despite it all, however, these piteous souls will find a way to laugh and cry their way through it."

"My father always tells Roger a baron must care for those in his charge, as he would care for his own blood," Beatrice said.

"Does he now?" His body tensed, and he dropped her hand as if it were on fire.

She'd erred again. Her heart skipped a beat or two. How?

Garret's anger was clear in the tightening of his jaw. He rose and slipped into the darkness of the night.

The unfriendly dark closed in around her.

"A lover's quarrel?" Tom's voice startled her.

Beatrice clambered to her feet. Should she follow Garrett? Nay, men were best left to cool their anger in peace. That's what Nurse said. She glanced back, but Garrett was gone.

She walked with Tom back to the fire. The women spoke quietly amongst themselves. Their children were spread out beneath their blankets, lying like small cocoons a safe distance from the blaze. It hardly seemed fair that she had so much. She'd never questioned the appearance of food on the table or clothes to wear. These women's clothing hung by threads and many of them were barefoot.

Her father had gone to London to stop this. Her heart swelled with pride. These women mightn't know it, but Sir Arthur of Anglesea stood for them. Her mission was doubly important. There were people like this throughout the land. England needed men like Sir Arthur. Good men, who would speak against injustice. She understood, now, what Godfrey had meant when he'd said the kingdom needed her father. As soon as he'd put things at Anglesea to rights, Sir Arthur must return to his noble cause.

It didn't help these women this night, though. Beatrice approached the angry one.

* * *

Garrett had barely restrained himself when she spoke of her father, her eyes glowing. The stupid girl had no idea what her father was capable of. She spoke of the sod as if he were a shining, gleaming hero. His fingers tightened about the pouch.

She walked to one of the old crones by the fire.

Sweet Jesu. He couldn't conceive of a life as sheltered as hers, a life without want or need. Everything she desired, handed to her by her doting father.

He could tell her all about her father, the heroic Sir Arthur. He could speak of Sir Arthur's courage and valor as he'd tossed a woman and her young child out into the world with nothing but the clothes on their backs. How that woman had sold her body to feed herself and her young son. It had been justification enough for Sir Arthur that he and his mother were connected to his enemy. Aye, it took a rare merciful man to do such a thing. Let the goodly Sir Arthur taste of his, Garrett's, brand of mercy.

Garrett slipped deeper into the forest. Injustice clawed at his innards, demanding to be heard.

# Chapter Eleven

Garrett prepared the horses. Dawn would break in an hour or two. In the clearing, Tom gathered his belongings. Time to move on. Garrett tightened Parsley's girth.

Parsley groaned and stared at him balefully.

Across the banked fire from him, Beatrice stumbled out of her blankets and shivered in the predawn chill.

He had some work to do there. His anger of the night before had raised his companion's guards. Beatrice wasn't stupid, and Tom's eyes were keen.

The travelers had left early that morning, slipping away with barely a sound for such a large group. The ashes of the campfire were the only sign they'd shared this space with their small party.

Beatrice accepted some food from Tom and looked around. Her brow puckered before she located him. She slid her gaze away.

He read the uncertainty on her expressive face.

Garrett slapped Parsley on the rump. The huge gelding stumbled a few steps out of his way and shot him an aggrieved glance. "Good morning," he greeted Beatrice with a smile.

Relief chased across her face. She returned his smile without hesitation.

The girl had no instinct for preservation. It didn't occur to her not to return his greeting in kind.

She nibbled on a wedge of hard cheese. Her cheeks were lightly flushed.

It was almost too easy. Garrett put the bridle on Breeze. The mare stood at least sixteen hands. A large horse for a young lady, but Beatrice handled her effortlessly. The mare whickered and pressed her nose against his chest, blowing a moist gust of horsey breath on his tunic.

"How are the horses?" Beatrice stood just beyond his reach. She shifted her weight from one foot to the other.

Breeze swung her head toward her rider.

"Well rested." Garrett slipped the saddle over the mare's back. She stood dead still for him. Her eyes fixed on Beatrice.

From her pocket, Beatrice pulled an apple and held it to the horse.

"Hello, sweetheart." The horse's ears flickered as she chomped on the apple. "They will know I am gone by now." Beatrice dusted her hands against her tunic. The fabric pulled tight across the generous swell of her breasts.

Garrett could only imagine the furor at Anglesea when they discovered their youngest treasure missing. "Will they come after you?" A brother in hot pursuit wouldn't suit his plans at all.

Beatrice shrugged and rubbed her hand gently down Breeze's cheek. "I am not sure."

"Then we shall have to ride hard to lose them. I know a little-used way to London that could help us."

"You do?" She smiled at him as if he'd pulled the moon from the sky and handed it to her.

No veils or blinds with this one. Every thought she had, as she had it, right there on her face. She took everything he said as the truth. It irked him, especially as he was speaking out of the wrong side of his face. There was no other path to London. At least, not that he knew of. As he'd brooded through the night, it had occurred to him he needed to stretch their journey to London. He hadn't accounted for the horses or how much farther four legs could travel in one day. He'd also underestimated Beatrice's determination and how many hours she could spend in the saddle. The ache in his braies hadn't abated one bit from the day before.

"It might throw them off our path." He saddled Badger. The big gelding kept his snapping teeth in his nosebag.

Beatrice's tunic and chausses were rumpled. She appeared to be wearing half of the forest in her long braid. Yet her eyes were near dazzling and a pink flush brought color to her cheeks. A fine dusting of freckles littered the bridge of her nose.

"The fresh air becomes you." He meant it. She looked tousled and beautiful.

More color flooded her face. "You are a smooth-tongued liar." She laughed and touched her braided hair self-consciously.

It was such an innately feminine gesture it caught him there momentarily in its simple grace. "Never." He leaned his elbows on Badger's broad back. "You look like a girl who should be kissed."

"Indeed." She tucked her hands behind her back. Her lips were pursed as if she were picturing the kiss he wanted to give her.

Beatrice liked his touch and was too artless to conceal her reaction. She responded to him with an enthusiasm that made his task a pleasure.

Out of the corner of his eye, Garrett saw Tom had finished packing up their camp.

The man strode toward them. Tall and broad, he shouldered his pack and Beatrice's.

Tom may carp and whine at Beatrice, but the lad's heart was in the right place. He still didn't know what he was going to do about Tom. He'd have to find a way to lose her faithful watchdog.

"Ready?" As usual, Tom didn't waste words on him.

Garrett nodded and took Beatrice's gear from him.

Tom strode away to stow his own gear.

"He does not like me." He secured her pack to Breeze.

"He is always looking out for me. He is intimately acquainted with my ability to lead us both into trouble." Beatrice wrinkled her nose at him.

It was enchanting. The middle of his chest warmed. Garrett dropped his voice, low and intimate. "Am I trouble?"

She giggled and looked down at her feet.

"We could slip amongst the trees while he is busy." He moved around Breeze until he was close enough to whisper against her ear. Wildflowers, the scent clung to her hair. "And I could show you what sort of trouble I am."

"Hush." She tried to look stern but failed.

"As we did at Anglesea." His shaft stirred in his braies. He wouldn't mind a small side trip amongst the trees with Beatrice this morning. It was too long since he'd kissed her. Her skin was like buttermilk, smooth and creamy. He stroked her cheek.

"We cannot," she whispered breathily.

She wanted to.

He was hard enough to tent his braies. "Aye, we can." Garrett touched his lips to the curve of her ear. "The question is, will you, sweeting?"

"Beatrice." Tom brought him rudely back to the present.

He slipped behind Breeze, placing the mare between himself and Tom's sharp eyes.

Beatrice jerked and her face flushed with guilty color. She put some distance between them before turning to look at Tom. "Is there aught amiss?"

Garrett chuckled. Her mind was with his, somewhere amidst the trees.

* * *

Beatrice avoided Tom's gaze as he checked his pack before mounting.

Tom rifled through his pack, frowned, and dug some more. He looked up, his face a dull sort of angry red. "Those hags have robbed us. My purse is missing and it was right here." He held up the bag. "It was in a pouch, right here."

Garrett cursed softly.

"We must go after them." Tom swung into the saddle. "Most of them are too old to have gone far. We must ride them down and demand our coin."

"They left hours ago," Garrett said. "We could lose most of the day trying to find them."

"It matters not. Our money is stolen." Tom shook his pack like a dead rat. "It is despicable. After we shared our food with them and—"

"Nay, Tom." Beatrice was truly dreading what Tom would have to say when he found out the truth. For a craven moment, she almost lied, but she couldn't. Tom would hunt those poor women to the ends of the earth. "The women took nothing. I gave them the purse."

Tom's mouth dropped open.

Beatrice shifted and braced herself for a storm.

Eyes starting out of his head, Tom went rigid. "Say again."

Garrett merely watched, his elbows braced on Parsley's back.

"It was my money." And she'd done with it as she saw fit. "You were merely keeping it safe."

"You gave our money to those women?"

"They needed it, Tom." Beatrice moved closer to Breeze's reassuring bulk. "You saw how thin some of them were. And the children, Tom, how could you begrudge coin to those tiny, starving children?"

"You gave them our money?" Tom's jerked on the reins.

Badger tossed his head, snorted, and carried Tom into a nearby bush.

Tom cursed and fought his way clear of the grasping branches, arms flailing, his face alarmingly red.

"Aye." Beatrice winced as he tugged twigs out of his tunic. Inside she quaked like a pudding. "They were hungry."

"I am hungry." Tom flung greenery at the ground. "What coin will you use to feed us?"

"I have more. I did not give you all our coin to hold."

"How much?"

"Enough."

"How. Much." Tom's lips compressed into a tight line.

"Have done," Garrett said. "The sun will break soon, and I do not like the look of those clouds." He pointed above the trees.

Gravid, pewter clouds rested above the treetops, streaked with dawn's colors.

"We should find shelter before the storm breaks."

"And how shall we pay for shelter?" Tom soothed Badger, stroking the bay geldings neck.

"I told you," Beatrice said, her patience worn thin. "I did not give them all our money."

"I do not believe you."

"Jesu." Garrett shook his head. "You squabble like children."

"We do not."

Garrett kept his gaze level.

"Much." She squirmed a bit. "All right." She mounted Breeze, so she wouldn't have to look at the knowing expression on his face. "We have been friends since we were children. Old habits are hard to break."

Garrett scrabbled onto Parsley's back.

Beatrice opened her mouth to give him a hint. She snapped it shut again. Garrett couldn't ride, but he hadn't said anything. She suspected he wouldn't take well to her giving him some instruction.

"Are you coming?" He glanced at Tom over his shoulder. "For myself, I do not care what you decide."

Tom went redder and clenched his fists by his sides.

Beatrice tensed.

Tom looked ready to launch himself at Garrett and drag him to the ground.

She said a quick prayer that Tom's usual common sense would prevail. He'd be no match for Garrett's steely bulk.

"Come, Tom." She plucked a leaf from the top of his boot. "We still have more coin. We will have to use what remains more sparingly."

"You had no right to give away money without discussing it first." Tom scowled, but at least he guided Badger onto the small bridle path behind Garrett.

Danger averted, for now. Beatrice mounted and followed him. "If I had asked, what would you have said?"

"I would have told you not to be an idiot," Tom replied.

Beatrice smirked at him. "You see?" She clucked to Breeze. "Which is why I did not tell you."

Garrett choked. He turned his head toward the woods beside them.

"Come along." Beatrice guided Breeze behind Parsley.

With Garrett bouncing around on Parsley's broad back they followed the bridle path along the wood line to where it opened onto a wider road.

She'd love to give him a hint or two. He'd be rattled black and blue if he kept that up. The day was still and oppressive. Even the birds were quiet, other than the occasional thrush busily calling from the treetops.

Poor Parsley. He wasn't accustomed to having an inexperienced rider jar his back. It was a good thing the horse was sweet-tempered. Badger would have had Garrett off by now.

They moved inland. A low line of hills hid the sea, and meadows dotted with the yellow, pink, and red of wildflowers stretched beneath the heavy sky.

Tom's silence weighed heavier at her back. She hadn't heard the end of the money. And Tom didn't even know the whole story.

Low, stone walls carved allotments in the landscape. The summer crops were good this year. There would be food for the winter if the harvest yielded this promise.

Those women wouldn't starve whatever the harvest, because she'd given them instructions to Anglesea. Her mother and Nurse would see those poor souls fed. Those who wanted to stay would be welcomed.

Tom would shout the birds out of the trees if he knew. By sending the women to Anglesea, she'd almost drawn her family a map to find her.

She didn't care, however. Those children were starving and the women nigh desperate.

It was done.

The storm Garrett spoke of gathered behind a smear of purple mountains against the horizon.

Garrett made a more interesting view. His back was much broader than Tom's. She'd had her arms around his hard body. A tiny tendril of heat snaked through her. Garrett had held her in his lovely, strong arms. Could arms be lovely? But his chest and the march of ridges across his belly had definitely been beautiful. She'd like to see more of those. She lingered over the interesting swells of muscle beneath his tunic. Beads of perspiration formed beneath her tunic and slithered between her breasts. The air was terribly sultry and close. Nurse would pin her by the ears for her wanton thoughts. Best to think of something else. "Do you have any brothers and sisters?"

"Nay." Garrett's spine stiffened.

That was not an answer. The mystery around him irked her, and she was thoroughly bored. "You do not speak much of family or where you came from."

"Mayhap because I have not many happy stories to tell."

"I beg your pardon." Beatrice bit her tongue until she flinched. Nurse always told her to watch her tongue, and here it had led her into trouble again.

"No need, sweeting." He turned. "Mayhap, it is because the last thing on my mind is talking when you are near."

"Oh, Garrett." She giggled.

He grinned at her.

She did this a lot with Garrett. He appeared to enjoy making her giggle, which was partly why she did it when he was around. She didn't usually giggle. Giggling women were annoying. Which brought another thing to mind about Garrett. He was changeable. One moment terse and angry and the very next smiling wickedly enough to make her forget all reason. And when she questioned him, he was always quick to deflect her with charm and an easy smile.

"There is a crossroads up ahead," Tom said from behind them.

"Aye." Garrett and Parsley plodded forward.

"I spoke to one of the oldsters last night." Tom came up beside her.

"Indeed," Garrett drawled. "Were you actually speaking to a thief? Good Lord, Tom, what will become of you?"

Beatrice giggled and choked off the ridiculous sound.

Tom threw her a hard look. Perspiration darkened his blond hair to brown around his face.

She shouldn't laugh at him, but Tom needed a prod every now and then. He was solid and dependable, like pottage for breakfast.

"He said we should follow the left fork if we want to reach London." Color stained Tom's neck and cheeks.

Garrett stopped and turned in the saddle. He pursed his lips as if considering whether to take him up on the challenge or not.

Tom looked thunderous.

Garrett stared back at him.

The air crackled between them.

Beatrice's belly fluttered. "Then we shall take the left fork." They mustn't fight. Garrett was bigger, and Tom might get hurt. She was in love with Garrett, but Tom was her best friend. And she might never get to London if they came to blows.

The men remained locked in their staring battle.

It all seemed a bit pointless to her and she clapped her hands to get their attention.

"I thought you wanted to take the other path?" Garrett raised an eyebrow at her. "The one we discussed this morning."

"What other path?" Tom puffed up his chest.

"Garrett says there is another path, a lesser-known one. We are concerned my family might be trying to catch up with us."

"I do not know anything of another path." Tom perched atop Badger like a wooden post, his brow wrinkled.

"Which is why you are not leading." Beatrice nudged Breeze forward. "Come along then."

* * *

A woman's scream split the calm morning.

Garrett went cold. The skin at his nape crawled.

Beatrice rode slightly ahead of him. She gasped as she stared at something over the rise. Her hand flew to her throat.

Garrett couldn't see from here. He needed to get closer. "God's bones."

Beatrice careened down the road toward the scream, her braid streaming behind her like a blasted war banner.

## *Chapter Twelve*

reeze responded instantly to her demand for speed. The ground blurred beneath her as they shot down the rise. The woman's scream came from a huddle of people near the bottom. The sound still rattled around her brain.

Two men were shouting and waving at a third, on the ground, his chausses about his knees, his buttocks pumping.

The woman flailed beneath the man, so much smaller than the brute atop her.

They had no right. Anger surged and Beatrice's heart raced faster than Breeze's hooves. Her heart in her mouth. She was almost upon them.

The man on the ground stilled. He got to his feet, grinning. Smug, ugly, triumphant.

Pigs.

They scattered like pins as she bore down on them. The rutting sod tripped over his loose chausses, grabbed them with one hand, and stumbled back.

"Get away from her." She hauled Breeze to a stop.

The mare squealed. Her hind legs slid on the road before she gained purchase. Breeze fought for control, tossing her head and rearing.

"You get away from her, you whoresons," Beatrice screamed. She wheeled Breeze in a circle before the horse would relinquish control. The mare lunged against the bit.

Keeping well away from Breeze's flashing hooves, the men spread out, advancing on her from three directions. "What are you doing here, girl?"

She struggled to catch her breath. "Get back." Beatrice tried to keep them all in sight, jerking on Breeze's reins.

The one in the middle was the biggest. Arms held out, his face split in an ugly leer. "Do you want some of the same?" His arms were great cudgels, raised to grab her. "Get her."

Beatrice spun Breeze.

He laughed and leaped out of the path of the horse's hind legs.

She had no weapon. "Get away" she yelled.

The man lunged.

Breeze sidestepped suddenly, and Beatrice slipped in the saddle. The mare was panicked, she wasn't a destrier, and the shouting and ugly swirl of emotion unnerved her.

A blur of black and Badger slid to a stop. Dust swirled around his hooves.

Tom leaped from his back, bearing the big man to the ground.

Beatrice's hands went limp on the reins. Her breath sawed through her lungs in small pants.

A hand grabbed the bridle, and Breeze squealed.

Beatrice froze.

Small eyes above a dark, unkempt beard leered up at her. "I have you now."

Beatrice kicked at him, but he dodged the blow and sneered.

Out of nowhere, Garrett appeared behind him.

The man spun, swinging his fist.

Garrett ducked the blow and stepped in.

Breeze scrambled away from the grappling men. She plunged and bucked, the whites of her eyes showing.

Beatrice clung to her mane desperately.

"Get off that bloody horse." The third man grabbed her tunic and hauled her from the saddle.

"Garrett," she screamed, fighting to stay in the saddle.

Garrett's head whipped toward her. His eyes were wild, feverish.

A body dove at him. He went down.

Breeze bucked, and Beatrice hit the ground. The impact knocked the breath from her body. Breeze's hooves flashed above, and Beatrice threw up her arms to shield her head.

Pain exploded across her scalp. Her hair wrenched at the roots.

Garrett had his assailant in a headlock. They writhed and twisted together.

Tom rolled, fists flying.

They couldn't help her. Terror choked her. She fought and lashed out with her legs, each movement sending more pain through the grip on her hair. Her nails raked the hand in her hair.

"Bitch." He yanked her neck at a sharp angle.

Her vision wavered. Agony seared her scalp, like her hair was coming out at the roots. Her neck felt as if it might snap.

Boots appeared in her vision, kicking up choking dust.

The grip on her hair disappeared and she was free. Collapsing onto her hands, she sucked huge breaths into her chest.

Lips curled in a feral snarl, Garrett seized her attacker by the nape, jamming his head down into his rising fist. Blood sprayed, spattering her face.

Beatrice jerked back. Her stomached heaved. Desperately she wiped the sticky warmth from her face.

A body dropped at her feet.

Beatrice scrabbled backward. Small stones dug into her palms.

The man tried to stem the flow of blood from his face with a hand. Steamers of blood and saliva dribbled down his chin. He hawked and spat. The gory remains of a couple of teeth hit the road near her feet.

Beatrice retched.

Garrett and the big man circled each other.

The one with the bloodied face clambered back to his feet. He threw himself at Garrett from behind as Garrett lunged.

Garrett stumbled to his knees.

The ground shuddered beneath her.

Garrett disappeared beneath a tangle of limbs.

"Are you all right?" Tom's face was in front of her, red and sweaty. Blood streaked his cheeks; spittle flecked his lips.

Beatrice nodded.

Whirling. Tom grabbed one of the men on Garrett.

Grunts of pain, fists and feet flying, it all blurred in a grizzly spectacle.

Beatrice stumbled to her feet. Her legs shook so badly she could barely stand.

The fight was an ugly, brutal affair of hands, feet, even teeth used to exact the most damage. A thin spray of blood arced through the air.

Beatrice stumbled back as it nearly touched her. She'd seen men fight before, but those men had been knights. It wasn't this scrabbling, grunting, bloody scramble for supremacy. Her stomach heaved as another teeth jarring crunch sounded.

The third man lay on the ground, unmoving, as Tom and Garrett battled on.

His eyes were open and staring.

Beatrice jerked away. A flash of white caught her eye. Her heart leaped into her throat. *Please God, not another one.*

Not much bigger than a girl, the woman crouched beneath a small hedge, her arms around her raised knees. Her eyes, large and staring, were fixed on the fight as if she was somehow separate from all that was happening. Her dress was torn, her breasts pressed to her thighs.

Beatrice blushed for her.

The woman's eyes flickered up to Beatrice and away again. Wounded eyes.

A feral desire to inflict pain rocked through Beatrice. She turned, but it was over.

Two men stumbled back down the road.

"I'll find you, you bitch." The big one yelled, dragging his friend with him. "Do you hear me, Ivy? I'll find you."

The woman flinched and tightened her grip on her knees.

Garrett's breathing cut hard through the air.

Hands on his knees, Tom's chest heaved as he sucked in air.

The man in the road lay there, jaw slack, eyes wide.

"Is he dead?" Beatrice's legs buckled as she went to Tom and Garrett. She needed to see if they were hale and unharmed.

Garrett shrugged and spat blood. Gore and perspiration streaked his face. His lip was split and there was a deep red mark beneath his eye. Other than that and the damage to his clothing, he seemed fine.

Tom staggered beside him, his fist bloodied and his tunic torn.

They were well. She stood and sucked air into her tight chest.

Garrett stooped to the body. He dug around in his clothing, jostling the inert form from one side to the other like a macabre poppet as he searched.

It was horrible. Beatrice wrapped her arms around her waist. "What are you doing?"

Garrett came away with a pouch. His knuckles were split and bleeding, so he struggled with the ties of the purse.

"You are taking his money?" Grave robbers did this at battles. Her father had told her. Awful, desperate people who picked over the bodies of the dead. Beatrice went cold to her core.

Garrett calmly shook the contents of the purse onto his palm. Coins glittered as he poured them back into the purse.

"He does not need it," the woman said.

Her nerves on edge, Beatrice jumped.

The woman's dark hair was snarled and ragged. Ugly patches of red mottled her skin and an angry scratch dissected her cheek.

"Here." Garrett threw the money pouch at Tom. "Now you can stop whining about lost coin."

He strode over to Beatrice and tugged her close.

Beatrice stumbled before she regained her footing.

Still scorching with the heat of the fight, Garrett's eyes were ferocious.

He was a frightening stranger to her. "Do not, ever, do something that bloody stupid again."

"I—" Beatrice tried to step back from him.

"Ever." He held her fast.

He shook her, hard enough to make her teeth rattle before his hands dropped away from her.

Her legs sagged. Beatrice took a deep breath and tried to steady herself. Nobody had ever been that rough with her. That the men Garrett had found would have done worse made her shiver.

Garrett crouched down in front of the woman.

The woman reared away from him. Her eyes went huge with a kind of terror Beatrice had never seen.

She wanted to do something to take that fear away, but she knew not what. She had no experience, no wisdom to offer.

Drawing a slow, careful breath, Garrett waited until the woman grew still and then said, "It is over."

"Aye." The woman looked at the fallen man with her face devoid of expression. "They are gone?"

"Aye." Moving slowly, Garrett pulled off his tunic and handed it to her.

She eyed his offering and then snatched it and tugged it over her head. Slowly, as if she were hundreds of years old, she got to her feet. She was a tiny, slight thing beside Garrett.

"They knew you." Beatrice reached out to aid her

The woman jerked away. "Aye." She turned from the body and pulled her hair free of the neck of the tunic.

Beatrice expected tears.

Instead, the woman carefully rearranged her hair.

A fine tremor shook Beatrice as reaction set in. She had

witnessed this poor woman being brutalized, and yet, the victim appeared to be carved from stone.

"Who were those men?" Tom stood at Beatrice's back.

His familiar, solid presence gladdened her. She grabbed his hand. Tom's sweaty fingers gave hers a brief squeeze and let go.

"Does it matter?" Garrett methodically cleaned his hands against his chausses. His face was cold, distant. Bruises marred his chest and arms.

Beatrice offered him her water skin.

Taking it with a nod of thanks, Garrett swilled the water around his mouth and spat.

"Your lip is cut." She touched her finger to his mouth.

Garrett jerked away. "I am well."

Her hands were shaking and she clasped them together.

Tom stepped over to Badger and rummaged through the bags. He handed a spare tunic to Garrett. "I asked who they were because I want to know if they will be back."

"He will be." The woman huddled between Tom and Garrett. "He thinks he owns me."

"Is he your husband?" There'd been a man at Anglesea who'd beaten his wife. Father had seen to him.

The woman gave a rough snort, completely at odds with her delicate appearance. "Men do not marry the likes of me. They rut on me and go their way."

Beatrice's gaped. The woman was a—

Beside her, Tom reeled. "You are a—"

"A whore." The woman glanced at Beatrice. "You rescued a whore, my lady."

All eyes turned to Beatrice and she couldn't gather her thoughts into coherent speech.

Tom looked thunderous, the woman resigned, and Garrett—

Garrett's arms were crossed, his face wore a mixture of outright challenge and contempt.

It was as if this were some sort of test that she didn't understand the rules to. She didn't know what to make of it.

"You cannot stay here," she said. "Can we escort you somewhere safer?"

"I lived with him." She nodded toward the two men who had disappeared.

"Well, you cannot go there." Beatrice shuddered at the idea. "Is there anywhere else? Anybody able to protect you?"

"Nay." The woman clutched her arms as if she were chilled.

"Beatrice." Tom beckoned with his head.

She waved him away. He'd have to wait until they found somewhere for this poor soul. "You have no family, then?"

"Nay." The woman winced and tucked Garrett's tunic about her.

They needed to get her to safety, where she could heal. But where? The road stretched in either direction, empty. No village or even small cottage interrupted the green expanse beside it. There was only one thing Beatrice could think to do. "Can you ride?"

"If I must."

"Beatrice?" Tom jostled her shoulder with his. "I must speak with you."

"Not now, Tom."

"Aye, Beatrice, now." Tom's face was set.

Beatrice stumbled after him. Her trembling legs wouldn't cease, but Tom would only create a commotion if she didn't hear him out.

He gripped her arm and tugged her farther away from the other two.

Garrett ripped a section of his tunic, doused it with water, and handed it to the woman. He kept a careful distance from her.

"Beatrice, get that idea right out of your silly head." Tom spun her around to face him. He drew his shoulders back and stared down at her. His blue eyes blazed angrily.

"I have no idea of what you speak, Tom."

"Aye, you do." Tom jabbed a finger at her. "You are thinking of taking that...that woman with us."

"We cannot leave her here for those men to find again. You saw what they did to her." Beatrice knocked his hand away.

"She is a whore." Tom jerked straight. "It is what she does."

Beatrice clenched her hands so hard her nails dug into her palms. She wanted to smack Tom until his teeth rattled. "I do not think her being a—I don't think that has anything to do with what happened to her."

"Of course it does." Tom paced to the side and back again. "You have no understanding of these things. Your father would be horrified if he knew what sort of low person you were—"

"My father," Beatrice glared back at him, "would never, ever, ever leave a woman here, alone and in danger."

"He would a trull." Tom's lip curled over the word.

"Nay, he would not." Beatrice was sure, and if her father had contemplated such a thing, her mother would have set him a-rights immediately.

"It is my duty to protect you." Tom drew himself up taller. "And that means protecting you from your own innocence."

"I have never disliked you more in our lives." Beatrice stepped nose to nose with Tom. Except, he had grown quite a bit and it was more nose to chin. "I am going to help her, and you will not stop me." She couldn't keep the quiver out of her voice. If she stared at Tom much longer, she might box his ears. Or cry. Beatrice stalked away. She didn't care what Tom said.

The poor woman had been raped. Whores fornicated for coin, but many of them did so out of pure necessity. Her mother had explained it to her once when she had asked about Lilly. What had happened here today was wrong, even if it happened to a woman who sold her body. Those men had taken something the woman hadn't wanted to give.

Garrett held Breeze. The mare still quivered, her nostrils slightly flared.

Running his hand over her neck, Garrett kept his face to Breeze. "What now?" The terrible anger had receded and he appeared calm.

"We ride." Beatrice turned to the woman. "I am Beatrice."

The other woman tucked a strand of dark hair behind her ear. "Ivy."

"Will you come with us?"

"Aye." Garrett's tunic hung to her knees.

"Garrett?" Beatrice took Breeze's reins from him.

"Aye, my lady?" His fingers brushed her hand.

"Would you help Ivy onto my horse? She is hurt."

"Aye, my lady." This time, he used her title with no mockery. He approved of her actions, his smile told her. It warmed her from deep, deep within.

Garrett approached Ivy slowly. "I have to put my hands on you, lass."

Ivy nodded, and then he moved toward her.

# Chapter Thirteen

The road blurred before Beatrice, and she wiped her face. Wind and rain whipped the tree branches into a dizzying dance. Garrett's storm had hit them. A spiteful wind lashed cold rain into their faces. Travel had been slower with Beatrice and Ivy riding double. Garrett and Tom were hunched shapes to her right. Breeze plodded through the nasty weather with her head lowered.

Ivy huddled behind Beatrice, keeping her back warm, but there was no respite from the driving needles of rain in her face. Their small party sloshed on miserably until an old crofter's hut appeared a little ways off the road.

Garrett signaled their party to stop. Shouting over the storm, he pointed to the hut. "We should take shelter until the storm passes."

Beatrice halted, fisting her hands on the reins in frustration. He was right. They had to stop. The road beneath them was slippery mud, slowing them further. They were gaining almost no distance and merely exhausting animals and riders alike. The delay was like a tight band about her throat. London was miles away still. In her imagination the thunder of hooves coming from

Anglesea rang loud and pressing. Even now, they could be closing on her.

Tom slid from Badger, pushing rain-soaked hair off his face. She couldn't share her concerns with him. He would only lecture her and tell her he'd told her so.

The hut was old and abandoned, but it also promised some respite from the rain.

Beatrice dismounted before turning to assist Ivy.

Ivy's pale face gleamed stark white in the gloom. She hissed and bit her lips as Beatrice steadied her descent. Beatrice wanted to soothe the hurt, but Ivy moved away the moment her feet touched the ground.

Garrett led them inside.

The relief was immediate, and Beatrice pushed back her hood. She stamped to clear the mud from her feet.

A couple of wooden stalls to one side indicated other animals had been housed here. Tom took the horses, his shirt plastered to his broad back. Steam and the smell of wet horse seeped through the hut.

The place hadn't been lived in for a long time. There was no furniture and the thatch had worn thin in patches, letting a steady seep of water form small puddles on the earthen floor.

Opposite the door was a broad stone hearth and the floor was dry on either side. Beatrice moved farther inside, and Ivy trailed her.

Nobody spoke much. Everyone was relieved to be out of the rain.

Garrett shook his head like a dog, droplets sprayed around him. "We best get dry." His borrowed tunic, tight across his broader form, clung to the ridges of his chest and belly.

Beatrice dragged her eyes away and shrugged out of her cloak. With nowhere else to drape it, she settled for a rusted hook against the wall. Her clothing had escaped the worst of the wet, but still, she was chilled to the bone. Her plait hung in a soggy rope down her back, making her shiver.

With no cloak to shield her, Ivy's dark hair clung wetly to her head. She sat curled around her knees beside the hearth. Bare, mud-splattered feet peeked out beneath her hem.

She must be freezing. Beatrice searched for the words to make it all seem better and came up blank. Everyone getting warm and dry would be a start. She tugged her plait forward and rung water from it.

Garrett crouched by the hearth.

A small stack of wood rested against the stones, dusty but dry. It wasn't much, but any sort of warmth would be welcome.

Why did he not light a fire? She couldn't remember ever feeling quite this cold or damp.

Ivy concerned her more. The girl's teeth chattered.

"I think it is blocked." Garrett peered up the chimney.

"How would you tell?" Beatrice crouched beside him.

"I can light a fire and we can see if we are smoked out."

Their faces were close enough she could see the lighter flecks of brown in his eyes. His smile was like the sun through a miserable day. Of all the smiles he gave her, this one she hadn't seen. It warmed his chiseled features and invited her to join, open and guileless.

"Do you have a second idea?" She wanted him to look at her this way always. It made honey of her insides in the most wonderful way.

His easy smile disappeared, and his expression grew sensuous. "Aye." He cupped her cheek with his palm. "But I do not think Master Tom would find favor."

The change bothered her. He went so quickly from one to the other. She searched his face for the answer. "You have many faces, Garrett."

He dropped his hand. Tilting his head, he studied her.

"I am concerned about Ivy." Beatrice grew uncomfortable under his gaze and she didn't know what to make of the uneasy pinch in her chest. She needed to think about it. "I believe she is hurt."

"Poor lass." Garrett looked past her to the other woman. "The hurts done her will take a long time to heal." He cleared his throat and stood. "She will want to bathe. I will fetch some water and Tom and I will make ourselves scarce."

"I will help her." Beatrice rose to stand shoulder to shoulder with him.

Together, they looked at the huddle of flesh and bone that was Ivy.

Beatrice got the uneasy sense Ivy wasn't really with them. Bodily, for certain, but her tightly closed expression was as effective as miles of distance. "If she will let me," Beatrice said, more to herself than Garrett.

"She will need time. And a gentle hand to help her put back what they took from her." He strode over to Tom.

The depth of his empathy surprised her. He shifted and changed like a free streaming storm and left her befuddled in his wake.

Garrett conferred with Tom in low tones. His spine snapped straight suddenly.

Tom glowered and shook his head.

Oh, dear, trouble brewed again. Could they not see now was not the time for one of their disagreements?

Garrett straightened his shoulders, seeming to swell in size. The frightening stranger from the fight was back.

Tom and Garrett's current argument appeared a mite more serious and Beatrice's shoulders tensed.

Garrett spoke again, thrusting his hand toward the door.

Puffing out his chest, Tom narrowed his eyes and set his jaw in a stubborn line she knew well.

Garrett stepped into Tom.

Gathering violence prickling over her skin, Beatrice hurried closer to them. They had all the storm they could manage happening outside. They did not need a tempest within.

"It is pouring," Tom said.

Garrett's voice was implacable. "We leave, now."

"I will turn my back."

"Nay." Garrett snapped. "Stand beneath a big tree."

"We can take shelter right here. I am not going out in that storm for a—" Tom caught Beatrice's gaze and dropped his head.

"For shame, Tom." Anger rose up, swift and strong. "Look at her. Look what they did to her. I only ask you to give her a private moment to clean those men from her skin."

He took a step back at her vehemence. "I already fought for her. How much more do you want?"

Beatrice followed him, struggling to keep her voice down. "You have no idea what she has suffered."

"She is a whore, Beatrice. There is not enough water to clean all the men off her."

It was like a blow to her middle.

Tom's eyes widened. Color flooded his neck and crept onto his cheeks.

"You dare to say such a thing." The air rushed out of her lungs.

"Get out." Garrett's eyes were dead, his face frozen, his expression pure menace.

The air snapped tight between the two men.

Tom took a reflexive step back.

Rage throbbed from Garrett's rigid muscles.

Fear swept away her anger, and Beatrice leaped between them. Her heart thundered in her ears.

"You did not mean that, Tom." Her voice shook. Garrett looked ready to kill. "I know you could not have meant to sound heartless."

Garrett's menace pulsed against her back.

"Move, Beatrice." He went to step around her.

Beatrice whirled and blocked his path. "Go, Tom. Return when you are more yourself."

Tom paled. He clenched his fists by his sides as he glared over her head at Garrett, taunting.

Garrett jostled her shoulder to get by her.

"Now, Tom." Beatrice held fast in front of Garrett.

He kept coming.

Desperately, she grabbed both of his arms. Her hands couldn't encircle the breadth, but she dug in her fingers and clung. "Leave, now." She hoped to God Tom listened because she couldn't hold Garrett much longer.

For a heart-stopping moment, Tom hesitated. Then, he spun on his heel and stalked outside.

Beatrice kept her grasp on Garrett. He could chase down Tom and pound him into the mud. "He does not mean it." Beatrice dared not look at him. Fury pulsed through his clenched muscles. She aimed her words at his chest. "He is not himself. I have known him all my life, and I know he does not mean what he said."

"You can let go now." Garrett's arms flexed beneath her fingers.

Beatrice dug deeper. Her fingers ached from the effort to contain the power clenched beneath them. "I think not. If I let you go, you will go after Tom."

"He deserves no less."

"Aye." Prickly heat broke out over her body. "You are right, but I still cannot let you go."

"And you intend to hold me here and stop me?"

"Aye."

He twisted and his arms came free. Snatching her around the elbows, he hauled her up onto her toes. His face was stone.

Beatrice's mouth went dry.

"What did I tell you about putting yourself in the path of danger?"

Images of Garrett battling Ivy's attackers flashed through her mind. "Tom does not always mean the things he says."

"Then he should not say them."

"You are right. Of course, you are right. But he is angry with me. He is upset by all of this. Tom is not an unkind person. When I found this puppy left behind the keep near the midden heap, I could not get to it and Tom, he was kind, because he is kind, and he took off his boots—"

"Hush." He gave her a slight shake.

Beatrice hushed.

He released her elbows.

Her feet sank back onto the floor. Beatrice peeked up at him.

His face was still set but not as rigid.

Angry but not murderous was a definite improvement. Her legs went limp with relief.

Shaking his head, Garrett stalked toward the door.

"Where are you going?" Beatrice scrambled after him.

"Nay." He whirled around, and she slid to a halt. "I am going to fetch water."

"Water?"

"For Ivy."

"Oh."

"Go and see what you can do for Ivy. I will bring her some water." He dropped his head forward. When he looked up again, the awful grimness had receded from his expression. In truth, the tiniest of smiles threatened to take possession of his face.

Thank God, the immediate danger had passed. She wanted to sit on the floor and cry. This was not, however, the time for indulging. She raised her shoulders and lifted her chin. "Beatrice the Brave," she muttered.

"What did you say?"

"Nothing."

His mouth definitely softened before he slipped into the wet evening.

Beatrice approached Ivy carefully. "Garrett will fetch some water for you to bathe."

Ivy shivered.

"We are afraid to light a fire for fear it will smoke us out. So, I am sorry to say, the water will be cold."

Ivy gave a stiff nod.

"Come." Beatrice held out her hand to the other woman. "Let us get you tended."

Ivy used the wall to push herself up. She swayed and recovered her balance.

They must be close in age, but Ivy looked no more than a defenseless, broken child. Beatrice trusted her instinct. "Tom and Garrett will remain outside until you are settled."

Ivy stared at the doorway and bit her bottom lip.

Tom and Garrett were nowhere in sight. The trees outside strained in the direction of the wind.

One of the horses stamped and whickered.

The door had long since rotted and caved in. Slanting rain stretched across the opening and splashed up from the ground.

Of course, how could she not have seen it? Ivy was worried about the exposed doorway. "I will stretch one of our blankets over the beams here. See." Beatrice pointed to a row of nails, which had probably held household implements. "I will string it between those and you will be quite snug within."

"He is right," Ivy said. "The flaxen-haired one. I am a whore, and I deserve no more than what happened to me."

Beatrice was halfway toward where Tom had stacked their belongings, but she jolted to a stop. If Tom were here, she would strangle him. She took the time to calm herself before she turned. "Nay." She wanted to yell the words, but Ivy looked as if the force of her anger would blow her out of the room. "Tom could not be more wrong. No woman deserves to be so ill-used."

Ivy uttered a strange, guttural cry as if a sob caught in her throat. Her eyes narrowed, and her mouth worked. Moisture flooded her eyes and Ivy blinked rapidly.

Beatrice stepped toward her. She ached to comfort the other woman.

"Nay." Ivy held up a shaking hand. "I cannot." Ivy's jaw clenched, her chest heaved. "You must not."

"I cannot imagine how you must feel."

"Nay, you cannot."

Suddenly, Beatrice understood. Ivy didn't want compassion. Compassion would weaken her. So she forced herself to remain where she was while Ivy fought for composure.

Thunder rumbled overhead. A heartbeat later, lightning flickered. The horses whickered nervously.

Ivy's face stiffened into hard and bitter lines. Her eyes went dead as the tears disappeared.

Beatrice fetched the blanket and secured it to the hooks. Tears would've been better than Ivy's unnatural stillness. Nurse would've known what to say to Ivy. Mother or Faye would be better than she at this. None of them were here, however. Ivy had her. She would have to do.

Garrett had found some old buckets behind the hut. Most were broken and useless, but two were in fair enough condition to contain some water.

At Anglesea she had a big, linen-lined tub. It took three men to fill it with water. Nurse would've put soothing herbs in the hot water. As it was, Ivy would have to make do.

Beatrice took the buckets behind the blanket.

Ivy hadn't moved. She allowed Beatrice to help her remove Garrett's tunic.

Beatrice dragged her eyes away from dark, angry bruises against Ivy's smooth skin.

"You should not see this." Ivy looked down at her body. "A young lady like yourself."

Beatrice couldn't speak. Her throat was so tight, and her chest so full of conflicting feelings. Even drawing breath was hard. She motioned Ivy to turn around. Dull, russet streaks ran the inside of Ivy's thighs. Blood. Those evil men had done this. The horror of the morning nearly overwhelmed her. Beatrice's hand shook as she dipped a rag in the water and handed it to the other woman.

Beatrice slipped to the other side of her makeshift hanging, giving Ivy her privacy. She needed to do something, anything, or she would burst with the welter of emotion within. She scooped up the remains of Ivy's dress. The bliaut was ripped beyond repair and blood stained the fabric brown in spots. It made her shudder just to hold the bliaut, a visceral reminder of what Ivy had suffered.

Beatrice had two dresses within her belongings. Ivy was a much smaller woman, but she could tighten the laces.

Garrett huddled beneath the eaves, trying to keep out of the rain.

Beatrice handed the bliaut to Garrett. "She cannot wear this."

He nodded and jogged out into the rain.

Outside, the storm turned the ground to mud.

Water swished from the other side of the blanket. Beatrice pushed her dress and a chainse around the barrier. The noises stopped.

"I cannot wear these." Ivy's voice held the tiniest bit of animation.

"The gown will certainly be too long," Beatrice said. "And you look to have more bosom than I, but the clothes are clean and warm."

"My lady, these are too fine."

Fine? Beatrice's heart twisted. It was a plain wool gown she'd passed to Ivy. She'd brought it because it was the simplest of her gowns, and she didn't want to draw attention to herself with the fineness of her raiment. Her life was leagues removed from the people she'd met. Not two full days traveling and she was in an entirely different world. "I am more comfortable riding in my chausses," she said. "And you cannot wear your old gown."

Behind the blanket, the gentle swish of water began again.

Beatrice lost count of the buckets of water she passed between Garrett and Ivy. Garrett steadfastly replaced the used water with fresh.

Finally, Ivy emerged dressed, with the gown trailing about her feet. Her skin was reddened from scrubbing, and her hair hung wet down her back.

Beatrice found a comb and handed it to her.

Ivy got to work on her long, dark hair.

Beatrice tried not to stare.

With her delicate face scrubbed clean, Ivy was still pale and a large bruise marred her cheek. Her hair was near black and her eyes a deep, mossy green. She was beautiful enough to rival Faye. Faye's beauty had earned her a powerful husband. Ivy's had led her to a different sort of fate altogether. The result had been vastly different, but their path hadn't been dissimilar—Faye's and Ivy's. Both were lovely women whose beauty had been traded like coin.

Of course, Faye had been given some choice in the matter by an indulgent father. But Beatrice knew many girls, of noble birth like herself, who'd been given in marriage without their opinion being sought. For the first time, Beatrice was glad for her three failed betrothals. She'd accepted the notion of marriage to each of the three men, but hadn't sought it or welcomed it. One of those men could've been a brute like the one who had attacked Ivy. Brutishness didn't confine itself to serfs and the poor.

With her hair neatly braided, Ivy turned to her. "The others can come in now."

* * *

Beatrice peered at the darkening day. All she saw was rain and more rain. There was still no sign of Tom. He'd been gone for hours.

"He will be back." Garrett sat on the other side of the hearth from Ivy with his back against the wall.

Ivy had retreated behind the blanket. When Beatrice last checked, her eyes were closed, and she'd appeared to be sleeping.

"What if he is not?" Beatrice willed the darkness to form the shape of Tom.

"You are here," Garrett said.

Sadness weighed at her. She loved Tom dearly, but the Tom she'd witnessed this day left her shaken and unsure.

"You must not condemn him on a few moments of poor judgment." Garrett correctly interpreted her thoughts. "It has been a difficult day for all of us. Tom is merely reacting to it in his way."

"Earlier, you looked like you might rip his head off his shoulders."

"And you stopped me." He grinned. "You have more courage than good sense."

That was closer to the truth than he knew. Beatrice pulled a face. "My brothers will tell you I have no sense." It had been a long day, and the weather matched her mood.

"I would not go that far." He chuckled. "But I would suggest you stop throwing yourself in front of men with violence on their minds. Come." Garrett patted the ground beside him. "It is a miserable night with no fire."

She didn't need him to ask her twice. Beatrice crossed the space and sat beside him. His body heat drew her like a lodestone. She wanted to wriggle closer to him and wondered if she dared to be that bold. Things were altered between them. Uncertainty corroded the edges of what she understood about Garrett. Just when she saw the glimmering of an understanding, he shifted and revealed something more. The charming, passionate lover made up only one portion of the man. And yet, at Anglesea, she'd nearly given her virtue to that man. Her head was crowded with the new things she had to fit into place. Her heavy limbs, however, wanted to close the tiny distance between them. None of it made much sense to her.

Garrett dropped his head back against the wall and closed his eyes.

The strong column of his exposed throat was dark from working in the sun. The dull purple of a bruise shadowed the harsh line of his jaw.

She traced the mark with her finger. He'd got it in defense of her.

His eyes popped open at her touch.

"Does it hurt?"

"Not much." He lowered his head. The charmer lurked in the depths of his eyes. "You could kiss it better, if you had a fancy to."

Beatrice was not of a mind to be charmed. She pushed her shoulder against his.

"Did you suffer any other hurts today?"

"Nothing to speak of." Garrett shrugged. "Who is Beatrice the Brave?"

Heat rushed up to her hairline.

Garrett laughed.

"Nobody."

"Tell me."

His laughter disarmed her. "I am." She shifted against the hard pack of the floor. "At least, it is how I imagine I should be." She waved a hand, mortified to be admitting such a thing. "This journey is about Beatrice the Brave."

Garrett raised his arm and encircled her shoulders. He drew her, unresisting, against his side.

Beatrice immediately felt better. He was a solid, warm presence beside her.

"Was that Beatrice the Brave today? Riding to save Ivy?"

"Nay. Today was me."

"Were you hurt?" His arm tightened until her entire side pressed against him.

It was a lovely feeling. Beatrice sat absolutely still and enjoyed it. "Nay, you were there before he could do me much harm."

"Do not do that again."

"Aye, Garrett." She lay her head against his shoulder. He was wondrous warm. She curved toward him and fidgeted to get comfortable. "I wish this rain would stop." Right now, the rain wasn't bothering her one whit, but the need to get to London pressed against the back of her mind.

"We will leave when it does." Garrett's voice rumbled against her ear. "We will try to regain the time we have lost."

The thump of his heart was steady beneath her ear. The Garrett smell surrounded her. Things did not seem so impossible anymore. Ivy would go with them. She would rather send Ivy back to Anglesea, but after today, she couldn't ask Tom to take her. Leaving Ivy alone wasn't to be thought of. Beatrice's head fit perfectly into the hollow beneath Garrett's collarbone.

His hand dropped from her shoulder to her hip and pulled her closer.

The small pouch around his neck rested near the tip of her nose. She wanted to ask, but weariness dragged her eyelids down.

* * *

Her body cleaved to his, and Garrett smiled. Tom's petulance had given him the opportunity he needed to press his case. Of course, with Ivy here, he'd be limited in what he could do. Still, it wouldn't hurt to stroke the fire in Beatrice a bit higher.

He inhaled the scent of her hair. Wildflowers. He'd give it a few moments more until she was perfectly relaxed.

She sighed.

He enjoyed her weight resting against him, trusting and warm. His.

She moved, and his shaft gave a lazy stir. Her breath sent warm puffs of air down his neck.

Slumping, she made a soft, snuffling noise, like a tired puppy.

Garrett glanced down.

Lashes dark against the pale of her cheeks, full mouth open in a soft pout, she was dead asleep.

Garrett wanted to laugh and howl at the same time. He edged down the wall until he made a better pillow for her. Careful not to wake her, he shifted Beatrice into a more comfortable position. It mildly concerned him he didn't mind that she used him as her pallet.

She fit right in his arms.

It had been a whore of a day. Things had gotten murky in his head. The lack of clarity sat ill with him, like an itch beneath his skin he couldn't scratch.

Beatrice had flipped his thinking inside and out. He hadn't, for one instant, thought she'd behave as she had done with Ivy. Truth be told, the boy's reaction was closer to what he would've expected. The image of Beatrice charging down the rise on her horse taunted him. Garrett's gut tightened. She was a danger to herself.

What was her family thinking to allow her out without a constant guardian angel to keep her clear of trouble? Ludicrous. Unfortunately, it seemed he'd volunteered for the duty merely by being in her presence. His heart had nearly stopped when he saw that sodding whoreson reach up and pull her off her horse. His anger had been barely contained as he fought. Garrett shook his head at himself. There'd been three of them. Three. He needed his wooden head examined.

And Ivy.

She brought his mother clearly to mind, as if she were in the room with him. Ivy had the same bone-deep weariness that had beset his mother. It rested in the bruised depths of their eyes and carved lines of disappointment around their mouths. Once, his mother had been beautiful enough to catch the eye of the powerful lord of the demesne she lived within and alluring enough to establish her place as his only leman. She had laughed then, sang to him, and told him stories of valor and glory.

Then a marauding knight called Sir Arthur of Anglesea, shouting the name of King John's justice had torn their world asunder as ruthlessly as he had razed the castle, their only home, to the ground. His mother had taken years to die, piece by piece. He lived to bring her justice. And what better justice than to render a whore, the daughter of the man who had torn his world apart?

Except, and here was the thing that wouldn't rest easy within him, Beatrice would have condemned such an action had she been there. She might have even ridden to their rescue. A man didn't have to spend more than an hour or two in her company to see what she was made of. It was right there, on the surface, written across her expressive face. Every thought she had and every emotion she experienced. There was no cruelty in her.

For the first time since he'd put his feet on the road toward revenge, Garrett was torn. The inherent rightness of his actions didn't seem quite so certain anymore.

He was a maudlin dolt. It was right what he did. Sometimes it was mete the innocent suffer along with the guilty. Less than a day's hard riding from London, life had handed this opportunity to him and he would be a fool not to take it. When the rain let up, he'd lead them into the night.

The boy would be too busy nursing his own self-righteous grievances to take note of their direction. Through the door, the rain lessened. He'd have a few solid hours of darkness to work with. He should wake Beatrice and tell her to get ready.

Her arm lay across his belly.

She was so trusting it made his teeth ache. There was no need to wake her right away. She was tired, and Tom wasn't back yet.

* * *

"Beatrice." Tom's voice intruded on her sleep.

Beatrice lay with her cheek against a blanket, and her limbs were cold. She shivered and blinked at the hut. Then she remembered where they were. It was dark all around now, but the rain had stopped.

"Beatrice, it is time to go." Tom shook her by the shoulder.

Beatrice sat up. The last thing she remembered was cuddling up beside Garrett. "Where is Garrett?"

"Outside with the horses. We let you sleep as long as we could."

"Where were you?"

Tom rubbed the back of his neck. "Walking, thinking. Sitting and more thinking." He cleared his throat. "I was wrong, Bea. I need to beg your pardon."

Sweet relief flooded Beatrice. This was the Tom she knew and loved. "Aye, you were."

Tom gave her a sardonic look. "I am not sure what came over me. You were right to chastise me."

"Garrett nearly did worse." Beatrice turned to look for Ivy.

The other woman perched on the folded blanket Beatrice had used as a screen. Her hair was neatly braided and her skirts carefully tucked around her legs. She waited.

"Bea." Tom helped her to her feet. "I want you to be careful with Garrett."

A glib answer rose to her lips.

"I do not think he is as he appears to be."

Tom's words echoed her thoughts too closely. Beatrice squeezed his hand. Tom loved her. He only wanted to protect her.

"You are too quick to trust, and I am concerned for you." This was her Tom, sweet, caring, and hopelessly stubborn, but a good man.

She threw her arms around his neck. "I do not like to fight with you, Tom."

"God's wounds, Bea." He went bright pink but gave her a rough hug.

Chapter Fourteen

A long ride through the night regained some of the time lost. They'd stopped a few hours before dawn to get some rest. The women huddled together for warmth in the early hours before dawn.

Beatrice woke with Ivy stiff as a board behind her. The bright sunlight stung her eyes. She shifted and groaned. Her body was full of tired twinges and aches. Today would bring more hard traveling.

"We are lost." Tom's voice broke the still morning. "How, in the name of God, can we be lost?"

Beatrice sat up and rubbed the sleep from her eyes.

Behind her, Ivy did the same.

Near the horses, Tom and Garret stood and glared at each other.

Garrett looked irritated but not murderous. A horse whinnied over his reply.

"You said you knew the way." Tom thrust his chest forward.

Beatrice scrambled to her feet. Being lost would be an unmitigated disaster. Her family was counting on her to reach London. Assuming Henry hadn't suffered a rush of blood to the head and decided to come after her. Henry wouldn't do anything quite so impulsive. The most impulsive thing Henry had ever done was take an extra cup of mead.

"What is it, Tom?" Every one of Beatrice's limbs ached. She was unaccustomed to riding as many hours and sleeping rough. Her steps lacked any semblance of grace as she stumbled to Garrett and Tom.

"He says we are lost." Tom pointed at Garrett.

Garrett spread his arms wide and grimaced.

Dismay flooded through Beatrice. "We cannot be." His sheepish expression irked her. "You know the way. You said so."

Garrett stroked her cheek. "I am sorry, sweeting. I must have taken the wrong path in the dark."

She jerked away from his touch. "How can you be sure we are lost then?" Beatrice tried to be sensible, but she wanted to shake him until he admitted it was all a silly misunderstanding.

"The sun." Garrett pointed to a low line of crags on the horizon. "It rose there and if we were on the right path, it would have risen above yonder hill."

"Nay." Beatrice glared at the soft, green hills. Disappointment welled into her throat. She pushed it down. "Then we must simply retrace our steps and get back on the correct path."

"Going back will take us almost half a day out of our way." Tom stamped over to his blanket and snatched it off the ground. "We are running out of time. We had barely enough time to reach London as it was. This will cost us everything."

"Stop it, Tom. You are not helping." She had to make London. There was no choice. Beatrice turned on her heel, grabbed her belongings and shoved them into her satchel.

Ivy scrambled to her feet and blinked at her.

"I have not done everything I have done to be told nay now." She struggled with the blanket. The cursed thing defied her, spilling over the edges and refusing to make itself small. Beatrice punched it into the satchel. "I will reach London. I will warn my father. And he will reach home in time to save us."

"Beatrice?" Garrett was warm beside her. "I am truly sorry, sweeting, but we have lost too much time."

"Nay." Beatrice trod toward her horse. "I will not accept it."

"Where are you going?" he called after her.

Of all the stupid questions. Beatrice nearly exploded. She hadn't time to stand and argue with stupid men. "I am going to London."

"You do not know the way." Garrett's hand on her arm burned like a brand against her skin.

Beatrice yanked her arm away. "Then I will ask someone who does." She loaded her satchel onto Breeze. The animal sensed her mood and danced a few steps away from Beatrice. Beatrice focused on the white blaze between Breeze's eyes. She forced herself to take a deep calming breath. This wouldn't defeat her.

"Where are you going?" Garrett asked.

"With her," Ivy replied. "If she wants to go to London, I will go with her."

"Jesu, save me from illogical women."

His hands hard on her shoulders, Garrett spun her around to face him. "You cannot go traipsing off with no direction."

Beatrice thrust her chin out. He could glare all he wanted. "You said it was that way." She pointed to the hills. "Then such is the way we will go."

"I said that is where the sun should have risen." Garrett rubbed the bridge of his nose. "I have no idea where we are."

Beatrice glared at him. She didn't want to hear it.

"We could ask someone." Ivy slipped to her side.

Of course. Hope flared. It was the most sensible thing to do.

"There is nobody here." Garrett stuffed his fingers through his hair.

"I see smoke." Ivy nudged her and jerked her chin. "And where there is smoke, there is bound to be a person tending it."

Above the tree line, a thin wisp of smoke rose before disappearing into the cloudless sky.

It was a blessed sign. Beatrice loved Ivy in that moment. People nearby meant help.

"It could be anyone." Garrett moved to take the saddle from her, but Beatrice fought him. He was stronger than she. She tugged harder at the saddle, not caring how undignified the tussle. "Remember what happened last time you tangled with strangers?"

"Let go."

"Nay, I cannot allow you to go tumbling into trouble again," he said with infuriating calm.

"He is right," Tom spoke.

The knife twisted in Beatrice's chest. Of all the people she had thought to side with her, Tom was foremost. She lanced him with a look shrieking his betrayal. She gave up the saddle so abruptly Garrett had to catch his balance.

Bareback it was, then. She snatched up Breeze's bridle and tugged. Breeze sensed she was past discussing the issue and quietly fell into step behind her.

"Beatrice?" Garrett called.

She kept walking, searching for a likely stump or rock to help her mount. Rapid footsteps came after her. Beatrice quickened her pace, but his legs were longer and he got in front of her.

"All right." He held up his hands. "We will ride toward the smoke and ask directions. Get on the damn horse."

Her pride demanded she tell him to go to the devil. She looked at Ivy.

Ivy shrugged.

It was her decision to make. Beatrice spun, clasping her dignity about her, and pulled Breeze's saddle out of his hands.

* * *

Garrett should have been livid. Outflanked by a stubborn girl and her henchwoman. He stared at Parsley's neck and fought the grin threatening to spread across his face. By God, she had spirit. He could still see her, marching around their camp with her hair flying and her jaw locked tight. Why he found this amusing remained a mystery, but he did. At best, his attempt had bought him half a day. He should be galled it hadn't gained him more time.

* * *

Beatrice stared down at the scurrying figures. The smoke had materialized into a small village resting in the crook of a river. A squat stone steeple marked the end of the village. It was no more than a handful of whitewashed cottages around a green, but the green bustled with activity.

"It must be a market day." Tom drew rein beside her.

Ivy stiffened against her back.

Markets meant lots of people and lots of people with wagging tongues. Beatrice understood Ivy's reticence. However, people meant knowledge. Someone in that throng must be able to set them on the right path. Even knowing the name of the river would help.

"I shall go down and see what I can find." The road meandered through some planted fields and into the center of the village. "Ivy needs to stay here, and you can keep her company." Her glance encompassed both men.

"Nay," said Garrett and Tom, a hairbreadth behind him.

Beatrice gaped at them.

Male jaws hardened and, as one, they shook their heads.

"Nay." Garrett didn't shout, but authority ringed his voice.

Beatrice's hackles rose. It was all very well for him to be puffing up his chest like a bantam rooster, but he'd got them into this pickle in the first place. Needs must. She raised her chin and braced for a fight. Men could be so illogical at times.

"We are lost." She kept her tone civil. "We do not have time to wander around the countryside, hoping we find our way onto the right road. Ivy cannot be expected to go amongst a group of people. That lout could be looking for her."

"He will be looking," Ivy added.

"There." Beatrice patted Ivy's hand. "And she cannot be left here on her own." She suppressed an eye roll as Tom and Garrett's expressions didn't change. In fact, they looked more resistant.

"Beatrice." Tom fixed a stare on her. All Tom needed was the wimple and he would be his mother.

She narrowed her eyes at him. He needn't think it would work on her.

"You cannot go into a village on your own and ask the way to London. For a start, you are a woman traveling on your own, and those folk will make any manner of assumptions about you and secondly..."

The self-righteous ass was back to carping on the Ivy incident. Tom's first point, however, had enough validity to warrant some thought.

"We must split up." That would fix the problem. "Tom can come with me, and Garrett must stay with Ivy." She would much rather Garrett came with her, but given Tom's demeanor toward the other woman, Beatrice didn't want to burden Ivy with him.

"Nay." Garrett's jaw clenched. "You and Tom would stick out like a sore thumb. I have some experience of how not to draw too much attention to myself as a stranger."

It made sense to Beatrice. "Fine."

"I will go with Beatrice and do the talking." He turned to Tom. "If there is trouble, it is more likely to come from down there. You and Ivy can stay here, concealed by the trees. If matters go awry, hide or run for it."

Tom opened his mouth to argue, but Beatrice had heard enough from both of them. She looked at Ivy.

The woman gave a reluctant nod.

Tom grumbled as he dismounted. Stomping over, he stood beside Breeze and held his arms out to Ivy.

Ivy froze and stared at his hands.

"I only want to help you," he said gruffly. "It is a long way down." Tom gentled his voice. "And you are tiny."

Ivy slipped from Breeze's back.

Tom removed his hands the moment her feet were steady beneath her. "We will find somewhere in the shade and wait."

Ivy led the way back into the trees. Tom followed, hovering just out of arm's reach.

"Come along." Beatrice spurred Breeze toward the village.

Garrett fumed along in her wake. He knew some nasty words and had an inventive way of stringing them together.

She slowed Breeze and waited for him to catch up.

He was a dreadful rider. His arms and knees stuck out like bristles on either side of Parsley.

Beatrice swore Parsley gave her an aggrieved look as his rider flopped around like a sack of meal on his back.

"You need to stop that." Parsley carried him past Beatrice before Garrett was able to halt him.

With a grin, Beatrice fell in beside them. "Stop what?"

"Come along," he mimicked her. "I do not 'come along.'"

"And yet, here you are." Beatrice laughed and spurred Breeze forward.

The village was bustling. More than one set of eyes turned to stare as she and Garrett entered through the end furthest from the river.

"Like a bloody sore thumb," Garrett muttered. He dismounted with her. They left the horses tied to a water trough.

"Remember." He caught her arm, halting Beatrice from joining the steady trickle of folk heading toward the green. "Let me do the talking. Follow my lead. Do nothing else."

"Aye, Garrett." She made for a collection of tables set out across the grass. People were sitting, drinking from tankards and it seemed rather convivial. They looked like her best chance to gather information. "Come along," she called over her shoulder.

He caught the back of her tunic. "You, my lady." He reeled her in. "Are in sore need of having your ass paddled." His dark eyes danced good-humoredly. He slipped an arm around her waist and drew her up against him. "And I am just the man to do so." He was hard and warm.

Her skin tingled. She brought her hands up to his chest. A teasing Garrett was impossible to resist.

"Now, behave." His voice grew husky as his arms tightened. "Before these nice people think I am manhandling a boy."

Beatrice's face heated. She'd given no thought to her boyish attire.

"Although, no red-blooded man would think this belonged to a boy." He gave her bottom a ringing slap.

Beatrice didn't know whether to laugh or protest. Her bottom stung and she put her hand on the offended area.

Garrett strolled away from her. "Come along."

* * *

It made sense to replenish their supplies with an extra mouth to feed. It pleased Garrett how readily Beatrice agreed with him. With a bit of clever handling, this detour could become more time on the road.

The market was small but thriving. Loud calls, hawking everything from bullocks to hair ribbons filled the air. Young bucks, dressed in their best tunics, hair neatly slicked back, paraded about. Eyes flashing brighter than their bliauts, a giggling huddle of girls looked them over from the stone cross central to the green.

Garrett drifted from stall to stall, sharing a word or two here, testing the produce there, but all the while steadily working his way toward the tables outside the tavern. He tugged Beatrice out of the way of a small band of children, shrieking with excitement and chased by a pair of barking dogs. He and Beatrice appeared precisely as he wanted them to: two unremarkable travelers stopping for supplies. The beefy rich smell of meat pastries tempted Garrett into parting with some coins.

Of course, Beatrice in her chausses caused more than one

passing comment. A rotund farmwife huffed indignantly from behind her baskets of greens. He should've thought to get her to put on a gown, but he'd been too intent on preventing Beatrice from descending on the village with her lavish smile and her noble accent. If her family was looking for her, and they damned well should be, he didn't want to lay a trail for them.

As she followed meekly behind him, munching on her pie and confining her comments to him, he wasn't displeased with the way things were going.

Beatrice had forgotten her haste, for the moment. Her expressions held him captive, shifting in constant response to what she saw and thought.

Moving amongst the press of people, Garrett allowed time to lag.

He stopped at a baker's stall. Large, golden loaves spread across the table, their yeast smell making his mouth water.

As long as no abused whore, starving orphan, or whipped dog stumbled across their path, they should get along without making too much of a ripple.

He should've known better than to toss temptation to fate. His nape pricked and he turned. His shadow was no longer where he'd left it. He caught sight of Beatrice stomping across the green. Her destination? Where else, but to the ragged creature confined to the village stocks. Jesu, have mercy. He dropped the bread he was buying and dashed after her.

"Hey," the baker shouted after him.

"I will be back." He narrowly avoided crashing into a crate full of live chickens.

The crown of Beatrice's head shone like a beacon from the far side of the green. The girl had accursedly long legs, which carried her quite a distance when she was intent on it.

Garrett reached her before she opened her mouth. He sweated freely as he clamped a hand around her already opening lips and hauled her back. He got a kick in the shin for his troubles.

"Settle down," he whispered in her ear. "Do not speak."

"Garrett." She turned, her eyes big with outrage. "Did you see who is penned up like an animal? He is nothing more than a child."

"He's a thief, Beatrice." He wrapped his arm about her shoulders and put some distance between her and the curious glances from the men drinking at the tables.

"But he cannot be. Look at him; he is only a baby." Beatrice gazed at the puny miscreant in the stocks. Tears welled in her eyes.

Garrett glanced at the boy.

He was young, or mayhap small for his age, but he did make a pitiful figure. His skinny legs were liberally decorated with an assortment of scabs. His arms looked thin enough to pick a lock. Fresh smears of blood spoke of rough handling. Someone must have hacked off his hair because bits of scalp showed through the patchy mess. Or the boy had the mange.

The boy's eyes met his.

And Garrett knew him. He'd been this boy and known such a boy in a dozen or more different villages scattered across England. The runt was as clever and resourceful as a rat and just as dangerous.

Unfortunately, the boy had already taken Beatrice's measure. Dismissing Garrett as of no use to him, the boy turned soulful orbs to Beatrice.

She clasped her hands to her chest.

Garrett dropped his arm to her waist to keep her clamped to his side. Over her head, the convivial group at the tables had all turned to watch them. From the market, more faces were looking their way. Visions of having to take on an entire village taunted him.

"The boy is a thief, Beatrice," he whispered. "He may look pitiful, but trust me, that boy has a better chance of surviving than a plague of locusts. Come away now." He tugged on her waist.

"I cannot leave him like this." She raised her face to his and gripped the front of his tunic.

"Beatrice." Garrett drew a measured breath. "The boy has, no doubt, stolen from one of these good, honest people. Look around you. Do these look like the sort of people who would lock a boy away without reason?"

To his relief, she did look around her and remained unresisting in his grasp. Then, she looked back at the boy. Her lips trembled, and she pressed them tightly together.

Garrett cursed.

"I do not care." Up went her determined chin and her eyes shone with the fervor of a born Samaritan. "No child deserves to be treated in this manner. And if he did steal, I will wager it was because he was hungry."

"Not all children are innocent," he said.

"Well, they should be."

He might've saved his breath to cool his pottage because Beatrice had found another unfortunate to gather beneath her wing. Why had her family not curbed her of this? He vaguely remembered the pack of ugly dogs that sometimes followed her about Anglesea. He would lay his last coin he knew who'd acquired those.

"Please, Garrett."

He steeled himself as she pressed closer to him. She didn't intend the action as provocative, but his body reacted anyway. He'd had too many days of watching her ass in the saddle, the way her chausses clung to the long sweep of her legs. There was a bloody good reason why women should be put in gowns. Her breasts molded against his chest and her thighs pressed against his.

Garrett disentangled himself. He was beaten. "What is the boy's fine?"

Heads swung to a large, authoritative man sitting atop a table. His tunic was richer than his companions. He lumbered to his feet, wiping his mouth with the back of his hand. A big man, most of it girth, the sod was also as cunning as a fox. Garrett noted how his beady eyes moved in his face, florid from drinking in the warm sun.

The man took it in: Beatrice, him, and the scraggly creature in the stocks. The big man put down his tankard and adjusted his belt. "Three marks."

Garrett laughed. "What did he take, the king's bloody horse?"

The man studied him, and Garrett let him. The conniving dog had read the situation correctly, but Garrett hadn't spent his life surviving on his wits for naught.

"I tell you what." Garrett studied the boy critically. "As he is such a scrawny little whelp, I will give you what I have. Five shillings."

"Nay, Garrett." Beatrice took hold of his tunic and tugged. "We have enough." She found her purse and opened the ties. "See here."

# Chapter Fifteen

eatrice glanced at Garrett and bit the inside of her cheek. He'd barely spoken to her since they'd left the village. She shouldn't have interrupted him, but she hadn't realized until she said the words that Garrett was bargaining for the boy. She'd only been relieved there was sufficient coin to see him freed. Of course, the villagers had been most unpleasantly insistent they take the boy with them and leave right away. After taking their entire purse.

"What, in the name of God, is that?" Tom rose as Garrett all but dropped the boy from his saddle.

Beatrice was glad they'd not left the boy there. The villagers were not such nice people. She didn't say as much to Garrett. He looked angry enough to bite her head right off her shoulders.

"He has a name." She dismounted and went to stand beside the boy. He was pitifully thin, and her heart ached all over again. "What is your name?"

"Newt."

"I beg your pardon?"

"Newt." He had a high, piercing voice. His dark eyes darted in his face as he took everything in about him. "I am called Newt."

"Surely that is not the name your mother gave you?"

"Do not know, never knew my mother." Newt hawked and spat, drying his chin with the tattered end of his sleeve.

That was a bit disgusting. Beatrice stepped back and threw a speaking glance at Garrett. The boy was an orphan, without the benefit of a proper Christian name or a proper rearing.

Garrett's glare made her shiver.

"You went for directions." Tom threw up his hand. "How did you come back with that?"

"Newt," Beatrice said. "He is not a that; he is a boy, with a name. Only, not a very good one."

"You can call me whatever you fancy, my lady." Newt sidled over and gazed up at her with limpid eyes.

Garrett growled, and Newt snapped his mouth shut.

"What is he doing here?" Tom loomed over Newt. The top of the boy's scraggly head barely cleared Tom's belt.

Newt tucked himself beside Beatrice.

"It was dreadful, Tom." Beatrice's heart twisted for the poor little mite. Tom was frightening him. "He was pinned up in these stocks and his poor limbs were protruding. See what those awful people have done to his hair." She reached out to touch Newt's head.

Tom caught her hand. "Do not touch him. Things are living in there."

Beatrice dropped her hand. There was definitely some movement in Newt's straggling remains of hair that couldn't be attributed to the gentle breeze.

"I still do not understand what he is doing here." Tom rubbed the back of his neck.

Beatrice hesitated, looking for the right words.

"Tell him." Garrett's hands clenched around his belt.

Beatrice sent him a mute appeal to tell it for her, but Garrett planted his legs apart and jerked his head at Tom.

"I paid his fine." She got it out as quickly as she could.

"You did what!" Tom's bellow made her wince.

Newt ducked behind her.

Goodness, the boy was fast. "I could not very well leave him there." Beatrice looked to Ivy for support, but Ivy was eyeing Newt with distaste.

"Aye," Garrett said. "She paid his fine."

"With what coin?" Tom's turned to Garrett

"This is the good part." Garrett strode back toward Tom.

Now, the two men chose to be in perfect accord?

"She paid his fine with the coin we were supposed to use to replenish our food."

"All of it?"

"All of it." They stood shoulder to shoulder, legs braced, and hands tucked into their belts.

"He is filthy." Ivy wrinkled her nose a little.

"Aye." There was the tiniest glimmer of sympathy in Ivy's face. Another woman would understand. "And see how thin he is. I do not think he has eaten in days."

"I have a powerful ache in my belly." Newt placed his hands over his middle and hunched over.

"I have a powerful ache in my ass."

"Garrett." She didn't think he should use such language in front of the boy. "He is just a child." Beatrice tried appealing to his sense of justice. Garrett wouldn't let a child suffer. Not her Garrett.

Her Garrett turned his back on her and strode over to Parsley.

"That child, I will wager, knows more curses than you do," Tom, the betrayer, said.

"Mayhap if we bathed him?" Ivy suggested.

"I am not touching him." Tom folded his arms over his chest. His top lip curled back.

"We could do something about his hair?" Beatrice suggested to Ivy, turning her back on the two men.

"Have you thought what you will do with him now?" Garrett rested his arm on Parsley's back. His pose was relaxed, but his eyes glittered at her dangerously.

"He must come with us." It was difficult to meet his eyes when he was so angry with her.

"How?"

She opened her mouth to argue and shut it again. Her belly hollowed as she did the mental tally. They still had only three horses and, now, five people.

"I thought you were in a hurry to reach London?"

Garrett was right. She was pressed; her family needed her to reach London, and too much time was already lost. Her confidence wavered. She'd acted hastily. But the boy was here now. "I don't suppose you have anywhere to go?"

"Nay." He gave her a cheerful grin.

"He can ride with me." It wasn't a perfect solution, but it would do at a push. "And when we stop for the night, we will... do something with Newt. We can make him more presentable and find somewhere to leave him. A farm in need of another hand."

"I do not think I should bathe." Newt licked both his palms and drew them down his face. "There."

"Sweet mother of God." Tom pressed his fist to his mouth.

Beatrice shuddered in distaste. Newt looked more disreputable than before his tongue bath.

"And I would not do well on a farm." Newt shook his head. "I'm not much on the tilling and the plowing. Not much with animals either."

"Another sort of place, then." Desperation closed in around Beatrice.

"If he is riding with you, with whom will Ivy ride?" Garrett was ruthless in his anger.

Beatrice's shoulders drooped. She couldn't ask Ivy to ride with one of the men.

Confirming her fears, Ivy paled and worried her bottom lip with her teeth.

Tom and Garrett still wore their identical smirks.

"I know." She tried valiantly to keep her voice chirpy. It

sounded high and strained. "I can walk, and Newt and Ivy can ride."

"You are going to walk all the way to London?" Tom raised an eyebrow.

Garrett cursed liberally.

Tom looked impressed.

Beatrice's heart sank. She'd created a dreadful snarl. She'd only wanted to save the boy. Tears stung the back of her eyelids and she blinked them away.

"Besides which," Garrett said. "Your act of martyrdom will ensure you are remembered here. If anyone is looking for us, we are leaving them bloody waving flags."

It got worse. "I did not think of that."

"Nay, you did not." Garrett straightened; his frown deepened. "And we still do not know the way to London."

"London? You are going to London?" Newt's head snapped from one to the other.

"And is that not exactly like you, Beatrice." Tom thrust his fists onto his hips. "Henry is always saying if there is a thought in your head, it must be lonely, for it lacks company."

His words stung, and Beatrice blinked faster. She would not cry. Not with Newt looking at her as if he were regretting her rescue.

"I think Henry sounds like a right horse's ass." Ivy touched the edge of her sleeve.

Only it made Beatrice want to cry more. Henry did say such about her, often enough for it to have become a phrase within the keep. And he was right. Tears made her sight swim, and she turned her head. She hadn't thought any of this through, and now she was here with Ivy and Newt looking to her to take care of them. Tom was furious with her, and Garrett would probably never speak to her again. He'd see her for what she truly was and want nothing more to do with her. Just like her three betrothals. Her betrothed had, to a man, changed their minds once they'd gotten to know her better. The damn tears insisted on creeping down her cheeks. She pretended to push her hair back and swiped them away.

"Do not cry, my lady." Newt slipped around her and tugged on her tunic. "I know the way to London."

Beatrice's tried to control her voice, but it came out in a choked gasp. "You do?"

"Of course I do." Newt thrust his shoulders back. "I was born in London."

"I thought you did not know where you were born?" Garrett's voice came from much closer.

Beatrice turned her shoulder. She didn't want to compound her error by appearing weak and silly.

"I said I did not know my mother." Newt peered up at Beatrice, twisting his head when she tried to duck and hide her face. "But any fool knows where they were born, because they were born there."

"Get on the horse." Garrett grabbed him by the back of his tunic. "And if you so much as breathe on me, I will wring your neck like a chicken."

Newt scampered away.

"And if you steal the misbegotten beast, I will hunt you down and use your guts for garters." His large hand cupped her chin, turning her face up to him.

Beatrice tried to evade his grasp, but his fingers tightened.

His fixed look bored into her. His lips were drawn in a tight line.

More tears welled in her eyes and trickled down her cheeks.

"No tears." He rubbed moisture away with the calloused pads of his thumbs. "You began this, Lady Beatrice, and you must finish it." Garrett dropped her chin and strode over to his horse. There was a short altercation as he positioned Newt before him, ensuring the boy barely brushed against him.

"Come on, my lady." Ivy gave the sleeve of her tunic a tug. "Who will rescue us if our champion is weeping into her kerchief?"

"Buck up now, Bea." Tom swung onto Badger's back. "He is no worse than the three-legged cat you found, the one that now only has one eye. I can always trap us a rabbit or two."

"And I know which greens we can eat." Ivy stepped a bit closer. "Your man will get over his pet in a mile or two."

"He's not my man." Saying the words aloud threatened to open the floodgates.

Ivy snorted. "He is your man, all right. Or I do not know men. And I do know men."

# Chapter Sixteen

Beatrice was relieved when the rest of the afternoon passed quickly. Newt rode with Garrett and pointed the right direction. Either the boy was an accomplished liar, or he did know the way to London. Beatrice stayed silent. She'd drawn enough fire down on her head for one day.

As the afternoon bled into evening, Garrett's anger remained unrelenting. He kept his back firmly to her as he rode.

She hadn't noticed before how many times in a day he would turn and smile at her, or say something outrageous when Tom couldn't hear. His continued anger chipped at her, and she teetered on the brink of a dejected slump throughout the afternoon.

The evening stayed clear, and the travelers kept moving. Nobody suggested a stop for the night yet. Yesterday's rain had drained away, and the road was good. The horses managed a slow but steady pace.

She'd almost reached London and her father. It should've made her feel better. It didn't. Instead, her eyes kept straying to Garrett's stiff back.

* * *

The boy stank. Garrett breathed through his mouth. He must've smelled as rank when he was a youngster, before he was introduced to lye soap and water. Forcibly. He'd fought like the very devil, but One-eyed Bets had an arm stronger than any blacksmith and a determination to match it. Too old and scarred to make her living on her back anymore, Bets had eked out an existence caring for the children of the other whores in exchange for a meal and a place to sleep.

She'd taken a shine to him.

He might have smiled at the memory had he not been so livid.

The boy wriggled. "My ass is getting sore, and I am still hungry."

"Shut your cakehole, or I will shut it for you."

Newt was a smart lad and knew when to keep his tongue between his teeth.

Garrett was done with this. Tonight he'd leave. Newt knew the way. Beatrice had her guide to London. She had Tom to protect her and Ivy to keep her out of trouble. He'd reached his limit.

And he'd been so close. Frustration seared his guts. He'd been within a meeting or two of tossing up her skirts and burying himself between her lady-white thighs. If they'd remained at Anglesea, he would be on his way by now, Beatrice deflowered and his revenge a sweet aftertaste.

Where was he instead? Plodding down the road to London, sharing a carthorse with a reeking gutter brat. This idiocy was actually taking him further from his goal. He now had not only a glowering boy chaperone, but a whore, and a baseborn brat firmly entrenched between him and Beatrice's virginity. There had to be another way to bring Sir Arthur down. If it took the rest of his days, he would find it. But trailing along in this caravan of fools wasn't the way.

Tonight then. Once the others were asleep, he would disappear. He gripped the pouch around his neck. It almost alleviated the tugging within his chest.

* * *

Garrett still hadn't spoken to her. He'd helped set up their camp for the night in a small clearing beside the road. The distances between woodland lengthened as they traveled. It had taken some time to find a good place to rest for the night.

Tom had only managed to bag one rabbit. All in all, it had been a miserable meal, with a handful of greens to accompany the rabbit and only water to wash it down. Their paltry fare could be laid at her feet, too. They'd ridden late into the night to try to make up for their slower pace. There'd not been time to lay more traps for dinner.

They all sought their blankets shortly thereafter.

Garrett was a dim shape at the edge of the woods. The low flicker of the fire bathed him in long shadows. He was just at the edge of their camp, but the distance yawned wider and wider.

The sky above her was clear and littered with stars. The chirp of crickets rose and fell as sleep evaded her.

Ivy lay at her back, so still Beatrice thought she slept. Then, she would turn and see Ivy's eyes wide open, staring at nothing. Ivy didn't invite sympathy, and Beatrice pretended not to notice.

Across from them, the pale flames of the small fire illuminating his features, was Tom, and a little farther on, Newt slept.

Garrett had offered to stand guard. They were getting closer to London, and the road had been busier than before.

She should've been sleeping. They would reach London tomorrow, and she'd need to find her father and impress upon him the urgency of returning home. He wouldn't be happy about her secret journey. Roger would be unhappier, and Roger didn't have their father's years to mellow his responses. William would probably find the entire thing greatly amusing.

Tomorrow she would reach the end of her journey. What would happen with Garrett then? Judging by his manner toward her now, he would drop her in her father's lap and leave. And thank the Lord for his deliverance from her. The thought was like a noose about her neck.

Beatrice gave up on sleeping.

Garrett's stiff posture bade everyone stay away.

Yet, she had to speak with him. She couldn't rest until this matter between them was settled.

Ivy's eyes were closed and her face slack.

Barely breathing, Beatrice inched away.

Tom snored softly from the other side of the fire.

Beatrice slipped past.

With the alacrity of one who sleeps light, Newt opened his eyes. He saw her and closed them again.

Gaze fixed on the night, Garrett kept his voice low as he said, "What is it?"

"I have wanted to speak with you all day." Beatrice slipped between the trees until a large trunk shielded her from view. Now she stood here, Beatrice couldn't find the right words. This was harder than she'd thought.

Garrett stared forward, his back propped against a tree, his long legs stretched before him.

Not knowing whether to sit or to stand, she crouched beside him.

"Go back to sleep, my lady."

Her courage faltered. His voice was chilly enough to freeze her where she crouched, and he was back to calling her "my lady" with that hateful sneer. The craven part of her wanted to take her dismissal and leave. She straightened her shoulders. Any daughter of Lady Mary's did not shirk when something unpleasant needed attending. "I cannot sleep until I beg your pardon."

He went still, like a hind scenting trouble.

"So." She rubbed her damp palms against her thighs. "I do beg your pardon."

He stared into the night.

Mayhap she should return to her spot beside Ivy. Except, she'd not done what she'd come here to do. The dull ache in her chest wouldn't go away. She needed to breach the distance he'd placed between them somehow. "I did not think today when I saw Newt in the stocks. I should have spoken to you first, before I acted."

Still the unnerving silence.

"I do not always think." That was only the half of it. "Indeed, I rarely think if you ask my family. But I did not mean to embroil you in any of this." She thought only of the thrill of being alone with him. "I only wanted to go to London. I suppose I should have waited and spoken to my brother, Henry. Or my uncle. Tom has been saying as much since I first went to him."

It wrenched inside to admit any of this, but it weighed on her and he deserved her honesty. "I wanted to do something, for once, which made me special. Every member of my family is known for something. Me?" A small laugh escaped her and she hushed it. "I am known for three failed betrothals and a slew of unfortunate incidents. I know it was silly of me, but, just this once, I wanted not to be *Oh, Beatrice!*" She imitated her mother.

He shifted and stilled.

Beatrice plunged forward. "We are taught pride goes before destruction and I should know that by now. Except, this time, I have dragged you and Tom and Ivy and Newt with me. And I have no idea how to fix it."

She wobbled and put her hands on the ground for balance. "You have been so good to me." After all Garrett had done for her, she'd repaid him with heaping a greater load on his shoulders. "I asked, and you dropped everything and agreed to lead me to London. Tom has not been fair to you, but you have not allowed him to provoke you. I am grateful for that, too. When I rushed in to help Ivy, you saved both of us, and you were tender with her. And today, when you were ready to wring my neck, you rescued Newt and did not, once, threaten to box my ears."

Garrett tightened his jaw.

Her chest ached. She'd only made him angrier. "You are a good man, Garrett, and I do not deserve any of the kindness you have shown me."

She'd said what needed to be said, but it was cold comfort. With Garrett still sitting as if he'd been carved from the tree. Nurse always said doing the right thing was its own reward. Nurse was wrong. Her misery was like a dull blade sawing through the center of her. "I am done. I wanted to thank you for your kindness and beg your pardon for causing you all this trouble."

She shifted away.

"Stay."

* * *

Garrett was speechless. What had she bloody done? He was done for. Nobody had demanded an apology of her. Yet Beatrice had come and thrown herself on his mercy. *Jesu.* Her sweetness ran right the way through to the bone. It tied him in tighter and tighter knots. He'd made the mistake of thinking her lack of guile worked to his advantage. And it had. Up to a point. It also completely disarmed him.

*You are a good man, Garrett, and I do not deserve any of the kindness you have shown me.*

He ground his teeth together until his jaw ached. *Nay, I am not. I am a bastard and a whoreson. I am a conniving churl, looking to use you to exact my revenge.*

*You are a good man, Garrett, and I do not deserve any of the kindness you have shown me.*

And as she'd said those words, he'd known it—for one moment—the sharp need to be that man. What was he to make of any of this?

He latched his hand behind her neck and tugged her forward. Her face inches from his, he could read her eyes. All she was, right there for him to see in its purity. He soiled her merely by touching her, and yet his hand wouldn't uncurl from her nape and release her. She ran like a fever through his blood.

"Beatrice, what am I to do with you?" He hadn't intended to speak.

"I am not sure."

Garrett bit off a short bark of surprised laughter.

"I think, mayhap, you should leave me here to my own devices and go back to your life. I did not want you to leave me in anger though."

Garrett's groan rose from the deepest part of him. Where was his anger now? She said the very thing he'd been brooding on. God's bones, but she invited him to go. Perversely, it made him reject the notion. "And what would happen to you if I left you here?"

"I should get along." She gave her chin a valiant lift, but the pillowy softness of her lips trembled. "I might not reach London, but I should get along."

"Beatrice the Brave." Christ, she was killing him. She had such courage, just no understanding of where her true strength lay.

She dropped her gaze to the ground.

He couldn't see in this light, but Garrett was willing to bet his right arm her cheeks were flushed with color.

Garrett marveled at her; at the same moment, he wanted to shake some sense into her. She had no weapons to ward off predators. She was like a hedgehog without its prickles or a rose without its thorns. It wasn't his job to be her protector, his mind screamed at him, but the rest of him wasn't listening. It was looking at the clear lines of her face. There was no artifice to Beatrice. She concealed nothing.

She'd known he was angry with her. Instead of puffing up with feminine outrage, she'd slunk over here and offered him the sweetest apology he'd ever heard. Not because of it being lyrically worded, but more because she made no excuses for herself. How did one fight someone who kept scattering flowers in your path?

"Beatrice." He'd never been as she. Not even when he was a small child. "You give away pieces of yourself too easily."

Look at how she was with him. Never once had she questioned his intent. She refused to take note of Tom, her best friend. She'd opened herself to him like a flower before the sun. It had made her an easy target for such as he. A nasty shock sparked through him. What would happen when he was gone? Would she be as vulnerable to the next sod with murky intentions? And suddenly, he couldn't bear the thought. Or worse, the idea Beatrice would grow bitter and hard. That she would lose the wondrous, openhearted embrace with which she viewed the world.

"I am a big girl. There are enough pieces to go around." She squared her slim shoulders.

Nay.

He wanted to gather up the parts of her she scattered around and keep them just for himself. The thought was like a rusty blade to his vitals. He craved all the pieces of Beatrice for himself.

He fastened his hungry mouth on hers.

She came without resistance.

*Fight me*, part of him wanted to shout. *Open your beautiful eyes and see me for the rotten, miserable whoreson I am.*

She sighed and opened her mouth beneath his.

A better man would have chastely saluted her lips and sent her back to bed. But he wasn't a better man. He was the son of a traitor and a whore, and the rot went right to the core of him.

He thrust his tongue into her mouth, bringing his hands to cup her face and drag her closer to him. He wanted all of her, to grab the sweetness that was Beatrice and drink until he grew sick with it.

And, sweet Jesu help him, but she gave, as she did everything else, freely and wholeheartedly.

* * *

Garrett kissed her like he was desperate for the taste of her. His mouth devoured hers.

The woman in her thrilled, as the girl grew shy. She almost pulled back, but as if he sensed her withdrawal, his mouth grew hotter and hungrier.

He wanted her.

It was intoxicating to know he felt it, too. This yearning for each other.

His hand tangled in her hair, demanding she yield to him.

There was no resistance. She was his for the taking. She slid her hands around his neck, pulling him to her. That awful chasm between them closed. Still, too far. She inched closer to him.

He groaned.

The sound tugged at her matching need.

His hands were rough on her legs as he pulled her onto his lap.

This was where she needed to be.

His thighs were hard beneath hers. His chest rubbed the aching points of her breasts. He parted her legs until she straddled him.

It was beyond improper, but Beatrice exalted. Her thighs were spread across his. Her aching core met his hardness. The intimate contact rippled through her. She should be shocked, but she had to have this. She wanted much more, and she had no thought of how to ask for it with words. Small, needy sounds escaped her to get swallowed in the heat of his mouth. Her body knew what to do.

Garrett rocked her against him. There. He pressed her where the ache was keenest.

Her skin was too tight to contain the restless hunger. "Aye." She pressed harder; she was where she had to be.

"Beatrice, you should stop me." His chest heaved.

"Nay." She could not get enough of him. More. She wanted more and more. Beatrice moved on him of her own accord, trying to assuage the clamor driving her on.

His hands tightened around her bottom before slipping beneath her tunic.

They were fiery on the bare skin of her back. Beatrice tugged her belt. She craved his touch on every part of her. She wanted to feel his skin on hers.

He closed his hands over her breasts. His long fingers stroked her nipples.

The ache grew. Pleasure shot to the place where they were joined. Beatrice exalted in it. Her breath came ragged and harsh, as if she'd been running. Nothing else existed for her, except the pressure of where their bodies rubbed and his hands upon her breasts. She was wicked and wild and free. The sensation built until she vibrated to the ends of her fingers.

She came apart into a thousand brilliant splinters.

He tightened his arms as she collapsed onto his chest.

She lay there, melted, panting, and acquiescent. Totally his.

He stroked her back as her heart slowed. The hard ridge of his flesh pressed her thighs.

She buried her head into the sweat-dampened heat of his neck. His pulse pounded beneath her mouth. For her, because of what they had shared. Beatrice traced the motion with her lips.

* * *

Garrett ached. He wanted her more than he had wanted anyone in his entire life. She lay spent and recovering atop his pulsing shaft and, damn him to hell, all he could think of was how good she felt in his arms. He burned to slide off her braies and ease his aching rod into her.

He beat back the frenzy raging in his blood.

*Take her*, whispered his body. *Get from her what we must have.*

And yet, he sat there and held her. Like some stupid sot, he was content to smell the slight floral scent of her. Her breath escaped in small puffs, tickling the sensitive skin of his neck. Her mouth branded his throat above his pulse.

She'd given herself completely over to the pleasure.

It humbled him.

It terrified him.

The woman in his arms was far beyond his experience.

*Take her.* Here it was, the opportunity for which he'd toiled for all these years. Here was revenge, laid before him, willing and ready.

And he couldn't.

He wrapped his arms around her so she didn't feel the chill on her fevered skin.

She'd come sweetly and completely for him. She gave herself with the sort of abandon that left other encounters feeling cheap and unworthy.

He didn't deserve the gift she bestowed on him. Some tiny part of him, still clasping a frail tendril of goodness, wouldn't let him abuse her gift. He would curse himself as the worst kind of sentimental fool for letting the moment pass, but he was equally sure he was going to do it anyway.

"Garrett?" She blinked up at him, and his chest ached.

She wasn't for him. And it had nothing to do with the cur who'd sired her or her title. He dropped a kiss on her forehead. "You should rest."

"That was," she wriggled, "marvelous."

Garrett's face split into an idiotic grin. Damn her and her honesty, it reached deep inside of him and tugged at the buried part of him. "Aye, sweeting, it was, and now you should go back to Ivy before I forget my good intentions."

The little vixen actually hesitated as if she was weighing her options, and Garrett groaned.

He wasn't noble. He was a dog with a throbbing shaft and a desirable woman perched right on it. There was a limit to how much he could take. He shifted her hips until she clambered off him. The relief and the disappointment robbed him of coherent thought.

"Garrett? You will still be here when I wake?" She stood beside him, her face soft and beautiful.

He'd put that look on her face. His chest swelled with pride and something else; he dare not put a name to it. "Aye, Beatrice, I will be here."

He should've left when he had the chance.

Garrett snorted. What a sodding liar he was. He'd never been going anywhere. He'd been sitting here brooding, looking for the smallest excuse to stay.

"Beatrice?"

"Aye.

Not one more day of watching her glorious ass in those chausses. "Put your skirts back on."

* * *

Garrett's eyes burned and he rubbed the grit from them. He hadn't slept all night. The same fledgling part of him that had sent Beatrice back to her blankets had flickered into life as he kept watch over the sleeping camp. It struggled for purchase against the rage and bitterness he had nursed since his childhood and won. He welcomed the new day.

As the sky lightened about them, the camp woke.

Ivy was first. She caught sight of him, froze, and nodded. Ivy knew instinctively what he had fought against. Beatrice had rescued more than her body from those men. As the days passed, if she stayed close to Beatrice, his lady would work her magic for Ivy, too.

Ivy fussed with the smoldering ashes of last night's fire.

His much larger form almost dwarfing her, Tom joined her.

Ivy tensed, but she didn't move away. It would be some time before she lost her fear. She cried out and sucked her fingers into her mouth. She must have burned them.

The boy nudged her gently out the way and took her place.

It was such a small action, but Garrett saw it for what it was. Ivy had a protector, whether her protector was aware of it or not.

What would his mother's life have been if she'd had Beatrice to bring back the joy and Tom to watch over her while she did?

Garrett untied the pouch from his neck. His fingers shook as he released the tiny knots that held it closed. He hadn't looked inside in years. Not since the day he'd tied it around his neck as he left his mother's grave.

A flash of color fluttered to the ground. Garrett picked it up and cradled it in his palm. A red velvet ribbon, it had once been bright scarlet but was faded brown with constant use. His mother had clung to this tiny remnant of happier times. She kept it tied to the bodice of her chainse, close to her heart.

She hadn't loved his father. Wulfric had been a heavy-handed, vicious lout, but he'd kept her and Garrett well fed and comfortable. The ribbon came from before. She'd been wearing it when she left her father's house as a young maid.

Her father had turned his back on her when she took up with Wulfric. She'd been too shamed to return to her family after Wulfric was dead. Or too proud. Garrett was never sure.

The ribbon fluttered in his palm as a gentle breeze rippled through the clearing. Garrett's fist closed around it instinctively.

Instead, he stopped the motion and opened his fingers.

The wind picked up the ribbon and it floated to the ground beside him. It rippled once, twice, and then lifted to be carried into a nearby clump of gorse. It hung there a moment before another light gust took it higher.

Garrett left the pouch on the ground as he rose.

"Newt is gone," Ivy said as he walked toward the fire.

He looked back to where Newt had spread his blanket the night before. The boy was gone, but the blanket remained, sprawled across the ground like a stain. He wasn't surprised.

"Beatrice will worry herself over him." Ivy folded her hands in front of her.

"Beatrice." Tom shook his head. "She will not believe the worst of anyone."

"Aye." Ivy's hands clenched. "It is a unique gift."

"Or a curse." Tom strode over to the blanket and snatched it up. "Did he take anything?"

"Not that I can see." Ivy's mouth tightened. She rose and moved to where Beatrice lay.

Tom's face fell.

Clapping a hand on his shoulder, Garrett gave him a sympathetic nod. Women! They tied your tongue into knots.

Tom started and straightened his shoulders.

"I would check to see what the little turd has taken," Garrett said.

# Chapter Seventeen

Shyness beset Beatrice when she faced Garrett in the morning. Her cheeks burned hot as she returned his greeting.

Tom gave her a sharp look but carried on packing the camp.

She and Ivy found a small stream and insisted on bathing before mounting. The stream gurgled through low rocks, hidden from view with the bright green of new leaves. The water was biting cold, but it felt good to be clean once more.

Beatrice eyed her dirt-encrusted chausses with dislike and wriggled into a dark blue bliaut. It was square-necked and plain, made of serviceable linen, but after her days spent in chausses, the dress made her feel softer and more feminine. As did the look she earned from Garrett as he helped her mount Breeze.

"Are you well this morning?" He adjusted her stirrups for her. His hand lingered on her calf.

"Aye." Beatrice smiled down at him. She was better than well. She was alive to the ends of her toes.

"We should make London by nightfall." Muscles bunched beneath his tunic as Garrett mounted Parsley.

Her fingers tingled. She's touched all that male power. Her cheeks heated, and she ducked her head. She followed his lead out of the clearing and onto the road. The road was paved now, and the horse's hooves clattered over the stone.

It might be her fondness for him, but he looked less awkward atop the large horse.

"We will need to reach London soon." Tom rode behind them. "We are short on supplies."

"When we find my father, he will see us fed." Beatrice smiled at the rest of the party.

Ivy looked doubtful, and Tom merely rolled his eyes. Garrett's face almost dispelled her cheer entirely.

His expression remained carefully blank. He returned her smile, but it was one of his practiced, clever smiles. Not one of the others she hoarded to herself.

It was like a slap. The Garrett of the night before had disappeared. So quickly, between one moment and the next, her Garrett was gone and in his place, this smooth stranger. Unease crawled over her skin like ants.

As with the day before, the road grew busier. All manner of people slid past them. Great wagons loaded with wheat and hay, herds of cattle or sheep, and people from lords to paupers, all heading for London.

"I have never been to London." Beatrice looked forward to her first sighting of the city. "I hear it is very large."

"Aye." Ivy's tone was curt.

"We will not be there long. I must get home." Beatrice peered over her shoulder.

Ivy pursed her lips and frowned.

"When I have found my father, we will return to Anglesea." Ivy need not be concerned with staying in the city long. "I would like it if you came with us."

Ivy's arms tightened about her middle. "You would have me come home with you?"

"Aye." Nurse would take to Ivy. God help Ivy then because Nurse could fuss and coddle a soul to death.

They wove their way through a small group of travelers with

large baskets strapped to their backs. The baskets were filled with wrapped bundles. Wares to be sold in London.

"My lady," Ivy said. "I realize you intend only to be kind, but surely you can see, you cannot arrive home towing one such as me."

"I do not see anything of the sort."

"I am a whore." Ivy sighed.

"Nay, Ivy, at Anglesea you can be what you wish to be. I shall not tell them anything other than we found you on the way to London. The rest is up to you to tell."

"And Tom?"

Beatrice looked at Tom.

He raised a brow in question.

"Tom will honor whatever I say." Beatrice patted Ivy's knee. "He behaved badly toward you, and I know he is sorry for that. Tom has lived a simple life. Everything to him is either right or wrong. He knows what you suffered was wrong. It just took him a bit of time to sort through the other part."

"Me being a whore?"

"I do not like that word." Swift irritation spiked through Beatrice. Ivy should not denigrate herself in that manner.

"It is the truth."

"It was the truth." A new life awaited Ivy. She would see to that. "What happens now is up to you, and Tom will not do or say anything to make it otherwise."

"He disapproves of me." Ivy sniffed.

"And me at times."

Ivy chuckled.

Beatrice guided Breeze past a small herd of goats. The mare snorted at them and sidled.

"Tom is very moral, and his morals sometimes war with his big heart. But his strict principles are also what make him the best sort of man. The sort a person can rely on. He has been my rock since I was a girl."

"Do you love him?"

"As one of my brothers." Beatrice laughed. "Perhaps even more than my youngest brother, Henry."

"And you were never in love with him?"

"Tom?" The notion was so silly. Tom sat atop Badger, outwardly a man, but always the boy to her. Good Lord, they'd gone tadpoling together. He's pushed her into the stream. "Nay. Tom and I are great friends, but any more than that, and we would likely bludgeon each other to death."

The horse's hooves rapped against the stone in a steady rhythm. They passed a family. A stout father and mother herded a large group of children between them. A small girl glanced up as they passed. She smiled and waved her little hand.

"Will you come with us to Anglesea?" Beatrice waved back.

"I shall think on it," Ivy said.

It wasn't the firm "aye" she sought from Ivy, but Beatrice had time to work on her.

For a stretch, the road was empty. It wove through cultivated land. Villages dotted the hills here and there. The road dipped, and they followed it between neat hedgerows. Sparrows argued in the top branches.

Suddenly, Breeze tossed her head and sidled away nervously.

Beatrice tightened her grip on the reins.

"What is it?" Tom pulled Badger out of the skittish mare's path.

"I do not know." Beatrice searched the road to see what disturbed Breeze. "It could have been a wild animal."

Breeze whickered, and Beatrice ran a soothing hand down her neck.

Parsley was his normal stolid, and Badger, as per usual, merely looked annoyed.

Newt slid out of the undergrowth and into the road before them.

"Look, a feral beast." Tom crossed his arms over the pommel.

Newt. Whole and well. Beatrice was glad. She kept it to herself. Neither Tom nor Garrett had said a word to her about the boy's disappearance, but Beatrice guessed what they were thinking.

"Where did you get to?" Garrett drew rein beside Newt.

For once, Parsley didn't carry him a good ten paces beyond where he wished to stop. It wasn't her imagination. Garrett was improving on horseback.

"Here and there." Newt shrugged. He gave her a lavish bow. "My lady." He held up a large sack. "I bring you something to fill your noble belly."

"And where did you get that?" Tom rumbled behind her.

Newt's sack bulged. She was hungry, they all were, but she didn't like to think of some poor family going without this evening.

"I gave him some money," Garrett said.

Garrett stared at Tom.

Tom gave Garrett a hard look, then nodded. "Aye, Garrett gave the boy some coin."

"I did not know you had money with you." Beatrice glanced from one to the other. There was something between the two men. Their faces wore such a studied lack of expression.

"Only a small amount, if we should need it." Garrett shrugged.

A little too cool and dismissive. But the sack was full and her belly wasn't. "I will repay you." Except she'd already given away all her coin. Her cheeks heated in mortification. "When we get to my father, I will make sure he returns your coin."

Garrett's lips tightened, and his eyes went cold.

The uneasy feeling shivered through Beatrice.

"Have we time to stop and eat?" Ivy peered around her shoulder, her eyes locked on the sack. "I, for one, am starved."

"What a fine idea, my other lady." Newt jabbed his grubby thumb in the direction he had come. "There is a small stream back a short ways. It would be a fine place to feast."

All eyes turned to her.

Beatrice's stomach grumbled. With a flush, she signaled Newt to lead on.

Newt's bag was like a treasure chest. He drew forth fresh bread, apples, cheeses, a couple of long sausage links, and a small ham. He spread the food on a cloth Beatrice handed him.

She wanted to ask, again, where he'd found this. The more she thought on it, the less likely Garrett's explanation became. She opened her mouth.

A hand on her arm jerked her back.

Her back met with the resistance of Garrett's front. His arm slid around her waist to keep her in place.

"Do not ask, my lady." His lips were warm on her ear, and it distracted her from what he was saying. "Just this once, will you not let that conscience of yours rest?" His fingers stroked lightly over her belly.

Desire stirred beneath where he caressed.

His tongue touched the skin behind her ear.

The spot tingled. Beatrice shot a quick look at the others.

Tom watered the horses, and Ivy sat on a log with her back to them, rearranging the food.

"I am no saint." Certainly not when Garrett was doing such things to her, she wasn't. Beatrice delighted in the tease of his lips against her neck. She leaned into him.

His chuckle vibrated against her ear and sent stronger prickles of sensation over her skin. "Do you think Tom would notice if we disappeared for an hour or two?"

Tom threw himself down beside Ivy.

"Aye, regrettably."

"Then, I suppose we should eat." He placed another searing kiss against her neck before he released her and stepped to the blanket.

It took Beatrice a few moments more to compose herself. She sank onto the log beside Ivy.

"I have news." Newt stuffed bread and cheese into his mouth with both hands.

Beatrice winced as he sprayed half-chewed crumbs every-where. He wasn't a winsome boy.

"Oi!" Tom cuffed him lightly. "Swallow before you speak."

With the speed of long practice, Newt ducked the blow. "Is someone looking for you?"

Beatrice froze.

Newt puffed his chest up. His dark eyes darted in his face, alive with delight. He took his time selecting a link of sausages.

Garrett gave him a swift prod with the toe of his boot.

"I was in a village." Newt wriggled away from Garrett's foot. He made a vague waving motion with his hand. "And there were some men asking after a woman traveling."

Ivy tensed.

Beatrice took her hand and gave it a squeeze. "It could be anyone." She dearly hoped she was right.

"Rudd will not give up until he finds me."

Neither will my family if they are after me.

Ivy's fingers trembled.

Beatrice tightened her hold. "He will not find you."

Ivy looked away.

"Do you know who they were?" Garrett braced on his elbow.

"Did not want to get close enough to ask." Newt filled his mouth with sausage.

"Then, what did the men look like?" Garrett's glance met hers before returning to Newt.

His expression told her nothing. She wanted him to reassure her. A chill rippled through her. Beatrice put aside her meal, no longer hungry.

"One of them was a knight." Newt shrugged and took another huge bite of sausage. "He was armored up and all."

"You will choke." Beatrice tucked her shaking hands beneath her thighs.

Tense, their faces grim, Garrett and Tom were intent on Newt.

"I do not know any knights." Ivy gave a soft sigh of relief.

"And you still do not." Newt grinned at her. He rubbed his filthy hands together. Leaning forward, he let his eyes linger on each face in turn. "Because those men were looking for the lady." He sat back with a brisk nod. "They described her and everything."

Beatrice's belly clenched. Newt's knight was looking for her. Her pace was slow, and their path clear for any searching eyes.

Newt pointed a scrawny finger at Tom. "They said you might be with her. Or a man what looks like you." He paused for effect.

"How many?" Garrett asked.

"Do not know." Newt turned his attention to the apples. "Cannot count, but there was a knight and some men."

"Lots of men or a few?" Garrett snatched the apples away from Newt.

"Only a few." Newt kept his beady eyes on the apple.

"Garrett?" Beatrice turned to him. She was icy cold inside.

He tossed the apple at Newt. "Could it be your father?"

Newt snapped it out of the air and grabbed another hunk of cheese. He skittered out of reach with his horde.

"Nay. He does not know I have left." Beatrice's thoughts clattered about in her brain. Faye must have shown her note to the family. Did her mother know? Henry?

"It must be your brother." Tom got to his feet, his hand rubbing at that infernal spot behind his neck. "He has come looking for you, and there will be the devil to pay when he finds you."

"Then," Garrett got to his feet, "we will make sure he does not find her." He stopped and turned to Beatrice. "If that is what you want? We can stop now, and you can wait for your brother and go home with him."

"Beatrice, it would be better to wait here until Henry catches up with you." Tom loomed over her. It made her head spin even faster. Tom might be right, but it didn't sit well. "He will be even angrier if he has to chase us all the way to London."

"If it is Henry." Beatrice forced herself to breathe slow and deep. At last, her brain started to sort through what she knew. She stood. "We do not know if it is him. What if it is not my brother? Henry would not send a man to London before, and he does not have enough men to send a mounted party after me. What if the king has heard of what I am trying to do and those are his men?"

"What would the king want with a girl like you?" Tom frowned.

"To stop me from reaching my father." Beatrice looked back at Garrett. "How long until we reach London?"

"We will be there by sunset." He stood tall and strong, not telling her what to do, merely waiting to hear what she wanted.

"I want to see this done." Determination stiffened her spine. "I had a purpose, and that has not changed." Her mother would not miraculously recover, and the threat to Anglesea would not disappear. Her father must still come home with her.

Garrett nodded and bent to clear up their meal.

"You should leave us behind." Ivy rose, motioning herself and Newt. "We will only slow you down."

"Not me." Newt's eyes widened.

Ivy's words brought up something she'd not allowed herself to consider before. She had to think of the best course. For all of them. They were her band, disreputable and bedraggled, but they were all here because of her.

Garrett readied the horses. Her heart twisted viciously. Things wouldn't go well for Garrett if it was her brother behind them. She looked at Garrett as Henry would see him, and her insides went cold.

Beatrice hurried over to where he prepared to mount. "You should leave us." She kept her voice low, speaking quickly before her heart overruled her good sense. "You can take Ivy and Newt with you and point Tom and me toward London."

"You are right." A gentle smile tilted the corners of his mouth.

A lump lodged in her throat. Leaving Garrett sat like a bitter lead weight in her stomach.

"I should leave you. It is the most sensible thing to do. And yet," he ran his fingers lightly across her cheek, "I seem to feel the need to see you through this."

"Garrett, you do not understand." Beatrice caught his hand and held it against her cheek. "If my brother discovers you, he will—"

"He will do what any brother would do." Garrett leaned forward and kissed her softly on the lips. "And yet, I am still here. Now mount up before I change my mind. Let us see if we can outrun whoever is looking for you."

* * *

They kept the horses at a steady pace. The road closer to London was better, and they made good time. It wasn't fast enough, though. A mounted party on destriers would close the distance in no time.

Beatrice peered around Ivy for nearly the hundredth time. The road behind them was empty except for a large bullock cart.

"Do you fear your brother?"

"Nay. It is my youngest brother and he is hardly the most fearsome of them." She kept her eyes on the road in front of her. The skin of her back crawled with the fear of someone behind her, eyes on her.

"Then why do you not wait for him and let him take the message to your father?"

It was an excellent question. Aye, she was concerned about how Henry would react to Garrett. But Garrett could melt into the forest and Henry wouldn't see him. It was more than that which concerned her. She'd come too far in her adventure for it to end now. It seemed like failure to turn tail and run for home, leaving Henry to complete her mission. Besides, she couldn't trust that Henry would take the message to her father. He had flatly refused when Godfrey had been speaking to him.

The steady motion of the horse helped to settle her.

She was almost certain it wasn't Henry looking for her. The

ride had given her time to think it through. Her brother was a pragmatist. If she'd left for London, he wouldn't set out himself to stop her. Not if it meant endangering the keep and their mother. He might have asked her uncle to find her, but it didn't seem like something Godfrey would undertake. Besides, Godfrey had no men. The best of them were in London with her father and brothers.

So, who was it behind them? Not Godfrey. It would be more Godfrey's way to sneak up on her undetected and talk at her until she was left with no choice but to turn for home. Tom was right. The king wouldn't have time to bother himself with a mere slip of a girl. And it was doubtful he would even know. Henry would keep the knowledge contained within the keep. He wouldn't want the world to know of his sister's shocking behavior.

It could be Calder. Calder had a solid reason to prevent her from reaching her father. Might he already have arrived at Anglesea, found her gone and determined to stop her? Did Calder have Faye and the boys?

All the unknowns clattered about her brain and increased her anxiety. Before she'd embarked on this journey, she might've thought nothing of a knight and his men looking for her. She'd grown years in only a few days. She'd learned things about the world around her, things her family had sought to conceal from her. Only now did she grasp the enormity of what she'd done. Beatrice didn't think even Tom had truly understood the extent of the danger outside the keep walls.

People were not safe in King John's England. It was a lawless place, where justice lay in the hands of the strongest. The meek suffered, just like her group of women and children. She'd not understood hunger until she'd seen it written on their faces. She'd not known evil until she'd seen what those men did to Ivy. Nay, her eyes had been opened, and she wouldn't trustingly wait for whoever pursued her to catch up with her.

She urged Breeze into the lead.

Garrett sent her a reassuring smile. He would get her there, his smile said.

Breeze rounded a bend in the road, and Beatrice's heart leaped into her throat.

Three large men on horseback stood in the middle of their path. On the verge were two more men, and on the opposite edge, a coach sealed off any escape.

Beatrice drew Breeze to a halt.

"Easy." Garrett stopped beside her.

Together, they studied the men blocking the road. They were men at arms, but there didn't appear to be a knight amongst them.

"They are churchmen." Garrett shielded his eyes with his hand.

Beatrice sagged with relief. Newt had said a knight led the men looking for her.

"Churchmen?" Newt popped his head around Garrett and drew it back again. "Jesu."

Newt was deathly pale and his eyes darted like a cornered rat. "Turn about. We must turn about."

"Nay." Garrett gestured. "This is the road to London, and we need to get past them."

Tom drew rein beside them. "What is it?" He narrowed his eyes as he assessed the men.

The men on the road turned to watch. "Churchmen." Garrett tensed. "Going by their colors, I would wager there is a bishop or someone similar in that coach."

"Why are we stopped then?" Tom threw up his hand. "We have naught to fear from the church."

Newt whimpered and wriggled around behind Garrett. "Do not let them see me."

Genuine fear glimmered in his eyes.

A sense of foreboding crawled up Beatrice's nape. "Newt?"

"Do you know aught of this?" Garrett kept his eyes on the men.

Newt choked. He gave a half nod, stopped, and shook his head.

"What did you do?" Tom caught hold of Newt's collar.

From the road, the men approached. They moved slowly. For now, Newt wouldn't be visible to them.

"Please, my lady." Newt stopped trying to shake free of Tom's grasp. "If they catch me, they will hang me for sure."

Newt must've done something terrible to be hunted by a powerful churchman. If he'd sinned against the church, she would be sinning by aiding him.

"Drawing closer," Garrett warned her in a soft undertone. "We either give them the boy or let him go, but you have to make the decision and make it now."

"I knew this wretched creature was trouble." Tom wound Newt's tunic around his fist.

"What did you do?" Beatrice glanced at Newt and then back to the road.

The leader carried a sword at his hip. His hand rested on the pommel. Armor glinted beneath their surcoats.

They didn't look friendly.

"Nothing. I did nothing." Newt wriggled some more.

"Newt?" Beatrice fixed him with a hard stare. "If you do not tell me, I will ask them."

Newt's eyes darted from Beatrice to Ivy. He licked his lips.

"Beatrice?" Garrett rumbled. "Almost upon us."

She kept her eyes on Newt.

"I might have helped myself to some things." He was going red from the grip Tom had on his tunic.

"What sort of things?"

"I do not know what sort of things." Newt whimpered. "I have not been to church in my life. Things." His voice rose to a squeak. "Gold and silver just lies there." He licked his lips. "It was only one cup."

"You stole from a church?" Stealing from a church? It was unthinkable. Unconscionable.

"I said I might have." Newt's clasped his shaking hands over the neck of his tunic. "I swear to you, my Lady. You let me go, and I promise not to lay a hand on another thing that is not mine."

Ivy scoffed.

Beatrice was inclined to agree with her.

"Let him go," Beatrice told Tom.

Tom gaped at her in disbelief. "He sinned against the church."

Newt writhed under his grasp.

The horses stirred, and Beatrice moved her mount to block the view of the men at arms.

"His sin is between him and God." There was no doubt their party aroused suspicion by standing here. "But he is my friend, and he has aided me. Whatever he has done is on his conscience, but I will not repay his friendship with betrayal."

"You go too far." Tom's head jerked back.

"Let the boy go, or I will make you." Garrett's face was carved from stone, cold and relentless.

With a curse, Tom opened his hand.

Newt leaped to the ground. He used the horse's legs to shield himself, moving like a phantom and disappearing into the hedgerow beside the road.

"Now we have added blasphemy to our tally." Tom set his lips in a grim line.

"I think that can be laid at Newt's feet." Ivy poked her head out. "Along with his other charms."

Tom coughed. The smallest of smiles tilted his mouth.

There was a tiny glimmer of something between Tom and Ivy. She would keep an eye on that, but with men at arms bearing down, Beatrice had more pressing matters to attend to.

"Ho, there." The leader slapped up his visor. He was of middle years, his face stern and drawn. Deep grooves bracketed his mouth. His cold gaze swept them, keen and assessing.

Beatrice nudged her horse forward. Garrett inched Parsley in front of her. "Let me." She tugged on Parsley's bridle until he stopped.

Tom groaned and clapped his hand to his forehead. "She will make a tangle of it for sure."

Not the most encouraging of reactions. Beatrice's confidence wavered.

"Nay." Garrett smiled at her. "She will do beautifully."

Beatrice could topple mountains when he looked at her with quiet approval gleaming in his eyes.

"Good day," Beatrice called.

The crest of their bishop lay emblazoned across their surcoats in rich gold thread. Beatrice wasn't familiar with the crest, but Garrett's guess was correct. Newt had earned himself a rich and powerful enemy. She sent a quick prayer heavenward for the sin she was about to commit. Hopefully, the Lord would make the fine distinction between lying to him and lying to one of his servants.

"Who are you?" The leader rested his hand on the pommel of his sword.

How to get past him without arousing any more suspicion? Faye popped into her mind.

"I am the Lady...Brenda." Putting a sweet smile on her face, she looked past him to the men with him. "And who are you?"

The man blinked. He opened his mouth and snapped it shut again.

"I am going to London." Beatrice beamed at him. "Are you going to London?"

"Er...nay." He cast a swift glance over his shoulder at his men.

"Oh." Beatrice wrinkled up her nose. "Then why do you block our path?"

The man stopped his horse and motioned the men on either side of him. They halted beside him. "We are looking for someone."

Beatrice tilted her head and gave him a glance of gentle disdain. "I am certain it is not I for whom you search."

The man flushed. "Nay, my lady, we are looking for a boy, a dreadful miscreant of a lad. Spawn of Satan."

"Oh, dear." Beatrice fluttered her hand. She peered around her. "Is he hereabouts?"

"We have reason to believe he was heading for London."

Beatrice squeaked and clasped her hand to her chest. "We are heading for London."

"But he is a small lad, and we will catch up with him shortly." The man squared his chest. "You have nothing to fear, Lady Brenda."

"Oh, good." Beatrice heaved a sigh. "I should not want to meet with such a desperate character."

"Are you alone, my lady?" The leader's glance encompassed the entire party. A slight frown creased the skin between his eyes.

Blast.

"Goodness, nay." She gave a light trill of laughter. "I have with me my lady's maid. Only she is dreadfully afraid of horses and managed to lose hers on the first day. Now, she must ride with me. Is that not the most dreadful inconvenience?"

The guard's mouth turned down at the corners, and he clucked his tongue.

His companions stared unabashedly at Ivy.

"Good morrow." Ivy waggled her fingers.

"And here are my guards." She pointed first at Garrett and then Tom.

"Is it not a small party for such turbulent times?"

"Indeed it is." Beatrice warmed to her role. It was the tiniest bit thrilling. "And so I told my father. But he would not listen. So, I went to my brother, and I said to him, 'Brother, how is it you would allow your only sister to travel with such a paltry escort?' and do you know what he said?"

The man shook his head and looked as if he were regretting the question.

"He said it did not signify." She paused, her hand splayed across her chest.

The churchman stared back at her.

"He said it did not signify." Beatrice tossed her head. Perhaps more than a tiny bit thrilling.

"My lady, he did not mean you do not signify." Garrett inclined his head toward the guard and raised his eyebrows meaningfully.

"I believe that is exactly what he meant." Beatrice tossed her head again. Actually, she was enjoying herself. "He does not value me as a brother should." She widened her eyes. "Do you have a sister?"

"Er—" He shifted in his saddle.

"Do you value her as is her right?"

"I—"

"Exactly." Beatrice tossed her hand in the air. "My brother does not value me, and it is not right."

"Surely not, my lady." Garrett smiled at her toothily. "What man alive could not value one such as you?" He winked at the guard.

"Er...aye, indeed." The man's eye twitched. "We will let you pass." He waved to his men to clear the way.

An instant path appeared between them.

"I do not think I do not signify." Beatrice leaned forward in her saddle.

"Not a soul alive thinks as such," added Garrett.

"Well, not my father." Beatrice struck out her bottom lip. "He says I am the star in his firmament."

"Quite rightly so." Garrett motioned her forward. "The sun in his skies."

"My father is greatly attached to me," Beatrice told the three men as she passed.

The men blinked at her and nodded.

"He should not like to think I was being bothered by an evil boy."

"We will catch him, my lady. Never you fear." The guard's chest puffed up.

"I shall tell my father how brave you are." Beatrice let her benevolent smile touch each guard in turn. She kept the smile in place until they were past the carriage. She nodded a greeting toward the coach, but nobody emerged.

The four of them proceeded at a sedate pace down the road.

Beatrice maintained a steady stream of nonsensical chatter. The skin between her shoulder blades prickled. She waited for the shout that would call them back. Then, she spared a thought for Newt. She wished him as agile on his feet as always.

Garrett joined in gamely, but Tom merely glared at the two of them. Ivy remained silent, her arms locked around Beatrice's waist.

They kept their torturous pace until the churchmen could no longer see them.

"Jesu, Beatrice." Tom's breath rushed out of his chest. "You should have kept your mouth shut. It could have gone horribly wrong."

Beatrice reeled as if from a blow. She thought she'd done well, all things considered.

"I think she saved us." Ivy gave her waist a squeeze.

Some of the sting eased.

"That may be." Tom frowned. "But she nearly took it too far. What was all the stars nonsense anyway?"

"She was magnificent." Garrett grinned.

Pleasure blossomed inside Beatrice. The smile he gave her crinkled around the corners of his eyes and came from some place deep within.

"My sister once said men cannot abide a chattering woman." She lost herself in the warm glow of Garrett.

"Well played, my lady." He raised his hand and saluted her.

"Where do you think Newt went?" Ivy peered about her.

"The little turd." Tom stuck out his chin.

"And you are as cross as a bear." She'd handled the crisis well, and Beatrice wouldn't let Tom diminish her moment of triumph. "But we still love you."

Ivy made a muffled noise and shook.

Ivy's laughter made her triumph even sweeter. A warm glow filled her chest. "Am I the star in your firmament?" Beatrice batted her lashes at Garrett. "The sun in your skies?"

Ivy laughed harder.

"For the love of God," Tom muttered.

"Without a doubt." Garrett's face softened. "And much more."

Her heart galloped. He meant it. His face was easy to read, laid bare before her with his heart in his eyes. She became uncomfortably conscious of Ivy and Tom watching their interchange.

"And you, Tom?" Beatrice pasted a glittering smile on her face. "Am I your sun and stars?"

"Beatrice." Tom tried his best to look stern, but he lost the battle. His lips twitched.

Tom's eyes widened, and he jerked upright. He froze for a heartbeat before crumpling in the saddle. A red stain spread across his tunic.

Ivy screamed.

## Chapter Eighteen

"Tom." Beatrice reached for him, but Tom slid from his horse, stumbled, and dropped to his knees.

Badger plunged, his hooves flashed perilously close to Tom's head. Beatrice grabbed for his dangling reins.

Badger snorted, his eyes rolling as he lunged backward into Breeze. Breeze skittered out of the way, catching Beatrice off balance. She hauled on the reins to calm her mare.

Tom staggered to his feet. Bodies swarmed.

Rough, hard faces leered up at her. Two of them. Big hands, hairy and coarse, latched onto Ivy's bliaut and pulled. "There you are."

"Rudd." Ivy's arms tightened about her middle.

"I said I would find you." He yanked harder on Ivy's bliaut.

"Nay." Ivy kicked at her attacker. Her foot connected with his heavy chin. He stumbled back a few paces.

Beatrice dug her heels into Breeze's flanks. Breeze screamed and wheeled. The man was forced to let go of Ivy or be trampled.

Tom had found a branch and defended himself against another man. His motions were awkward and jerky, but he was standing.

Desperately, Beatrice looked for Garrett.

He had a knife in his hand.

Beatrice's scream stuck in her throat. Two men flanked him. She wanted to shout a warning, but she dared not break his attention.

Rudd lunged toward them again.

Beatrice dug her heels into Breeze. The horse shot from the mass of moving bodies.

A man cried out.

She didn't stop to see who.

Ivy clung to her as Breeze pelted down the road, the horse's nervousness lending speed to their flight. Beatrice pulled Breeze to a stop. Her heart pounded in her throat.

Breeze fought for her head, blowing hard and trying to flee.

Beatrice hung on grimly. Ivy's arms were like bands of steel around her waist. Breeze settled, still tossing her head but no longer resisting Beatrice's control.

There were four attackers against Tom and Garrett.

Tom and his assailant circled each other. One entire side of Tom's tunic was stained red. Tom stumbled.

Ivy gasped and squeezed her waist.

Tom regained his footing. The man he faced was smaller, but Tom was injured.

On the other side of Parsley, Garrett had one man on the ground.

The man struggled, and Garrett kicked him in the ribs.

Savage satisfaction coursed through Beatrice.

Two large men lunged for Garrett, and he turned to meet them.

"Rudd will kill him," Ivy whispered.

"We need to help them." Beatrice wanted to do something, but she knew nothing of weapons.

"There." Ivy pointed a shaking finger at a large branch. "You ride and I will swing it." Ivy slid off the horse and grabbed the piece of wood. It was almost too heavy for her.

Beatrice helped her clamber back into the saddle. "Make sure you hit the right one."

"You ride straight."

Tom dropped to his knees.

"Go," Ivy yelled.

Beatrice walloped her heels into Breeze.

Breeze tore down the road toward the grappling men. The combatants didn't turn until she was almost upon them.

"Move, Tom!" she bellowed.

Tom leaped out of the way with a yelp.

Ivy lurched, swinging the club. It hit the man with a sickening crunch. Ivy jolted and slipped.

Beatrice grabbed a handful of fabric and pulled.

Ivy righted herself.

Beatrice urged Breeze through to the other side before drawing rein.

Tom's man was on the ground. Tom's chest heaved as he staggered to his feet.

Ivy gagged, and Beatrice looked over her shoulder. The end of her club was a gory mess of hair and blood. A tooth stuck out of it and hung drunkenly to one side, the bits of gum clinging to the end.

Beatrice's stomach heaved and she forced her gorge back down. She turned back to the fight. "Curse it." The men were now too closely engaged for her to charge again. Not without risking hitting Garrett or Tom.

Tom raised a rock, stumbled forward, and brought it down on Rudd's head. The brute crumpled to the ground. Tom lifted the rock and brought it down a second time.

As one, she and Ivy jerked.

His face a brutal mask, he hefted his rock again and struck the man. Again and again Tom struck.

Beatrice stared at her childhood friend in horror.

Garrett pushed Tom off Rudd. He had felled two and the other was running down the road. One of the men on the ground moved. Garrett raised his boot and brought it down on the man's head.

He straightened, his head whipping around. He caught sight of them and his shoulders slumped.

Beatrice trotted Breeze forward.

Ivy dropped her weapon, and it hit the ground with a dull *thud*.

Staring at the man he'd pulverized, Tom swayed on his feet. He turned and ran to the side of the road. His retching broke the desperate silence.

"Well done." Sweat and blood streaked Garrett's face.

Beatrice ran her eyes over him as she fell from her horse. Thank you, Lord, he was well. She nodded and walked straight into his arms. He stank of sweat and the coppery tang of blood, but she didn't care. He was alive and unhurt. She shook and tightened her grip around him.

His arms were steel as he held her to him. "Are you hurt?"

"Nay."

"Thank, Christ." He kissed the top of her head.

Ivy stared at the body. "He must have followed me."

Beatrice shuddered at the mangled mess of the man's head. She buried her face in Garrett's neck.

"Tom," Ivy cried.

Beatrice whirled.

Tom had fallen to his knees.

*Nay, not Tom.* Beatrice lurched toward him.

Ivy crouched beside Tom. She pried the shirt away from him to look at his injury.

Tom pushed her hands away, his face a scary shade of white.

"Let me see." Ivy evaded his hands.

"I am fine." Tom clenched his jaw. He wobbled backward.

Ivy caught him and righted him.

Beatrice's chest tightened. She'd been so relieved it was over she'd almost forgotten Tom had been hurt.

"How bad is it?" Garrett crouched beside Ivy.

"He has been stabbed." Ivy sat back on her haunches. "I cannot see how badly. He won't let me."

"Let her see, Tom" Beatrice could barely stand to look. "Or I will come and tend your wounds."

"A knife." Tom pulled a face. "One of those curs threw a knife before they attacked. I am sure it is nothing."

"Let her see." Garrett sneered. "Or will the sight of blood make you faint?"

Scowling at Garrett, Tom moved his arm to allow Ivy to work.

Ivy peeled the soaked fabric away from the wound.

Beatrice grew woozy. There was so much blood. Tom's blood. Surely too much.

"Do not faint." Tom glared at her.

"I never faint." Yet. Her voice wobbled and spots danced before her eyes.

Garrett rose and slipped his arm about her.

"See to Tom." Beatrice wriggled in his hold. "I am fine."

"Hush." He tucked her against his side. "Ivy looks to know what she is about. He won't thank me for fussing over him."

He was warm and solid. Beatrice dropped her head onto his chest. She drew comfort from the steady beat of his heart beneath her ear.

Ivy tugged and whipped Tom's shirt over his head.

Tom grunted, the sound muffled by the shirt over his face.

His chest was streaked with red, more darkening the waist of his chausses. A long, ugly gash oozed from beneath his armpit.

It looked horrible. Beatrice's throat constricted. She couldn't bear it if Tom's wound...

Garrett's arm tightened about her. "It's the blood that makes it look worse."

"It glanced off his ribs." Ivy prodded Tom to lift his arm. "Which is a good thing because otherwise it would have been a lot deeper."

The wound continued onto his back. Beatrice shivered. It had to hurt, but Tom was trying so hard to be stoic.

"It is long though," Ivy muttered. "It will need to be thoroughly cleaned and stitched."

"I can stitch it." Beatrice hadn't thought Tom could get any paler, but he went ghostly.

"Nay." He turned to Ivy. "Do not let her near me with a needle."

"Tom." Beatrice stared at him. He was her best friend. She only wanted to help.

"Beatrice." Tom grit his teeth. His face contorted with pain. "Do you remember when I fell off the stable ladder?"

Tom was being monstrous unfair. It must be the pain. "Tom, I was ten. I knew nothing of stitching wounds."

"You still know nothing of stitching." Tom glanced at Ivy. "I have seen her embroidery."

"I will do it," Ivy said.

"Are you any good?" Tom frowned.

"Do you have a choice?"

Tom laughed, flinched, and gasped.

"Can he ride?" Garrett stroked Beatrice's back in long, soothing strokes.

"Nay." Ivy continued her examination. "It did not hit anything vital, but if he rides, it will jar the wound."

"I can ride." Tom clenched his teeth.

"Not if you bleed to death, you cannot." She looked up at Beatrice. "You and Garrett must go on. I will stay here with him and tend to his wound. We will join you as soon as we are able."

"I cannot leave Tom." Beatrice stared at her aghast. "Or you."

Ivy jerked her head at the man Tom had bludgeoned. "Rudd is dead. He will not be looking for me anymore. And whoever pursues you is still alive."

"We can wait until the morning." Tom needed her, and she wouldn't abandon him.

"Do not be simple, Bea." Tom winced. "I am not going to die. Ivy is right. You must go on now you are so close. You could be in London by nightfall. We shall be fine here."

"But you are hurt."

"And you are a terrible nurse." Tom uttered a short bark of laughter. "Go on, Bea. You cannot wait here for whoever is after you to catch you. You made me come all this way with you. Do not give up now. Otherwise, it will have been for naught."

"Ivy is right, sweeting." Garrett turned her chin to face him. "She will take care of him, and you and I can ride hard for London."

A lark called from the meadow beyond, mocking her dilemma with its cheer. In the distance, a small group of travelers wove into view. Beatrice had to make a decision. Around them, life was moving forward. "It does not feel right."

"That is your big heart talking." Garrett kissed her temple.

"More like her soft head," Tom said.

"Do not make fun of her." Ivy turned on Tom. "Lady Beatrice has the warmest heart I have ever encountered. It is not a weakness to care deeply for those around you. It is a weakness in those who would seek to use it to their advantage."

Beatrice's mouth dropped open. It was the nicest thing anyone had ever said of her.

"You keep that heart of yours," Ivy said. "There are too few of those in this world."

"Come." Garrett tugged at her waist. "All will be well."

"Tom?" Beatrice stepped out of Garrett's light hold.

"Go, Bea." He managed a wan smile. "And Ivy is right. Do not let others change you."

Tears prickled behind Beatrice's eyelids. "You are my best friend, Tom. I shall be mightily put out if you do not make a full recovery."

Tom went pink. "Only because you will have to tell my mother what you did to me."

"True." She strode forward and cradled his face in her hands. Her heart swelled with love for the familiar, broad planes of his face, his clear blue eyes that she'd seen all her life. She pressed a quick kiss on his forehead. "Take care of him. And take care of yourself."

"God be with you." Ivy pressed her hand.

Beatrice took a moment to check Breeze had come to no harm. Her hands shook as she stroked the mare's neck. Breeze quivered, still skittish, but otherwise well.

They split the remaining food between them.

Beatrice tried to insist it all be left with Tom and Ivy.

"You do not know what you will find in London." Tom pushed her half of the food back at her.

"Come along." Garrett stroked her cheek. His dark eyes were tender as he gazed down at her. "Let us get you to London before more adventure overtakes you."

Beatrice mounted Breeze. She hesitated a moment. Tom and Ivy were so vulnerable, huddled together at the side of the road.

"Go," Tom snarled at her.

* * *

With only the two of them, Beatrice and Garrett were able to quicken the pace. Breeze took the lead, and faithful Parsley slipped behind his lady. Beatrice concentrated on the steady hammer of hooves on the road beneath her, barely glancing up as the scenery flew past them.

Beatrice wasn't sure when it began, but it crept up on her slowly. It started as an uneasy feeling in her belly, radiated to her limbs, and set her fingers trembling on the reins. The road before Breeze blurred, and Beatrice blinked to clear her eyes.

The emotion inside her swelled so big she ached. She didn't want Garrett to see how weak and silly she was. Beatrice the Brave didn't cry. Except the blasted tears wouldn't cease. Now the danger was passed, the emotions building inside demanded to be heard.

Tom was hurt. Fresh tears flooded her eyes. She blindly trusted to Breeze's sight. Her best friend had been wounded and killed a man. How would she explain this to Nurse? A sob hitched in her throat. Garrett could've died. Ivy could've been taken. She could've ended up like Ivy. And all because of her.

*Cease being so weak.* She was a whiney, mewling baby. Nothing had happened. She and Garrett were safe. Tom would recover, and Ivy would see to it. Her mind tried to tell her heart, but her heart turned a deaf ear. It reminded her of how they had risked damnation by lying to a churchman, how she'd seen a woman raped and nearly suffered the same fate. Twice, Garrett had been forced to fight to save her. Blood had been spilled for her.

None of this had been part of her glittering vision of Beatrice the Brave, riding to London to save her family. And it should have. She'd blithely ignored the danger in her hazy dream of glory. There was nothing glorious about this, pushing her beloved Breeze for speed as they raced for her father. Behind her, a group of unknown men pursued, and ahead of her lay uncertainty.

Her grand adventure had become exhausting, dirty, and terrifying. It was built of blood and fear. When this was over, she'd return to Anglesea and take up sewing. She'd live out her days, safe in her father's hall. Except, now, she wasn't the blind, spoiled girl who saw only what she wished to see. Garrett had called her princess once and he was right. She'd been a princess. The misery and suffering she'd seen in these few days weren't new. It had been there in Anglesea. If she'd opened her eyes wide enough to see it. No more. She dashed at her eyes with an impatient hand.

Beatrice the Brave needed to retire to a disused corner and stay there.

"Hey." Garrett tugged on her reins. "Stop a moment." He leaned over to clasp Breeze's bridle.

He would fall for sure with his poor riding skills. Beatrice drew to a halt. Shame stained her cheeks. She hated that he saw her weakness. "We dare not stop." She kept her face averted from his knowing glance. "We need to reach London."

"There is time enough for this." He slid off Parsley and walked to Breeze's side. "Get down."

"Garrett, we need to press forward."

He held up his arms. "Get down."

She didn't want to, but his expression was set. With a groan, Beatrice slid into his waiting arms.

He lowered her to the ground, bearing most of her weight until she rested against him. "What ails you, sweeting?"

His gentleness undid her. Beatrice blinked rapidly to prevent more tears.

"Beatrice the Brave does not cry," he said.

"She does." It burst out of her like a river overrunning its banks. Once the flood began, it wouldn't stop. Huge, gasping shocks racked her. "I am not b-brave at all." She hid her face in her hands, but Garrett snared her wrists and wrapped them around his waist. Beatrice dropped her face into the sweet spot where his neck met his shoulder. "I got T-Tom stabbed. Tom has never been stabbed. The only thing he wants is a farm and some pigs and chickens to raise. I do not want to be Beatrice the B-brave. I want to go home and be a good daughter and take care of my mother and never do anything like this ever again."

Garrett murmured something against her hair.

It sounded kind and gentle and it made her cry harder. "I was stupid to think I could ride off to L-L-London and everything would be fine. I am a stupid, thoughtless, ridiculous girl and I have n-nearly got everybody killed."

"All right, then." Garret took her by the shoulders. He set her slightly apart from him and stared into her eyes.

* * *

She was a soggy mess. Her eyes were swollen and her nose bright red. Straggling bits of hair clung to her damp cheeks. Her bottom lip quivered as she gave another loud sob.

"Enough." Garrett gave her a small shake.

She raised her wounded eyes to him, and his heart turned over.

"I think you have punished yourself enough for one day." He pushed back the damp tendrils of hair and tucked them behind her ears. With the sleeve of his tunic, he attempted to dry her sodden face. "You are, without doubt, the sweetest thing I have ever encountered." He wrapped his arms around her.

She nestled like a chick against him.

Garrett felt twenty feet tall as he tucked her beneath his chin. "You are warm and generous and too trusting for your own good. Aye, you can be a touch impulsive and we have not been short of excitement. Or company."

She snorted against his tunic.

"But, Beatrice." He drew her away from him. He needed to see her eyes and be sure she understood. "I would not have changed one moment of the last few days." He pulled a face. "All right, for Ivy, I would change the past, but not for the rest. I have never felt so alive."

"You are being kind." She blinked at him mistily.

Garrett threw back his head and laughed. Jesu, if only she knew. "There is nothing kind about me, except this girl in my arms and she is so kind, it makes my head hurt." He surrendered to the temptation and touched his mouth to hers.

"What of Tom?"

"Tom will have a fine scar to show the girls." He kissed her hot, wet tears off her cheeks. "And a grand tale to go along with it."

She sniffed and scrubbed her cheeks with her palms. "We could have died."

"But we did not. Now." He squeezed her arms. "Get back on your horse, stop torturing yourself, and let us find your father."

"Aye, Garrett." She peered up and gave him a shy smile.

Garrett thought his chest might burst wide open.

# Chapter Nineteen

Garret had no more interest in why. His plan had changed and that was all that mattered.

Beatrice rode hard on his tail as he led the way to London. And he was going to London. Straight to London with no more delays along the way. He would take Beatrice to her father. The man whose life he'd sworn to destroy. How would it feel to look on Sir Arthur again, after all these years?

His recollection of the man was that of a small boy. Sir Arthur had seemed huge and terrible astride his great destrier as he shouted the orders for the castle to be set to the torch. Garrett could recall the play of the flames across his features as Sir Arthur watched it burn.

Beatrice resembled her father. The strong, sharp lines of her face were barely softened by her mother's beauty. Beatrice had a beauty of her own, both fierce and gentle at the same time. She didn't deserve to pay for Sir Arthur's sins.

Sweet Jesu. He was in trouble so deep he couldn't see the end of it. Somewhere along the line, he'd become trapped by his own coils and held fast. And he'd pay the price for his arrogance. When this was done, he'd have to leave her. There was no future for the Lady Beatrice and the son of a traitor and a whore. She wasn't for him. Her lineage aside, Beatrice had a goodness that had nothing to do with piety or kind deeds. It shone from within her, and if he didn't leave her, he would dull the purity of who she was. His last thought was almost more unbearable than the idea of not having her.

There'd been nothing in his life to compare to her. She'd be his one good deed, his one moment of nobility. She'd realized none of this. Beatrice took the day as it came. She didn't fret over the future or agonize over past mistakes. If she was happy at this time, she was happy. God, he envied her.

And he loved her.

He feared this lay at the root of the matter. Had some part of him loved her before this began? Had it been disguised as lust, only to raise its head and refuse to be denied now? There could be no other explanation for the other night. He could've taken her. She'd wanted him to take her. And yet, he'd held back, like some callow boy with stars in his eyes.

The road became more congested and they were forced to slow their pace. Ahead, like a great, dirty smear on the horizon lay London, the end of their journey. Where he would leave her. Garrett struggled to draw breath.

* * *

Beatrice eyed the throng around them. There were so many people trying to cross one bridge. And yet the flow kept moving forward.

"London." Garrett gestured unnecessarily.

Beatrice twisted in her saddle to take it all in. Dwellings and shops piled up along the bridge like a child's building blocks. All jammed together and seeming to fight their way toward the sunlight. The noise of so many people near deafened her as she tried to catch the various shouts and calls ringing in the air. The smell threatened to empty her stomach. She breathed through her mouth as she stayed close to Garrett.

Somewhere in this mass was her father. She hadn't given a moment's thought to how to find him. Her plan had been to race for London and find her father. Such was the extent of it.

A cart stopped in the middle of the bridge, forcing the flow of people to trickle around it. Beatrice heard words that made her cheeks burn.

The mighty walls of the city loomed before her, casting her in shadow as she drew closer. She marveled at their thickness as they passed through the gate. Surely, these had been many years in the making. She saw men at arms among the crowds, relaxed, watchful but not wary. She searched their surcoats for Anglesea colors, but saw none.

At the far side of the bridge, the city split into myriad lanes, leading every which way. Garrett picked a quieter one and followed it.

The smell worsened on the far side of the bridge, and Beatrice put her hand over her nose. She let Breeze pick her way through the rotting food and human debris littering the way. A boy darted across the street, right before Breeze's hooves, and Beatrice forgot the stench long enough to calm her horse. Breeze and she were alike. They were used to wide-open spaces and clean air. Not the choking fugue of smoke hanging everywhere and pressing the stink against their nostrils.

Garrett moved toward a small square before a church and stopped. The back of the church abutted the city wall and opened onto the square at the front. Smaller dwellings huddled around the open space, jealously guarding the scant patches of sunlight that managed to breach the pale stone fortification towering above everything.

Garrett dismounted and waited for her.

Beatrice eyed the ground before sliding off Breeze. She placed her feet carefully amongst the befouled cobblestones.

He led the horses to a deep animal trough and let them drink. The horses were sweat-stained and tired. Beatrice gave them both a pat.

"We can start here." Garrett hauled her closer to him as a group of priests, head bent in prayer, jogged toward the church. Their sandals slapped against the cobbled ground. "The city is littered with churches and they are our best chance for information. I do not know London well, but if you give me your father's direction, I am sure we can find someone in that church to guide us."

Beatrice looked toward the church. A yellow stone structure with a steeple rising high into the afternoon sky. All manner of people clustered around the doors. She kept her gaze on the church as Garrett waited beside her. The time to confess had come, and he wasn't going to be pleased. She watched the shifting sea of faces and thought rapidly how best to phrase it.

"Beatrice? Your father's direction?" Garrett turned her chin up.

Beatrice gave a wan smile.

Garrett's face grew resigned and he dropped his chin to his chest. "London, right?"

"Aye."

"When this is done, my lady." A slight smile tilted the corners of his mouth. "We are going to have a long talk about planning and proper preparation."

"Aye, Garrett." Her gaze wandered past him. There was such a multitude of people to look at, a dizzying variety of different faces and garb.

He dropped his hand.

Beatrice missed the warm touch of his fingers. She pressed nearer to him. He was her rock amidst the churning waters of people swelling around them. "My father is known." Beatrice grabbed his sleeve. She didn't want to lose her rock.

"So he is." Garrett's expression tightened. He turned away before she could question him further.

She'd seen him do that before and it intrigued her. "Garrett?" She tugged his sleeve until he looked at her. "Do you know my father?"

A glib smile slid over his lips.

Beatrice almost stamped her foot. She knew that expression. It meant he would try to ease his way out of an answer with charm. She fixed him with a stern look. "Tell me true, Garrett."

The smile slid off his lips. Stark anger crossed his face.

Beatrice took a reflexive step back. His expression didn't bode well.

"What is it?" She braced herself for the worst, not sure what it could be.

"I know your father, Beatrice, but that is a story for another day." He turned back to Parsley.

Beatrice stared at his back. Outrageous. Did he think she would be content with such a meager scrap? His back remained to her. Aye, it was exactly what he thought. She would soon disabuse him of such a notion. "Garrett." She put a spine of steel through her voice. "I would like an explanation."

The muscles in his back stiffened. He glanced over his shoulder at her. "I brought you to London." A knot jumped in the side of his jaw. "I will take you to your father. You will have to be content with as much."

Would she now? Beatrice glared at his back.

"You there." A rude voice interrupted her swelling objection.

A priest strode toward them. His robes flapped around his ankles as he walked, making him look like a straggly crow. "You cannot leave your horses there." The priest waved his hands about, which sent Breeze sidling. Parsley merely rolled an eye at the man.

"Aye, Father." Garrett clasped his hands before him like a penitent. "We did not intend to leave them here. We were merely going to ask for directions."

"Directions to where?" The priest eyed them askance.

"The Lady Beatrice is looking for her father."

Beatrice bent her knee in deference as the priest's head swung toward her.

His face was angular, color high on his cheekbones. Beneath

the dark slash of his brows, his small, piggy eyes started at her toes and raked their way to the top of her head.

She must look a mess. Her hair was tangled by the breeze, her dress dirty and stained.

"Lady Beatrice?" He raised his eyebrows.

"Aye." Her cheeks heated. "Lady Beatrice of Anglesea."

"Very well." The priest sighed and tucked his hands into his habit. "If Anglesea is truly your father, then he is one of those rebel barons running amok through the town."

Beatrice wanted to defend her father, but a warning look from Garrett stilled her tongue. They didn't yet understand the lay of things in London. Tom would be proud of her. She was learning to think before she spoke. Dear Lord, she hoped he was recovering well.

"The lady does not know precisely." Garrett smiled at the priest. "But she is the daughter of Sir Arthur of Anglesea. He is well known throughout the kingdom."

Beatrice narrowed her eyes. Garrett's voice changed when he spoke of her father. An undercurrent of something like anger laced it when he spoke of Sir Arthur.

The priest rolled his eyes. "Anglesea is not in London."

"Aye, he is," Beatrice said.

"He is in Westminster." The priest looked pained. "You do know where Westminster is?"

"Aye." Garrett shifted.

The frown Garrett wore was not encouraging. Yet, Beatrice was greatly relieved not to have to admit her ignorance. This priest was nothing like Father Bernard, who ministered to their needs at home.

"But you will not reach there tonight." The priest nodded his head in dismissal. "The gates to the city will close at sunset." He stuck his head toward them. "And do not think to sleep here this night. I will remember your faces." He turned and started to flap across the square again.

He was a crow, Beatrice decided, and a bald one, at that. Some other crow must have plucked his feathers.

"Beatrice." Garrett rested his forearms on Parsley's back. "We will not reach Westminster tonight."

"Surely, the gates will not close precisely at sunset." The sky above her was barely streaked with sunset. There must be an hour or two before the sun went down. "We can reach them and be on our way to Westminster."

"Nay." Garrett shook his head. "I would not want to chance it with all these soldiers in the city. The gates to Westminster will, for certain, be closed before we reach there. I would guess your father is at the palace."

Disappointment pressed down on her chest. She'd been sure she would reach her father before this day was over.

"Do you have any coin?"

"Tom hid some from me." Beatrice reached for her purse. "He insisted I bring it with us."

Garrett grinned. "Tom knows you well." He took the purse from her. "We will need to see the horses safely kept before we go to Westminster in the morning. The quickest way is by the river and we cannot take them with us."

Beatrice stroked Breeze's neck. She wasn't happy with the thought of leaving her mare with strangers. Still, it wouldn't be for long. Tomorrow she'd find her father and soon after, they'd be riding for home.

Garrett peered inside the purse. "Well." He tightened the strings again. "We will not sleep rich tonight, but we should have enough to see us sheltered."

* * *

Beatrice's head ached. Garrett's words turned out to be optimistic. The city was full to the brim with soldiers taking up all the room. They struggled through the crowds as inn after inn turned them away. Full dark had fallen by the time they'd been

194

turned away from yet another establishment. The gates to the city were closed, and with them any chance of sleeping outside the city walls.

Beatrice tried to stay cheerful, but the last woman had turned them away rudely.

Around them, the city settled for the night. Shadows crept along the narrow streets, only dimly lit by flickering torches. With the night, a new population peopled the city. They slid out of the shadows to weave drunkenly in her path. Beatrice swore their eyes were on her. She almost ran into Garrett's back she walked so closely behind him.

He turned to look at her and winked. "I have an idea."

Beatrice sincerely hoped so. She was footsore and dispirited as she trailed him.

"Oi, my fine laddie." A raucous voice cut the air.

Beatrice whirled around to look.

A woman whistled through her teeth, her eyes on Garrett. "Look what I have for you." The woman tugged down her dress and jiggled her breasts.

Sweet Lord. Beatrice tripped over her own feet.

Garrett caught her. "Are you all right?"

"Aye." Beatrice craned her neck to stare at the woman. The woman had her breasts on display again, but she was looking at a different man. The next man paid no more attention to her than Garrett.

"Not long now." Garrett wrapped her hand in his.

Beatrice drew reassurance from his warm fingers entwined with hers.

The river glittered ahead of them. Garrett wound their way through the tangle of streets toward the waterfront. The expanse of water, silver in the moonlight, looked much better when she couldn't see the unmentionable things drifting along in the current. A stiff breeze tugged at her skirts and brought with it a welcome breath of fresh air.

She followed Garrett, trusting he knew where he was going.

The river was right before them, and yet the streets forced them to wind and turn before they reached it. Taverns clustered together as they drew closer. The oily tang of fatty meat and tapers hung in the air. Bursts of laughter and shouts came from behind the lighted windows. The reedy whistle of a pipe wound through the loud buzz of conversation as they walked past, yet another, tavern. Peering through the window, Beatrice didn't think it looked too bad. Rough men filled the tables, but there were women amongst them. Her belly was hollow with hunger and she spied coarse loaves of bread on the table beside wooden bowls.

Garrett tugged her forward.

Even Breeze's head hung when Garrett finally stopped before a large wooden shed.

Garrett tried the door. It was locked.

Her shoulders drooped. This was his grand idea? Breeze blew softly in her ear. Beatrice understood how the mare felt. She wrapped her arm beneath Breeze's jaw and leaned.

Garrett scrutinized the flickering dark.

"What are you doing?"

He went first one way, stopped and listened, and then turned. "Looking for a night guard." He peered around the side of the shed. "Or a water bailiff."

"What is a water bailiff?"

"Not someone we want to meet now." He grinned at her. "But the fact there is not one here is good news for us."

He handed her Parsley's reins.

"What is this place?"

"This is the wool district." He approached the door again. A stout chain and lock were wrapped around the latch. "These warehouses are kept full of wool waiting to be loaded onto barges."

"Garrett?"

He fiddled with the chain on the door. Light flashed off his dagger as he levered it inside the padlock.

"What are you doing?" Nerves fluttered in her belly.

"Finding my lady a bed for the night." With a flourish, he loosened the chain and stepped back. He caught it before it hit the ground. "We shall have to keep quiet, but I can think of no better place to rest than a nice, warm bed of wool."

"Is the chain not to keep people out?" Beatrice tried to look shocked. But the idea of a bed and an end to walking was too tempting.

"Only if such people were going to steal the wool." Garrett eased the door open with a slight creak. "As it is, we are only going to sleep on it."

"I suppose that is acceptable." Beatrice led Breeze inside. The shed was tall and stretched right over the water. A barge could be loaded from inside through a portal on the river. And, as promised, there was wool everywhere.

Garrett shut the heavy door to seal them in.

The inside of the shed smelled musty and dank. Beatrice wrinkled her nose and waited for her eyes to grow accustomed to the lack of light.

"We can stay here for the night. I will have to get some water and we can get settled," Garrett said.

Beatrice looked toward the river. She shuddered in distaste. The water would kill her faster than the thirst.

"Not from there." He laughed.

She heard Garrett open the door again. "Where are you going?"

"To get some water."

"And leave me here alone?" Beatrice glanced around the hut and shivered.

Garrett crossed the floor toward her. "Only for a few moments, sweeting." He gave her a quick hug. "I shall be back before you know it. Otherwise, let Parsley protect you. He is a real beast."

Beatrice giggled. It sounded too loud and she slapped her hands over her mouth. Noises filtered through the walls from the city outside. She stood where Garrett had left her and gathered up her courage. She was letting her fears get the better of her. "I will settle the horses," she said to the empty hut. Breeze stamped and blew through her nose as if to tell her to get on with it.

"You will have to eat light tonight." She slipped the nearly empty nosebag over the mare's head. "But tomorrow we will find father and you will have enough grain to fill your bellies five times over." She did the same for Parsley. The horses' eyes glowed in the dim light. Their smell floated above that of the wool and Beatrice breathed it in. It was the smell of the stables at Anglesea, and she drew comfort from it.

True to his promise, Garrett returned a few moments later. He carried some water for the horses and another skin for them.

She and Garrett didn't speak much as they dealt with the business of getting ready for the night. The bread had grown a bit stale, but Beatrice ate her half. Some cheese and apples and her belly was appeased.

"We dare not risk a fire." Garrett took a seat beside her.

It seemed an age since she'd enjoyed the comfort of a cheerful blaze. At Anglesea, even though it was summer, the great hearths would be lit and folk would gather about them. Conversation would fill the hall lit by the sweet-scented beeswax candles her mother insisted on. In their hut, the night closed in, the silence broken only by the slap of water against the dock. One of the horses whickered, and the other answered.

Garrett sat beside her, still as a stag scenting for danger.

"It grows late. We should sleep." Garrett spoke suddenly, startling her. His voice sounded odd. "We should be up before sunrise and get to the gates."

Beatrice nodded, realized he couldn't see her, and said, "Aye."

He shifted beside her and cleared his throat. "I will get the blankets."

He stood up, and Beatrice heard him moving in the dark. There were endless sounds of shuffling around before he returned.

"The wool stinks, but at least it's soft." He spread their blankets on the wool.

"I am becoming accustomed." Beatrice stood to give him room to work. "The river smells worse."

"Aye."

"I can do that." She stood feeling awkward, like she should do something to help him.

"I have it done." He settled onto his blanket, and they sat.

It was warm in the hut. The air was absolutely still. From the city beyond, the watch called the hour.

"It is because of what people throw in it," Garrett said.

"What?"

"The river. It stinks because of what people throw in it."

"Ah." It made sense. Beatrice raised her knees and wrapped her arms around them. If she stared hard enough, she could discern dim shapes on the other side of the warehouse. A horse slurped water noisily. "How did you know about these places?" She shifted her weight and froze. Every move she made clattered in the silence.

"I lived in London for a time." Rustling as Garrett changed position beside her.

"Ah." Beatrice tightened her arms and kept her eyes locked on the other side of the hut. She'd never been this ill at ease with Garrett before. Mayhap because she'd never been entirely alone with him. The thought caused her belly to tighten. Even at their secret meetings, there had always been people within hailing distance. There was nobody about now.

"God's wounds, this is foolishness." He chuckled, and the corners of Beatrice's mouth tilted in response. "Beatrice, you cannot sit there all night hanging on to your knees."

"I know." She was glad the dark hid her blush. "I just feel..." She didn't have the words for how she felt. Except, she wanted to explode from her own skin.

"I know," he murmured. "Would it help if I told you that you had nothing to fear from me this night?"

The knot in her belly drew tighter. It did help. And then, it didn't. She'd been poised for Garrett to take advantage of their situation. The knowledge he wouldn't was disappointing. Since she'd met him, Garrett had taken every small gap to press forbidden kisses and touches on her. Now, when presented with the perfect opportunity, he announced his intention to desist. It sat ill with her and made no sense. The dark gave her the sort of courage she wouldn't have had otherwise. "Why not?"

He choked and stilled beside her. "We may as well air this." His voice sounded resigned as he sat up. "Beatrice."

Beatrice shivered and hugged her knees tighter. She sensed she wasn't going to like what he said next.

"I will take you to your father in the morning." He drew a loud breath. "Once you are safe, we will part ways."

"What?" Her middle gave a sharp twist. She could see the glimmer of his eyes as he looked at her. "Why?"

"You know why." His fingers brushed against her cheek.

She did know why but she didn't want to admit the thought. Beatrice leaned her cheek into the light contact.

"You will tell your father Tom led you to London."

"Why?"

He groaned. "Your father will not like that we were alone like this. Your reputation will be damaged, and I am not the man he would have chosen for you. I will never be that man."

Beatrice wanted to deny his words, but she couldn't. "Nothing has happened," she said, instead.

His laughter was tinged with sadness. "Much has happened, Beatrice." His warm palm cupped her cheek. "Too much for words, but I am not the man who set out on this journey with you. The only thing I can give you is to return you to your father the same way you set out."

"You are speaking of my virtue." Beatrice didn't know how she could speak so boldly. Her face heated.

"Aye." His hand left her face.

She missed the contact immediately. Inside she felt bleak, desolate.

His shoulder pressed against hers. The water lapped against the pilings beneath the shed.

Part of her had known, all along, this couldn't last. Their worlds were leagues apart, but he'd been thrilling and exciting, and her soul had craved adventure. Now, she'd had her fill of adventure and the craving had changed. She pictured her life without him. Her mind veered sharply away from the image. It invented a slew of fancies in which she and Garrett could continue to see each other. Wild, implausible imaginings where he would live in the village, and she would come to him. It felt wrong. It felt sordid and underhanded. Discovery was only a matter of time. And Garrett would pay the dearest price. She had no words and leaned her cheek against his shoulder.

He found her fingers and intertwined them with his.

"I cannot bear to think on it," she whispered.

"Aye." He took a deep breath. "I am not a good man, Beatrice." He pressed her fingers to silence her when she would speak. "You know almost nothing of me."

"Tell me." Suddenly, she ached to know it all. All the questions she'd had when they first met and the hundreds of others that had gathered along this journey. Why was the pouch now missing from about his neck? Why did he look angry one minute and the seducer the next? She wanted to understand all the parts of him and carry them in her heart.

"Nay, Beatrice. I would have you remember me as we are now. As we have been on this journey. It is how I shall remember you."

Dear Lord, it sounded so final.

"Please. I do not want to speak of it. " Beatrice screwed her eyes shut. A giant hand closed over her throat. His words were like barbs. The morning would come, and she would reach her father. It was soon enough. For now, she had this, and it would have to last her for the remainder of the days coming.

"Be happy, Beatrice." He raised her fingers. His mouth was

hot across her knuckles. "Find a good man and have his babies. But for me, make sure it is a man who cherishes you as he should."

"Nay." She couldn't contemplate a man who could make her feel this way. If she pictured such a man, the face he wore was Garrett's. She pressed her face against the place where his neck and shoulder joined. Slowly, reverently, she drew in the unique musk of Garrett. Leather, fire, and man.

"I love you." So much that it hurt to even say the words.

Garrett circled her shoulder with his arm. "I wish you had not said that." He rested his cheek on her head. "Because, God help us both, but I love you, too."

He loved her. Joy shoved the hurt aside, and then it returned in a terrible rush. Tears sprang in her eyes. When he was gone, she would have the knowledge of his love to hug tight to her breast. Would it be enough? Would anything ever be enough again? Never. "I will not marry." Beatrice closed her eyes against the swell of heartache. "Not now."

"Do not say so." He turned her to face him. "It makes it harder to leave, knowing you are pining for something that cannot be."

The dark pulsed around them. The dull ache in Beatrice's chest grew with each beat of her heart. This night, this was the only one they had. She slipped her hands around his neck. "But we have now."

The muscles of his shoulders tensed beneath her fingers.

"We are here and we have this one moment," she whispered.

"Do not." His voice was hoarse.

"I must." His words were like a sharp dagger to her bruised heart. "Do you not want me?"

"Beatrice." His muscles trembled beneath her touch. "I want nothing more than to love you. I ache for you, but—"

"Nay." It was all she needed to know. Beatrice put her fingers over his lips. "The morning will come soon enough. Can we not pretend for one night?"

His eyes glittered down at her. A muscle jumped as he clenched his teeth.

"Please, Garrett."

With a groan, he reached for her, cupping her face in his hands. He stared at her for one endless moment before his mouth covered hers.

*Chapter Twenty*

Her final, ragged plea undid him. He could deny her nothing. Garrett found her mouth and plundered. This wasn't the artful kiss of the seducer, but raw and primal, as he sought to slake his need for her. She rampaged through his senses in a flood of heat, the taste and feel of her, the smell that clung to her skin.

She opened her lips to his demand, and Garrett was lost. He had to have her, even if it was only for one stolen piece of time. She made soft, needy sounds in the back of her throat. His head spun. She needed him as badly as he needed her and the knowledge drove him to the edge of insanity.

* * *

Beatrice clung to him like she might hold him to her forever.

Garrett lowered her to the soft piles of wool.

She met the bold thrust of his tongue with hers. She loved him and she poured her love into her kiss. For now, he was hers and she was greedy to have it all. Her hands dove beneath his tunic. His skin was hot against her palms. Hot and smooth over the strength of his muscle. She spread her fingers wide to imprint the feel of him on her hands.

He broke the kiss to rip his tunic over his head.

He was beautiful. Shades of darkness outlined the ridges and hollows of his body. He was different from her, big and male. Her beautiful, strong man. Hers. The knowledge was heady, better than anything. Impatiently, she pulled his head closer. Fastening her mouth over his, losing herself in the taste and feel of his mouth.

She arched her back into his strength. Her breasts against his chest. He was hard where she was soft, ridged where she was hollow.

His hands slipped over her rib cage, seeking her breasts.

She murmured her encouragement. His hands on her made her cry out with pleasure. The sensation shot straight from her rigid nipples to her core.

He pulled his mouth from hers to place it where his hands had been, dampening the fabric of her bliaut with his tongue until it clung to her breasts and she felt the heat of his mouth.

It was not enough. Not nearly. She writhed beneath him as his mouth continued to torment her through the cloth.

She pushed him up. The fabric between them had to go. She tore at the ties of her bliaut.

Garrett sat back on his heels and watched as she tugged it over her head.

Her chainse followed. The air was cool against her naked skin, his eyes flaming. She leaned back on her hands, letting him look his fill.

"Sweet Jesu, but you are beautiful."

She felt it, with his gaze powerful on her body. "Touch me, Garrett."

He reached for her with hard hands. His bare chest against her breasts made her whimper. Her skin was alive with thousands of prickling points, all demanding attention. It became more than want. She needed him. Boldly, she cupped his buttocks in her hands and pressed him closer to her heat. She loved the sensation, and she did it again.

"Beatrice." He tore his mouth away. "You are going to kill me if you carry on."

The power she held tingled through her muscles. She laughed and slid her leg between his. He was hard against her thigh. He'd done these wicked things to her and she delighted in doing them back to him.

He trembled against her. She made this strong man shake. It made her bolder.

"Nay." He caught her hands. Rearing back, he sat on his heels, breathing hard as he stared at her. "We need to go slower."

She didn't want to go slow. "Why?"

"You are a maid, sweeting. I do not want to hurt you."

"I am well, Garrett." Impatience had her reaching for him. She wanted all of him, and she wanted it now.

He raised her hands over her head and stretched above her.

She couldn't touch him if he held her hands. She moaned her protest and tried to work her hands free. His control irked her, ran contrary to her desire.

He tightened his grip on her wrists. "For the love of God, Beatrice. Will you please let me lead?"

"Aye, Garrett. But make haste. Or I am going to crawl out of my skin if you do not do something. Now."

He closed his eyes. "And try not to speak." He lowered his face to her neck. "You are only making this harder."

"This?" She nudged his hardness with her thigh.

"Aye, that as well."

She giggled and did it again.

He nipped her ear, then soothed the small hurt by sucking on the spot. "I have spent nights imagining this, and I will not be rushed." Hot, sucking kisses trailed her neck to her shoulder.

She delighted in the heat of his mouth. She wanted to show him how much. Beatrice writhed, but he still held her wrists in one of his large hands.

He moved down her chest to the tips of her breasts. He blew hot air against her nipples.

"Garrett." She bowed her back for more.

He obliged her by taking her nipple and sucking it deep within the heated cavern of his mouth. "Do you like that, sweeting?"

"Aye," Beatrice sighed, "more."

He laughed and moved his attention to the other breast.

Beatrice twisted beneath him, trying to free her hands, but he kept them fast. This was lovely, it was wondrous, but she wanted everything. She remembered her glorious release in the forest and she wanted it. Her hips bucked beneath him, grinding against his hard shaft.

He confounded her by shifting to the side. "Patience."

"Nay." Beatrice mewled her protest. She had no patience left. Every part of her demanded that he get on with satisfying her need.

His hand slid down her ribs toward her hip. His mouth continued to pay homage to her breasts as his hand nudged between her thighs.

Beatrice opened for his touch, eager to feel him where she ached the most.

Still, he tortured her, learning her body by feel as he caressed her hip, the top of her thigh, ran his fingers over her inner thigh.

So close and not nearly close enough. Beatrice growled and shifted her hips toward his hand.

And, finally, he slid his fingers over her swollen flesh. *Aye.* Beatrice cried out at the touch.

"Jesu, Beatrice, you are almost ready for me." He abandoned her breasts to kiss her.

Finally, he released her wrists, and Beatrice dug her hands in his hair. She held him fast and kissed him.

He met her passion.

Beatrice let the wildness grow within her.

His fingers caressed the pulsing nubbin between her curls before sliding into the core of her.

Her thighs opened wider in silent invitation, and Garrett eased between them. He took one of her hands and pressed it against his shaft.

Beatrice curved her fingers around his hardness. A twinge of trepidation pierced her abandon. He seemed overly large for her.

Garrett wriggled out of his chausses, and she touched his naked flesh. He was steel and silk in her hand. Beatrice tightened her grip.

"Like this." He guided her movement over him with his hand. Cursing softly as she stroked him. He moaned and dropped his head back. Beatrice grew bolder with her touch. She wanted to do to him what he did to her.

"Enough." He kissed her palm. "No more, or this will end now."

He sat up, and Beatrice drank in the sight of him. His shaft stood rigid from the apex of his thighs. He was a beautiful man. She wanted him to be hers and to make her his.

Slowly, Garrett widened her thighs with his hands. He looked at her. His eyes glowed hot.

She was momentarily embarrassed to be totally exposed to his gaze.

"Perfect." He caressed her, watching the movements of his fingers on her with hooded eyes. His finger dipped inside her.

Beatrice dropped back onto the wool as he continued to touch her. He stroked the sweet spot with his thumb, and any shyness was forgotten.

"I want to put my mouth on you," he said. "I need to taste you."

Shock and excitement bolted through Beatrice. She hadn't imagined such a thing.

Then, his mouth was on her, and she cried out. His tongue was hot and silky on her.

"Garrett." She bucked against his mouth. It was beyond

anything he'd done before. Sweet Lord, but she would surely come apart if he kept doing that.

He purred as he continued to lave.

Beatrice gripped his hair, an anchor in her careening world. He sucked on the place his fingers had found, and Beatrice shattered. She went rigid and arched hard against his mouth before collapsing, spent, against the wool.

He crawled up her pliant body until he hovered above her. "Now, you are ready for me." He kissed her.

She tasted her woman's taste against his lips. It was strange, but not unpleasant.

His shaft was rigid on her thigh. He slid over her slowly.

Beatrice's body awoke to this new possibility.

He reached down and guided himself inside her.

Beatrice stiffened at the invasion. The haze of pleasure surrounding her faded. She didn't think she could stretch to accommodate him.

"Trust me," he whispered against her mouth, pressing forward.

"I am not sure." Beatrice blinked up at him, she did trust him, but he was large against her.

"This will hurt at first." He thrust his hips forward.

It did hurt and Beatrice tensed. "I do not think I like this."

He stilled, framing her face with his hands. "Look at me, Beatrice." He placed a soft kiss against her lips.

Beatrice looked at him.

"I love you." He dropped gentle kisses to her lips and jaw, the tip of her nose.

The burning sensation between her legs eased slightly and some of the tension left her.

"Just like that. Be easy and trust me." He inched farther inside her.

It hurt. "Stop."

Garrett stopped, placed his forehead against hers, and screwed his eyes shut. His mouth was moving.

"Are you praying?"

"Aye, I am praying for the strength to live through this."

"Does it hurt you, too?"

He laughed, shaking against her. "Only you." He kissed her. "Only you could make me laugh at a time like this."

Beatrice experienced the tremor of his laughter all the way to the place where he joined with her. A much more pleasant sensation took the place of the uncomfortable stretching. Yet, it felt incomplete.

"Garrett?"

"Mmm?"

"It does not hurt anymore."

With a soft moan, he flexed his hips.

Beatrice noticed a brief smarting as her maidenhead gave way, but it was over quickly, and he was sheathed inside her.

Garrett stilled.

Her body cleaved to his and she grew accustomed to the feel of him within her. Still, she felt slightly cheated. She moved her legs and discovered if she raised her knees it brought him deeper inside her.

He caught his breath.

"Garrett?"

He raised his head to look at her.

"I feel sure there is more to it than this."

His eyes smoldered down at her. Perspiration beaded his forehead. The hunger in his expression called to something within her, a craving only he could appease.

There was much more to it, and Garrett showed her, moving slowly at first, letting Beatrice set the pace, then faster as need took over.

She met his thrusts, tilting her hips to take him deeper. A sensation started where they were joined and spread through her middle. It built until Beatrice couldn't contain it any longer. Harsh gasps and pants broke from her lips as she blindly sought her fulfillment. The end came fast and tossed her straight into a glorious release.

In the aftermath, Beatrice lay sated and replete beneath him. She listened to the sound of their breathing as it returned to normal, felt to the slow pulse of his heart against her as it grew calmer.

He eased away from her.

Beatrice shivered without the warmth of his body.

He rolled onto his back and pulled her tight against him.

Her head found a perfect hollow against his shoulder, and her legs twined with his.

"Beatrice?"

"Aye."

"I love you." He kissed the top of her head. "Whatever occurs in the days to come, remember I love you."

# *Chapter Twenty-One*

"**W**ake up."

Garrett's tensed. A man's voice woke him, smooth and refined. Beatrice was curled at his side, so vulnerable and trusting.

"Get up, or I will cut you from gut to gullet."

A stinging pain pierced his neck, and he opened his eyes. A length of steel rested against his throat. He traced it to the gauntlet, over the mailed arm, and looked into those eyes. Light eyes, some shade between brown and green. The man titled his head and smirked, his teeth white in his dark beard.

God's wounds. The whoreson had caught him unawares, for a second time.

Beatrice murmured in her sleep.

The sod's gaze drifted to her and went frigid.

Fear tasted like steel in his mouth. Garrett would die before he let the sod lay a hand on her.

"I said, get up."

"Move your sword."

The sword eased enough for Garrett to move. He turned to Beatrice and arranged her cloak over her nakedness.

The intruder had brought company again. He tucked Beatrice's leg away from view. A pair of ruffians flanked the door. Garrett recognized the same two as the last time.

Jesu. What were they doing here? And what in the name of God could they want?

He grabbed his chausses and tugged them on. This time, he wouldn't face them with his tackle hanging out.

The stranger watched him, his sword far enough from Garrett to allow movement.

His face was pretty as a girl's, but he held the sword like he knew what to do with it. The idea of that sharp steel anywhere near Beatrice terrified him. His hands shook as he tied his chausses.

"Over there." The stranger jerked his head.

*Not on your sodding life.* He wouldn't leave Beatrice within reach. His only chance of protecting Beatrice was to stand between her and the sword. "I will remain by my wife."

She stirred and her eyes fluttered open.

"We both know she is not your wife." The stranger's lip curled contemptuously.

"Godfrey?" Beatrice's voice was rough with sleep. Confusion and horror crossed her face as she blinked at the stranger.

Had she called him by name?

"Beatrice." The stranger clucked his tongue. "What would your mother say?" He shook his head at her.

Beatrice paled and dropped her eyes away from the stranger. Her hands tightened against the fabric of her cloak as she tried to hide her nakedness.

Garrett moved to shield her with his body.

The sword hissed through the air and stopped at his neck. "Do not touch her." The stranger's voice dripped with menace. "Or should I say, do not touch her again?"

"Nay, Godfrey." Beatrice scrambled to her knees.

Garrett studied the man's features. Christ on the cross. He saw it now, the similarity in the shape of their face and eyes. The same clean construction of their faces.

"Who is he?" He dropped his eyes to Beatrice.

Her head hung and her hair concealed her face from him, but he heard the misery in her tone. "My uncle."

Her uncle? He had so many questions. Her uncle played a deep game. Her shame cut through him far keener than any blade. "Beatrice is not at fault."

"I am aware of that," her uncle said. "Get dressed, Beatrice."

Beatrice's raised her head.

Garrett was glad to see her stubborn little chin come up. *That's my girl, sweet to the core with a backbone of hardened steel.*

"Not in front of them." She indicated the hulking figures by the door. "Make them leave."

"Modesty, Beatrice?" Godfrey raised one brow. "At this time?"

* * *

Shame hardened to anger within her. As if her uncle was without sin. She knew such not to be the case. His face had always made him a favorite with the women of Anglesea when he visited.

"Do not be an ass, Godfrey." Her uncle still held his sword to Garrett's throat. She glared at the men by the door. "Wait outside."

The men shifted.

"Do it," Godfrey called over his shoulder.

The men slipped out the door and shut it behind them. The thump resounded in the silence within.

"And you." Beatrice motioned her uncle to turn his back. "Drop your sword."

"You have grown a spine, niece." He rubbed his cheek with a long, elegant finger. "What a pity you had not grown some sense with it."

The insult stung. "I—"

"Spare me." Godfrey motioned Garrett with his sword. "I will not make the mistake of turning my back on you. Over there."

Godfrey gave her his back. He kept the tip of the sword

pressed to Garrett's neck. Blast. She would have to sneak across the length of the shed to surprise him.

"I underestimated you before," Godfrey spoke to Garrett.

Godfrey knew Garrett? She frowned over this as she wriggled into her chainse. Snatching up her bliaut, she pulled it over her head and began lacing it at the sides. Her heart thundered in her chest. There was no need to protest her innocence. Thank God, it was not one of her brothers who had discovered them. Godfrey was a reasonable man. Once she explained, he would let Garrett go. "There is no need for violence."

Decently attired, she approached the men. Her hair was a snarled mess from where Garrett had run his hands through it. She didn't care, though. At this moment, it was more important to get Godfrey's blade from Garrett's neck. It was very well for Godfrey to be defending her virtue, but they were all aware the horse had already bolted.

"I am sorry to be disobliging, Beatrice." Godfrey smiled down the length of his blade at Garrett.

Unease prickled across her nape. Something was amiss with this situation, other than the three feet of steel threatening Garrett's life. That was her first priority.

Garrett was rigid, his face a cold mask.

"There is every need, I am afraid," Godfrey said. "As you have, no doubt guessed, your friend and I have met before."

"Garrett?" Beatrice frowned from her uncle to Garrett.

"I did not know he was your uncle." Garrett's hands clenched and unclenched by his sides.

The air between the two men tasted thick with secrets.

"Put the sword down, Godfrey." Always secrets and veiled truths, and she'd had enough.

Godfrey smirked at Garrett. "I did not think you would manage it."

"Manage what?" It was as if they were having cake and ales together. Her uncle sounded so normal.

"That is not how it is." Garrett's shifted.

The sword pressed closer.

He stilled.

"For the love of God, you will cut him." Had Godfrey lost his mind? There was no need for this.

"I would do worse than that." The skin of Garrett's neck pressed inwards under the steady pressure of the steel. "Stay back, Beatrice. My hand could slip, and then where would your lover be?"

"Godfrey!" The unease blossomed into alarm.

Godfrey grinned, as if he enjoyed himself.

This was not the uncle she knew. His usual, easy demeanor seemed darker and more dangerous.

"He deserves no less." Godfrey's sword arm tensed. The blade pressed. "Shall I tell you who you allowed to rut on you, niece?"

"Do not listen to him, Beatrice." Garrett threw her a desperate glance.

"Allow me to introduce you to Garrett of Alethorpe." Godfrey waved his free hand. "Of course, the name will be meaningless to you because you, dear niece, pay little enough attention to anything."

The insult was a pinprick beside the larger concern. "Garrett?"

"Remember, Beatrice."

Remember what? "Why should the name mean something to me?" Dear, God. Her mind executed a quick jump. "Is it aught to do with my father?"

"Beatrice, you surprise me. It appears you are not as heedless as we thought." Godfrey chuckled.

The sound chilled her to the core. "You said you knew my father." Beatrice stepped closer to Garrett. "Is that what this is about?"

"Stay where you are, Beatrice." Godfrey twitched his sword. Light glinted off the blade.

She froze. Those blades were wickedly sharp.

Godfrey whistled, and the door opened admitting the two men.

They were of similar heights, roughly dressed in homespun tunics. One dark and the other's head closely cropped, they were both broad, although the shaved one leaned more to fat than muscle. Their faces were cold and merciless. The dark one had a vicious scar, cutting through his beard from his hairline to his chin.

Beatrice had never seen them with her uncle before.

Godfrey motioned toward Garrett. The two men moved swiftly. The dark one grabbed Garrett's hands and jerked them behind his back.

"What are you doing?" Beatrice's belly clenched in fear.

Garrett tried to wrench his arms free. The sword pressed closer. A thin trickle of blood snaked down Garrett's throat.

Beatrice couldn't drag her eyes from it. It was spiraling out of control. She had to stop it.

They forced him to his knees.

"Get your filthy hands off him." Beatrice had never been so angry. Not even when Rudd had attacked Ivy. She rushed to Garrett.

Godfrey grabbed her by the arm.

Beatrice jarred to a stop. She stared at his hand on her arm. Why?

"Tie him," Godfrey said. "The bastard is too handy with his fists."

One of the men lashed out and caught Garrett a glancing blow to the side of the head.

"Nay." Rage surged through Beatrice. She yanked at her arm. "Stop it."

Godfrey's grip tightened. His sword slipped into the scabbard with a hiss.

"Turn me loose." Beatrice pulled against his painful clasp.

"In a moment." Godfrey gripped her with both hands and hauled her toward him.

Her head snapped back on her neck.

"Let me tell you a story first."

"You lying sod." Garrett snarled.

The man behind him pressed his knee to his back, forcing Garrett's head down. He was on his knees, his hands bound behind him.

"Shall I tell her a story, as well?" Garrett's voice was muffled.

"Gag him," Godfrey snapped.

"Do not touch him." Beatrice couldn't free her arms. Tears of frustration clouded her vision. She had to get to Garrett.

One shoved a dirty rag in Garrett's mouth.

Nay.

Garrett retched and tried to spit it out.

The man tied it behind his head. Tightening the knot with a vicious twist.

Garrett's eyes beseeched her over the top of the gag.

"Let me tell you my story first." Godfrey shook her to get her attention. "And then we will see if you still care for your sweetly whispering bastard."

"I love him." If Godfrey understood that, he would stop hurting Garrett.

"How unfortunate for you." Godfrey's smile made her shudder. "Alethorpe is the name of the keep your father razed when King John first came to power."

"Garrett?" She had no idea who or what Alethorpe was. Why did this matter now?

Godfrey squeezed her upper arms and forced her to look at him. "It belonged to Sir Wulfric." He nodded toward Garrett. "His father. But Sir Wulfric had some trouble with loyalty to his king. He did not have any."

What was he talking about? She didn't need a history lesson.

Godfrey's grip bruised. "My brother was sent to deal with him, and he did. Did he not bastard?" Godfrey raised his voice over the last.

Garrett grunted against the gag. He struggled to free his arms, but the knee in his back prevented him from rising. The men yanked his arms tighter behind him.

"Why are you doing this? Stop it. You're hurting him."

"Listen, Beatrice." Godfrey pushed his face toward hers. "Arthur razed the castle and banished the inhabitants. Including Wulfric's favorite leman and his bastard son."

Godfrey's face swam before her. Her father wouldn't do that. Her father was a good man, a kind one. Godfrey lied, but why?

"Your father was much younger then."

Godfrey tormented her with his lies.

"He did not always think when his blood ran hot. You know what that is like, do you not Beatrice?"

"Why are you telling me this?" Beatrice didn't want to hear anymore. She didn't understand any of it. The only thing she understood was something was terribly wrong, and Godfrey's men were hurting Garrett.

"Listen, Beatrice." Godfrey shook her. "The leman became a common whore, and her son vowed to have his revenge on the man who had rendered her thus. Are you beginning to understand now?"

"Nay." She shook her head to dislodge her uncle's words.

"Aye, Beatrice. Who appeared in your life, sniffing about your skirts and whispering sweet words into your ear? Did he tell you he loved you, niece? Did he say he would die if he did not have you?"

"Garrett does love me." The words caught in her throat and sounded small and uncertain.

"He does not love you, you silly girl. He hates your father. It is not you that he sees at all. When he is swiving you, he sees your father."

A scuffle broke out.

The men struggled to contain him, but Garrett fought them.

"Garrett?" An awful tendril of fear took root in Beatrice's belly. She didn't want to feel it, and she tried to snuff it. "Is this true?"

"Do not be stupid, Beatrice," Godfrey said.

Garrett struggled wildly. Harsh noises rasped through the gag.

"Let him speak." Garrett would tell her true. He would explain this all and make it well again.

"And if I do, he will tell you the same lies he told you to get beneath your skirts in the first place. You cannot trust a word he says."

Godfrey released her.

Beatrice's vision darkened. She swayed on her feet. Her neck was stiff, like an old woman, as she turned to Garrett. "Garrett?"

Garrett surged to his knees. His shoulders bunched, color staining his face as he shouted through the gag.

"What are you doing?" She turned on her uncle. "How dare you treat him thusly?"

"He deserves no more." Godfrey took out his kerchief and wiped each finger with meticulous care. "This bastard came looking for his revenge. He came looking for you, Beatrice. What better revenge than to render a cheap whore the daughter of the same man who had done as much to his mother. It is almost poetic in its simplicity."

"Nay." Beatrice didn't believe it. She wouldn't believe it. Godfrey lied. She blinked at her uncle. Why did he tell her these lies? The awful, horrible lies that churned like bile in her stomach made her want to be sick.

"Thus is how I met him." Godfrey dropped the kerchief to the floor.

It lay there, like a broken bird against the rough stones.

Garrett strained against the men who held him. The gag pressed into his face, his skin white around the edges.

"I did not think he would get it right. It appears I underestimated him," Godfrey said.

Beatrice could barely lift the leaden weight of her legs. She did not want to believe, and yet...

Garrett had appeared suddenly in her life, charming and winsome and intent on her. She hadn't questioned, at the time, that such a man could be interested in her, when other men merely overlooked her. Such a handsome, beautiful man, and he wanted her. She thought of the times he had pressed her for more. Memories ran through her mind like beads on a rosary, slipping through her fingers as she counted them off.

"Tell me true, Garrett." She sank to her knees on the floor before him.

His shoulders slumped.

She tugged the gag from his mouth.

Godfrey's men shifted but made no move to stop her.

"Please, Garrett, no lies."

He closed his eyes, as if to look at her hurt him. When he opened his eyes again, Beatrice read such torture in their depths.

Pain pierced her chest and she gasped at the sharpness.

"It is why I came," Garrett whispered. "Wulfric was my father. That part is true."

"Nay." It made too much sense. The pain became almost unbearable. Her breath came in a ragged rush that caught in her throat.

"I came to avenge myself on your father."

"Oh, God." The sound was torn from her before she could stop it. Her being throbbed like a wound, open and raw.

"It is not why I stayed." Garrett's voice reached her from the end of a long tunnel.

It hurt so much. She could not contain it. Beatrice hunched her shoulders. If she could keep it inside her, she might draw breath in and out.

"Beatrice." Garrett's voice was dim through the storm raging around her. "It is no longer about revenge. Remember what I said last night. Jesu, Beatrice, please remember."

"Shut him up," Godfrey snapped.

A *thud* and a cry.

A part of her registered the men hit Garrett and wanted to call out in protest.

A warm hand cupped her elbow. "Come now, niece." Godfrey, warm and compassionate, as he put his arm about her. The smell of him was familiar and real, lemon and silk. Here she was safe and she leaned against Godfrey. How many times had he eased her hurts when she was a girl? Made her laugh when she cried.

He didn't love her. Garrett did not love her. Beatrice staggered, and Godfrey righted her carefully.

How she loved him.

* * *

"Can you ride?"

Beatrice nodded and clambered onto Breeze's back. Her horse was solid beneath her. She kept her hand against the warm arch of the mare's neck. They rode through a tangle of streets. Beatrice let them slip past, staring at the road before Breeze. Her mind revisited the past weeks. How could she have been so stupid?

Men didn't pursue her. Men pursued Faye. Courters lay in wait for Faye and sent her secret notes and trifles. Not Beatrice. Beatrice was the plain sister, the sister who'd scared off three suitors. They sang verse to Faye, but they told jokes about Beatrice.

She'd always known this. She'd been vain and stupid and allowed herself to be blinded to the truth. A part of her had wanted desperately to believe Garrett was enamored of her, stricken by her beauty.

Garrett.

The place he'd occupied was a deep hole through her middle. He'd set out to seduce her, and she'd aided him with both hands. Dear God, she'd tossed herself before him with this journey to London.

And last night. Shame sheared through to the bone.

Tom had tried to tell her how foolish this was. But, nay, she would hear nothing of it. The only thing she'd wanted was to get to London and the consequences be damned.

She bestirred herself. London. She was in London.

"My father." She turned in the saddle to find Godfrey riding silently beside her. They rode alone. She searched the darkness behind Godfrey for Garrett. She had no pride. Beatrice clenched her teeth in fury at herself. "I must go to my father."

"I have already seen your father, Beatrice." Godfrey sat straight and true in his saddle. Not like—

Nay.

"I rode for London the day after Faye came. I arrived here before you. It seems you went awry a time or two." The gentle reproach on Godfrey's face writhed within her. "Arthur is on his way back home."

"On his way back home?" Oh, God, all of this for naught. Self-loathing piled around her head and settled onto her shoulders until the weight was nigh unbearable.

"Surely you did not think Henry or I would allow your family to be sucked dry and tossed aside? Or calmly hand our fair Faye over to Calder?" Godfrey shook his head. "It is so like you, Beatrice, to go rushing in without thought. Now look what you have brought upon yourself?"

He was right. Beatrice's shoulders slumped. She'd brought this on herself, with her foolishness and her willfulness and her refusal to listen. Her family knew her well. She was troublesome Beatrice, thoughtless Beatrice, and impulsive Beatrice. She had a new name for them, Beatrice the fallen woman. Beatrice the whore.

She flinched, and Breeze moved restlessly beneath her. "I would like to go home."

"Soon. But the gates are still shut for the night." He leaned across and patted her knee. "Rest for what remains of this night, Beatrice, and I will take you home in the morning. You have suffered a shock."

Godfrey's kindness brought tears to her eyes. She didn't deserve his compassion.

"And this," he gestured the road behind them, "will remain our secret. There is no need to burden your father or your mother."

Oh, God, her mother. Guilt licked at her like flame. Her

mother would be ashamed of her. And her father? She couldn't imagine her father's reaction.

"It is done." Godfrey broke into her thoughts. "You cannot undo it. So, put it aside."

* * *

Godfrey took her to a large manor within the city. She was settled in a room and a warm bath prepared for her. Beatrice dismissed the maid sent to assist her. She didn't want the other woman to witness her shame. It must be writ across her, clear and bold, for all to see. The bath eased her sore muscles, and she scrubbed her skin to wash away the taint of Garrett.

Ivy's bath had been cold. Garrett had known what to do. He'd known because of his mother. He'd brought the water for her, so Ivy could wash the stain of those men from her skin.

A tear plopped into the bath. Her image wavered in the water. It was a pathetic sight, with her droopy mouth and sad eyes. Her hair hung around her face in wet tendrils.

Ivy hadn't crumpled like a linen napkin. Ivy had put back her shoulders and set her eyes forward. Beatrice hadn't suffered what Ivy had suffered, nowhere near the horror. She had a broken heart. It would mend. Nurse always said hearts mended easier than spirits. Beatrice wished Nurse were here. She missed Nurse's calm, good sense.

She missed her mother. Beatrice gave a huge sniff. The bath smelled of roses, Lady Mary's scent. She scrubbed at her cheeks with her fingers to take away the tears. She'd never wanted her mother more. The thought of her mother almost brought the tears back again. Beatrice pressed her palms into her eyes to force them away. How could she talk to her mother? Her mother would be disappointed in her. She didn't think her mother would cast her out, but there would be no more talk of betrothals. She was used and spoiled now, like last week's bread.

Enough.

Beatrice pulled a face at her woebegone reflection. This wouldn't kill her. When she left London, she would rebuild her life. Without Garrett. She pushed the hurt away.

She would ask her father for a small cottage on his demesne. Somewhere she could keep a cow and a pig and a few chickens. Tom would come and fix things for her and do the heavier chores. Mayhap, Ivy would like to come and live with her. Ivy didn't judge. They'd grow old together in their self-styled convent, where men were not allowed. When Nurse grew infirm, she could come to Beatrice's cottage to be cared for by the two younger women.

She would grow wise in her cottage. She'd learn to be patient, and perhaps, as time passed, young girls might bring their tales of secret love and bitter heartache and be guided by her. Kindly, she would warn them from charming men intent on lifting their skirts, steer them away from the liars and the cruel ones. An image of this future rose in her mind, and Beatrice cheered a mite.

The girls would whisper of her in secret. They'd wonder at the sadness in her eyes and the way her smile always held a hint of melancholy. She'd be called "The Lady of the Hills." Or, better yet, the "Lady of the Weeping Willows." There was a spot down near the river where the willows grew thick and green. That would be the place for her and her cow and her pig and her chickens. And mayhap Ivy, if she wanted to.

Beatrice climbed out of the tub. A large bed almost filled the room. The heavy woolen draperies had been drawn back and the linens turned down. She padded over to it. The crackling fire warmed the bare stones beneath her feet. Clean clothes had been laid out for her. The cheery red of the bliaut seemed obscene against the gentle vision of the Lady of the Weeping Willow. The Lady of the Weeping Willows wore gray. Beatrice pulled on the chainse, wrapping a towel about her wet hair. The problem with gray was it made her complexion look pulled. Blue. A soft blue was a much better shade for her. Or green, mayhap, to match the willows surrounding her.

Garrett liked her in blue. The thought popped her imaginings like a soap bubble, and the sadness crept back. Beatrice shrugged on the bliaut. The wool was fine against her skin. She had been dressing rough for days now and the beautiful fabric caressed her skin.

Like Garrett.

She didn't want to forget Garrett's caresses.

A wooden chest rested at the base of the bed. Beatrice found a comb and began to work through her hair. She wanted to remember his touch, and everything about him. The ache for him almost bent her double.

"Ivy," she whispered. "Ivy and the Lady of the Weeping Willow."

## *Chapter Twenty-Two*

Beatrice couldn't sleep. She lay, fully dressed, on her bed and tried. A maid had brought her a tray of food, and it lay spoiling beside the bed. Beatrice drank some of the wine. Earlier this night, she'd been so hungry she would have fallen on this tray like a madwoman. Now, the food merely made her feel ill.

It must be close to dawn. Godfrey was still awake. She could hear movement in the house and the soft opening and closing of doors. Always, when she was younger, Godfrey had a tale for her or a funny ditty to make the night pass. She wanted to feel like that child. If her father were here, she might have curled up in his lap, but Godfrey would have a story to pass the time.

She pulled on a pair of slippers and padded to her door. It opened onto a passageway leading to a cozy hall. She'd find Godfrey there, beside the fire. He liked to nurse his wine and stare at the flames. Beatrice slid silently down the passage.

"Are you certain she is sleeping?" It was a man's voice, but pitched high, almost girlish.

Godfrey replied. "Aye, the maid looked in on her."

He spoke of her. The maid had opened her door and Beatrice had wanted to be alone, so she kept her eyes shut until the woman had gone away again. Surely Godfrey wasn't sharing the tale of her ruin?

She stepped closer to listen and stopped.

She was doing it again. If she'd only stayed away and not spied on Henry and Godfrey, she would not have decided to rescue her family and none of this would have happened. Of course, Garrett had already appeared in her life. But perhaps she would have found the strength to resist his seductions.

*Liar.*

"I had a difficult time finding her," Godfrey said. "She took a detour or two. I had to retrace my steps a couple of times. Fortunately, London is the sort of city where there are eyes and ears everywhere."

So, it was Godfrey who'd been chasing them. Her silly imaginings had built a marauding army at her back.

"What will you do with her? She cannot go home." A pewter flagon clinked, and then the sound of something being poured.

Beatrice's heart missed a beat. Did her mother know of her disgrace and not want her home again? Did her father or Roger know she was ruined and had cast her out?

She half-turned to return to her room. She shouldn't listen to this.

"She will not go home." Godfrey was right. Her imaginary cottage was the place for her. If her father wouldn't help her, surely Godfrey would. He'd been kind and understanding tonight.

"I will miss her," Godfrey said.

She would miss all her family, but they might visit. A chair scraped, and a man laughed. High-pitched and light. Not Godfrey.

"I would have avoided this if I could," Godfrey said. "She is my favorite niece."

A warm glow lit her chest. He was her favorite uncle.

"I will regret her death."

Beatrice stopped in her creeping away. She wasn't ill. Did Godfrey think she would waste away because she didn't eat?

"How will you kill her?" the other voice asked.

Godfrey chuckled.

Nay. She'd heard that wrong.

"What an evil wretch you are?" Godfrey teased. "Is it the details you want?"

Part of her mind split from the other. It hung over her and looked down at her. There she stood, in a dim corridor, her hands pressed to her mouth. And she shook. Her uncle spoke of killing her. How peculiar.

Her head whirled. She trembled so hard she had to lean against the wall. The stone was cold on her back.

"Fortunately, Wulfric's bastard has provided the perfect opening."

Garrett. Wulfric's bastard was Garrett. Her breathing rasped and she kept her hands locked around her nose and mouth to silence it.

"Let me guess?" said the stranger. "Lover's tiff, he gets violent. Strangles her? Beats her to death?"

Beatrice's belly heaved. She fought the impulse to gag.

"Or drowning," Godfrey said. "It is much kinder, and she is my favorite niece. After that, the bastard will simply disappear."

Silently, Beatrice backed away from the door.

"And Arthur?" The voice pursued her down the passage. "Will he not seek justice for her death?"

"Arthur is in Westminster. He has no idea his daughter is in London, or the news she carries. By the time my brother gets word his daughter is dead, he will be in no position to seek retribution. And Wulfric's bastard will not see the light of day again."

"You have thought of everything." The voice warmed with praise.

"I have been planning this for some years." Godfrey's smugness made her shiver. He was bragging about killing her. "Calder played his part. He is poised to attack Anglesea. Arthur will be too busy dealing with his daughter's death to help them."

He'd planned it. Godfrey had it laid before him like a map. The only thing he didn't know was that she stood in the corridor listening to his plan.

Beatrice backed away, her slippers soundless against the stone.

She fumbled on the latch when she reached the chamber. The chamber she was meant to be peacefully sleeping within. While her uncle, her stomach dipped alarmingly, planned her death.

The inside of the chamber stared back at her dispassionately, ridiculously normal, while around her, the world tilted and dipped. The conversation rang over and over again in her head. A tiny part of her mind refused to believe it of Godfrey. Yet, she'd heard him say those things. She desperately wanted to know why. Godfrey was her uncle, a man she'd been raised to respect and love. Memories flooded her mind. Godfrey at table with them, laughing at a jest her father made, telling her long, improbable stories by the hearth.

It made no sense.

None of this made any sense.

Garrett.

Always, her mind insisted on returning to Garrett. Godfrey planned to use Garrett to blame for her death. The room did one of those belly-dipping swirls. It defied belief to be standing here thinking of her death. As if it were fated.

*Not bloody likely.* She raised her chin.

The whys and wherefores would have to wait. She wouldn't remain here, calmly and passively, waiting for her death to stalk her.

"Think, Beatrice," she spoke the words out loud. "For once in your life, think. It may be the last thing you do." Her throat closed, and she reached out a hand to steady herself. The wall against her palm was solid and reassuring.

The chamber sat on the ground floor of the manor. She regretted not paying better attention when she was brought here.

Then, she'd been still reeling from the revelations about Garrett. Her broken heart would also have to wait.

She crept over to the casement. It opened easily. The court-yard stood quiet beneath her, bathed in a benign moonlight totally at odds with her splintered life. Beyond the yard was a high wall. Her chausses and her tunic had been taken away with the rest of her belongings.

No matter. Beatrice crept back to her door and bolted it. She didn't want some inquisitive maid raising the alarm before she'd had a chance to put some distance between herself and the manor.

Quickly, she searched her chamber for anything to aid her. The chest was full of bed furs. The tray of food held a small eating dagger. Beatrice snatched up the linen napkin and fashioned a small pouch. Her resources were pitiful, and she had no coin. She grabbed the small loaf of bread and added it to her makeshift pouch with the knife. There was no cloak or shawl in the chamber and she dared not tarry any longer.

She slipped up onto the casement sill. The yard remained quiet. Outside the walls of the manor, she could make out the sounds of the city. Jumping into the yard, she clung to the shad-ows. She stayed close to the house as she moved, looking for a way over the wall. The gate would be manned. She felt sure of it. The wall was high and stout as she scrutinized its length. Finally, she found it. Beatrice let her breath out.

A large tree was planted near enough to the wall to be useful.

Pausing for a quick glance, she dashed across the open court-yard toward the tree. She rested a moment with her back against it. Her heart hammered in her ears. No cry broke the silence, only the sound of two voices passing close to the wall. Light spilled across the yard from the hall. Godfrey was still in there with his unknown companion.

Beatrice pulled the back of her gown between her legs and tucked it into her girdle. The top limb hovered beyond reach. Placing her foot against the bark of the trunk, she tried to get enough leverage to reach it. Her foot slipped, scraping her shin against the bark. She dropped back to the ground with a hiss of frustration.

The light in the hall flickered and went dim. Godfrey must be leaving the hall. Beatrice couldn't wait any longer. She tried again. Her legs scraped against the bark, tearing effortlessly through her thin hose. Any moment now, Godfrey might open the door to her chamber. What would he do if he tried and found it locked? Her fingers grasped the limb, and she scrabbled to gain purchase. Using her knees, toes, shins, whatever she could, she half scrambled, half walked up the trunk until she got her arms over the limb and hauled herself over.

She panted and took a moment to dangle across the limb and catch her breath. The house remained silent. A light flickered behind another casement and grew stronger. Godfrey in his chamber, she guessed. He'd not checked on her. He remained oblivious to the fact she'd heard him. It was a tiny advantage, but she'd use it. Beatrice swung her legs over the limb and edged forward. The bark abraded the inside of her thighs as she inched toward the wall.

The branch didn't quite reach the wall, but came close enough for her to get one foot on the top and then the other. She teetered precariously as she peered down. Her vision swam. She quickly lowered herself to a crouching position and then straddled the wall for safety. The drop to the ground yawned beneath her.

Beatrice stared at it in dismay. The wall hadn't seemed as high from the other side. She was likely to break something if she attempted the long drop.

"Stop it," she said. "You are going to end up with a broken neck anyway." Or drowned. Panic pressed against the back of her eyes.

Below her, a stone protruded slightly from the others. Her slippers were thin and she might gain a hold. She swung her legs over and found the stone with her toes. It gave her a pitiful ledge, but she levered her weight over. With her free foot, she searched the wall for another hold. Her toes barked against another small imperfection in the rock. She inched over the top. The second toe hole was farther away than she'd anticipated.

Her arms were wrenched to their fullest as she tried to keep grasping the top of the wall. One leg splayed to the side as she clung like a spider. She dared not look at the ground.

"Jump, Beatrice," she whispered. "Let go and jump."

Her hands slipped.

She hovered in a black void before her feet hit the ground. The impact shot through her legs and snapped her teeth shut on her tongue. The bitter taste of blood filled her mouth as she crumpled onto the street.

Pain shot through her hip, and she had to spit blood, but she was intact. The relief of it almost made her giddy.

"What are you doing?"

Beatrice jammed her fist into her mouth. She lurched away until her back hit the wall. A small form materialized out of the darkness and loomed over her. It was skinny and messy. Tufts of hair stood up unevenly on his scalp.

"Newt?"

"Aye, my lady, and what are you doing?"

Beatrice dropped her head back against the wall. A bubble of laughter rose up from her chest and broke over her lips. She couldn't seem to stop. Newt was here. She had no idea how or why, but suddenly the situation didn't seem as desperate.

"Are you addled?" Newt crouched beside her and peered at her face.

It only made Beatrice want to laugh more.

Newt frowned at her. "I will ring for the guard."

"Nay." She stopped laughing and grabbed the boy. "I am escaping."

"From what?" Newt shifted his arm away from her hand.

"My uncle is trying to kill me." Saying the words out loud only made them seem ludicrous.

Newt raised his eyebrows and glared at her doubtfully.

"I speak true." She tugged on Newt until he was close enough for her whisper. "I heard him tonight, talking to someone. Godfrey is planning to kill me." Her mind balked. It couldn't be true. But it was true, and she straightened her shoulders. "I need to get to my father, Newt. Will you help me?"

"I do not understand any of this." Newt straightened. "But I thought my eyes were lying to me when I saw you on yon wall."

"I can explain." Beatrice clambered to her feet. "But not here." She looked about her. A man rounded the corner and started toward them. "I must get away from here. When I'm safe I will tell you everything."

"Come." Newt motioned for her to follow.

Beatrice had trouble keeping up with him. Newt disappeared like another shadow in the night. He had an almost preternatural sense for when someone was coming and a sharp hiss would warn her to make herself invisible. He ducked and weaved through the cramped, winding lanes until Beatrice had no idea which end was up.

The smell grew worse as they moved, until Beatrice was forced to keep her hand over her mouth. She thanked God her stomach was empty enough to provide no threat.

Finally, Newt ducked beneath the struts of a house and motioned her inside.

Beatrice eyed the small opening. The boy had a lot less meat on his bones. An imperious hiss had her crawling on her hands and knees after him. It was a tight fit. Her hips scraped against the wood before the gap widened into a small bolt hole. Neither of them was able to stand in the tight space. A pile of old rags formed a pallet in one corner.

"Is this where you sleep?" Beatrice was appalled. The boy had gathered a small collection of odds and ends like a magpie. A tarnished buckle, a chipped jug, and a small pile of old tapers cluttered the top of an upended bucket. He owned almost nothing. Beatrice's heart gave a twist. The meanest churl at Anglesea lived better than this.

"Now." Newt waved her over to his pallet of rags. He took up position on the floor near the entrance. "Tell me."

Beatrice started with her arrival in London, skipped the bit about her and Garrett alone, and got to where her uncle had come to find her and hauled Garrett away.

Newt listened, nodding sagely every now and again like a small, dirty, wise man. "How did he find you?"

She stared at him. It hadn't occurred to her to ask. "I have no idea."

"Hmm." Newt dipped his head, gnawing his bottom lip like a rat.

"What?"

"Either he had a spy in your camp—"

Beatrice opened her mouth to deny it.

Newt held up one grubby finger to stop her. "Or he was following you the entire time."

"Those men you saw." Missing bits of the puzzle dropped into place.

"Mayhap." Newt shrugged.

"I must reach my father as soon as possible," she said. "Do you know how to get out of the city? If he found me before, my uncle will be able to find me again."

"My lady?" Newt's chest puffed up. "Not only do I know how to get out of this city, I know a man who can take you right to Westminster." His eyes shifted in his crafty face. "Nobody finds Newt when Newt does not want to be found."

For the first time in what seemed like years, Beatrice smiled. She made a jaunty motion toward the entrance. "Shall we?"

"What of your man?" Newt squatted by the wall. "I would guess your uncle has him stashed somewhere."

Beatrice flinched at his words. The pain throbbed like a raw ache, lurking beneath the urgency of the moment.

"He is not my man." She clambered off the pallet to hide her reaction.

"Your uncle will kill him for sure." Newt shrugged and turned to leave his burrow.

Fear rose up around Beatrice's throat. Garrett would die. It wasn't her concern. Garrett had lived his entire life by his wits and his devious brain. He could use those to save himself.

Newt shot out of the narrow gap.

Beatrice followed him. She grabbed for the rapidly disappearing tunic in front of her. "Wait."

Newt stopped and turned his head as far as the narrow passage would allow.

"How did you find me?"

Newt gave a soft chuckle. "I was waiting for you, was I not? I saw you and the big man enter the gates, and I followed you. It was quick thinking of him to find those warehouses."

"You saw us and you did not approach?" What a strange boy.

"Not my way," he grunted.

"So, were you there? When my uncle came."

"Might have been." Newt tried to scramble away again, but Beatrice held fast.

"So, you knew most of what I told you."

"Lady," Newt whined, "my knees are getting powerful sore on this ground. There is a rock right beneath me."

The ground pressed against her knees, too. "And if you knew where I was, you might know where Godfrey's men took him." Beatrice could not get his name past the lump in her throat.

Newt clamped his lips together.

"Newt."

"I might." He hunched his shoulders.

"I freed you from the stocks, Newt."

"And I helped you tonight."

Not so fast, Beatrice tugged his tunic again. "I fed you."

"I found food for us."

"I helped you escape from those churchmen."

Newt made a small huff of irritation. He screwed his face up in thought. "I know where he is."

"Where?" Elation coursed through her.

"Not far from where you were." Newt parceled out the information like a miser counting coins.

"We must rescue him." Garrett deserved everything that was coming to him, but she wasn't going anywhere and leaving Garrett in Godfrey's hands.

"You see." Newt glared at her, aggrieved. "This is why I did not tell you. I knew you were going to say something stupid. The girl was right about you." He sniffed. "You have a soft heart. It makes trouble for you."

"I cannot help that, Newt." Beatrice damned herself for a thrice-cursed fool. "It is my way."

"I will help you rescue him. Then you and I are even."

"Even." When Garrett was safe, Beatrice would never set eyes on him again. He'd brought her to London and taken care of her. It didn't mitigate against what he'd done to her heart or the virginity he'd taken from her, but there was no time to agonize about that now.

She followed Newt through the noisome alley outside his hole. She stretched her cramped back. Her knees ached, and her hip throbbed from where she'd fallen.

Newt led the way again. She kept her eyes locked on his back.

He stopped suddenly.

"What?"

He gave her a cunning grin.

Beatrice braced herself for what was coming.

"If we are doing a rescue," Newt rubbed his palms together, "we might need some help."

Beatrice crossed her arms over her chest. "What do you want?"

"I know something else. This thing will be handy."

"Name your price." She needed to get to her father. She already spent time she didn't have to rescue Garrett. He'd read Newt aright. She watched the conniving face in front of her.

"I do not have a price yet." He tapped the side of his sharp, little nose. "But I know something of great use. I know how to get help and if I give you that, you will owe me."

"I cannot pay you if you do not have a price."

"You will be in my debt." Newt nodded. "I may one day have need of a lady with powerful connections."

Beatrice was quite sure he would, some day when he found his neck in a noose. "I only owe you if you help me free Garrett and if you get me to my father. Now."

"Done." Newt hawked and spat and was off again.

* * *

Beatrice blinked through the smoke filling the small tavern. Her eyes must be lying to her. For there sat Tom, looking pale, tired, and disheveled. Right beside him, Ivy kept a sharp eye on the people around her. Tom's arms scythed through the air as he held forth.

Ivy paid him no mind.

"See," said Newt.

Newt had led her to a small, modest inn.

"Aye, Newt, this was worth knowing."

It had been a truly horrible night. Starting from the moment she'd woken to find Godfrey holding a sword to Garrett's neck. Now, new hope flared. Tom and Ivy were here, in London. She wasn't alone anymore. Newt didn't count. He would aid her only so far as is suited himself.

"Them two arrived earlier," Newt said.

"But the gates were closed."

He winked. "Beer carts have a way of getting through closed gates. Especially with a city full of soldiers."

"How did you know?" Beatrice would have offered Newt her entire chest of jewels for this.

"Newt has eyes everywhere."

Tom noticed her and stopped talking.

Beatrice walked straight at Tom.

His welcoming smile wavered, and he opened his arms.

Beatrice was never gladder to see anyone in her entire life. She pressed her face into his shoulder. Tom was her constant, her rock, her one patch of solid ground in her teetering life.

"Hey, there." Tom patted her back awkwardly. "Come now, Bea. Are you crying?"

Beatrice shook her head. She clung to the dear familiarity of his solid form.

"I told you we had to get to London," he said over her head.

"Aye, you did," Ivy replied.

"I knew there was something not right."

"Aye, you did."

"Her uncle wants her dead," Newt chirped.

Tom went still in her embrace. "I thought we had seen the last of you."

"Not me." Newt swaggered over to the table and grabbed a slice of meat off Tom's trencher. "I found her falling over a wall not too long ago." He stuffed it into his mouth, barely chewing before he swallowed.

"Beatrice?" Tom gripped her by the shoulders and put her far enough away from him to see her face. "Would you like to explain?"

"Not really." Ivy handed her a handkerchief, and Beatrice blew her nose. She didn't know where to start.

"Where is Garrett?" Tom guided her onto the bench.

It was as good a place as any to start. They sat at the table Tom and Ivy had been sharing. Newt hovered about, snagging bits of food. The tavern around them was filled to the brim with farmers and their broods. Tom wouldn't want to hear about her fall from grace, so she began with Godfrey arriving in the warehouse and the conversation she'd overheard.

"I knew he was up to no good." Tom snatched the bread out of Newt's hand.

"Which one of them?" Beatrice laughed but there was no

mirth behind it. Scoundrels were crawling out of the woodwork all about her.

"Garrett." Tom slapped his hand on the table. A large, round-faced churl looked over at them curiously. Tom lowered his voice. "I could tell, just by looking at him, there was something not right there."

Beatrice wished she could say the same. She'd remained in blissful ignorance right up until the end. Nay, that wasn't quite right. There had been signs, hints along the way she'd chosen not to question further. She'd desperately wanted to believe his love for her was true.

Tom heaved a sigh. "But, Godfrey? Are you sure you heard right?"

"I could hardly mistake his meaning."

"You have a strange family," Ivy said.

And getting stranger. Beatrice choked back a laugh. "How is your wound?"

"Good." Tom lifted his arm and rotated it at the shoulder. "It pulls a trifle, but Ivy did a fine job with her needle. She talked our way into a barn and patched me right up. The wife took a shine to her and fed us, as well."

"Newt said you arrived on a beer cart."

"That was Ivy's doing as well." Tom smiled at Ivy. "We had to leave old Badger at the farm, but we thought we could fetch him on the way home."

Beatrice placed her hand over Ivy's and gave it a light squeeze. She had taken good care of their Tom.

"Right." Tom got to his feet and shoved the remains of their meal into his sack. "So, now we go to Westminster."

Beatrice stood with him.

"I think not." Ivy glanced at her from the corner of her eye.

Beatrice's face heated.

"Of course we go to Westminster." Tom tied the ends of his sack with a decisive twist. "Sir Arthur must be told all of this and before Godfrey can make more mischief."

"Nay, Tom." Ivy rose. "I think we first go to rescue Garrett."

Beatrice was grateful to Ivy for saying it for her.

"What?" Tom's eyes stood out on stalks. "We are not going to rescue the scoundrel. Let the bastard rot." He looked first at Ivy and then Beatrice.

Beatrice shook her head.

Tom threw his hands up. "You cannot tell me you are seriously thinking of rescuing him?" His face grew quite red. "He tried to seduce you, Beatrice."

She barely kept the flinch from her face. Ivy's knowing stare pressed like a weight.

"He was going to use you to get revenge on your father. He and Godfrey deserve each other." Tom waved his arms as he spoke.

Ivy touched him on the arm, and Tom snapped his lips together.

Beatrice looked at Ivy in amazement. She needed to learn that trick from the other woman.

"I cannot leave him there," Beatrice said.

"Aye, you can." Tom stood, legs akimbo. "He got exactly what he deserved."

"Do you mean you will not help me?"

"Aye." Tom folded his arms over his chest. "I am standing firm. I should have days ago and we would not be in this mess, but it is not too late to begin now. I will not help you rescue that villein."

## Chapter Twenty-Three

"It will never work," Tom grumbled.

"Of course it will." Beatrice peered around the corner at the shed where Newt said Garrett was being kept.

Two men guarded the door. Actually, the men appeared to be doing more drinking than guarding. The shorn one was the same man from the wool warehouse. The other was slimmer and younger, his hair a middle shade of brown, his features pinched. The shed nestled close to where Beatrice had been taken. It was agreed she should stay out of sight in case one of the guards recognized her.

"It never fails." Ivy calmly rearranged her clothing. She had already taken off her chainse and now undid the laces to her bliaut, so it gaped and revealed a large portion of her breasts.

Tom's color was high. He studied the wall beside Ivy keenly. "I do not like it."

Newt showed no such forbearance and studied Ivy's neckline.

"You do not have to like it." Ivy shook her hair free of her wimple. "All you have to do is club the second guard. I will lead one of them around this corner, and Beatrice will deal with him."

"I still do not see why we are doing this." Tom rubbed at his neck.

"I will explain it to you later." Ivy patted his cheek. "Now, be ready. I do not want to deal with that man if you are not."

* * *

Garrett had been born fighting his way out of the womb, and he'd lived his life that way. Until now. The two louts at the door presented no challenge. He could have pried open one of the loose bars at the back of the shed, lured them inside, and brained them. An enterprising man could come up with any number of escapes.

Instead, he sat in the filthy shack and pined for Beatrice. Her face as her uncle gave her the truth haunted him. The knowledge he'd put that look there drove the dagger deeper. Godfrey's plan for him would involve his demise. He simply knew too much now. Godfrey couldn't afford to let him live.

Beatrice would be with her family. She would be safe with her father and brothers watching over her. Godfrey had played his game well. Her family was ignorant they harbored a snake in their midst.

What did Godfrey mean to do about Beatrice?

Garrett scraped his fingers through his hair. He got to his feet, but the hut was too small to pace and he shifted restlessly from side to side.

Outside, the guards talked to each other. They said nothing of Godfrey, so he gave up listening. These churls were hired muscle, nothing more. Not particularly costly muscle either, from what he could hear.

He wanted to go to Beatrice and explain, to assure her of his love for her. Garrett sat down and dropped his head in his hands. It would do no good anyway. She wasn't for the likes of him. If he were any sort of man, he would have left her with her virtue intact. It only went to prove what a miserable, lowly sod he was.

Jesu, but she'd come to him sweetly with her heart in her beautiful eyes and her entire being on offer. He hadn't been able to resist. Like Adam, he'd reached for one sweet taste of the forbidden fruit.

She was better off without him. She would be angry, hurt even, but she would recover and find…

Nay, he was not going to think on Beatrice and another man.

What was Godfrey's game? What had he said in the forge? They had a common enemy in Sir Arthur.

Jesu. His skin crawled. Godfrey coveted what his brother had. This had been played out since Cane and Abel. If Beatrice stood between Godfrey and his aims, she was no longer safe. The small hut closed in about him. His heart raced.

Jesu, he was a sapskull. So intent on his own misery, his brain had shriveled.

The city gates were still closed. Beatrice could not be with her family. Godfrey had her. Sweat broke out over his entire body.

He had to find her, just to assure himself she was well. She need never know he was there. And if she were in peril, his path was clear.

Beatrice. He'd been skulking here, not caring whether he lived or died now that he had lost the one good thing in his life. He prayed he was not too late.

One of the guards called out.

The man spoke to a whore. He exchanged a crude jest with his mate. It sounded as if the whore had offered the right incentive because one of them moved away from his post.

He surged to his feet. Only one guard remained at the door. He liked his chances. He pounded against the frame.

"Shut up in there," the guard yelled back at him.

"I need a piss."

"Piss in your braies, you stupid bastard."

Garrett banged harder. There was a thump as the guard drove his fist against the door.

"How much are you being paid to keep me in here?"

"Listen, you—"

A dull *thud* and something heavy hit the ground. The door rattled on its hinges and was ripped open.

Garrett leaped back and out of the way.

A tall figure stood limned by the torchlight.

"Just so you know," Tom stepped inside, "this was not my idea."

Garrett wanted to embrace him.

A meaty fist snapped his jaw shut and sent Garrett hurtling against the back wall of the hut. The wall creaked and listed. Garrett slid down the wall and waited for the ringing in his ears to subside. The boy threw an excellent punch.

Tom loomed over him, his hands bunched by his sides. "If it were up to me, you would rot and die for what you did to her."

Garrett stayed where he was. Tom looked ready to hand out some more of the same.

"Tom?" A woman called from outside.

Not any woman, but Garrett's woman. "Is Beatrice here?"

Tom turned and, with a growl of disgust, charged out of the hut, brushing past the figure in the doorway. "I am done."

Garrett clambered to his feet. She was here and safe. His heart hammered. He battled to think over the clamor. There was so much he wanted to say to her, he needed to say to her, but the words wouldn't form. He wanted to grab her and hold her to him. She'd rescued him. Beatrice had come to his aid. His chest ached with the knowledge. She believed the worst of him, and she hadn't left him here to die.

"Are you going to stay in there?" she spoke at last.

"Beatrice." He rushed after her and caught her arm.

Tom stood by, looking as grim as the grave.

"You should not have come. You have placed yourself in danger, again." Jesu, he got more stupid by the minute. They were the first words that had broken clear of the confusion.

She turned to stare at him, aghast.

Garrett wanted to pound his own thick head into the ground.

Of all the things he needed to say to her, he'd chosen to chastise her.

"I told her so." Tom half raised his fist. "But she would not listen."

Beatrice turned away from him. "You are free. Go where you will. I never want to see you again."

She walked away from him. For one, stupid moment he'd hoped she might have remembered he'd told her he loved her. He shook his head at himself. Of course she wouldn't remember that. He'd given her no reason to believe a word coming from his mouth.

"Are you going to stand there and let her go?" Ivy emerged beside him.

"I think it would be best." Inside, claws raked through his innards. He'd often scoffed at idiots in love, walking about with their faces down to their knees. He understood now. It felt as if he were slowly being torn to shreds from within.

"Coward." Ivy pinched his arm.

Garrett winced and yanked his arm out of her grasp.

"You owe her, and you know it. Now stop being such a babe and pay your debt. She goes to her father this night. It falls to you to see her safe."

"She has Tom for that."

Ivy made a rude noise. "Tom is as much an innocent on these streets as she is. Now stop standing there with your heart in your eyes and prove yourself worthy."

Could he?

"You could start by telling her you love her." Another sharp pinch from Ivy made him yelp.

Garrett put some distance between her fingers and his arm. "I have already told her."

"With your braies on?" Ivy gave him a hard look.

Garrett's dropped his chin onto his chest. The girl made an excellent point.

"I did not think so." Ivy sauntered after Tom and Beatrice.

"Wait." Garrett moved before the thought had fully formed.

"What do you want?" Tom was suddenly between him and Beatrice.

Behind Tom's shoulder, Beatrice's face was cold, unreachable.

Garrett had put the ice there. It fell to him to take it away. Because, behind her mask, flickering in the back of her eyes, was the hurt his Beatrice was unable to conceal. "I swear before God, Tom, if you do not get out of my way, I will end you."

"She does not want to speak with you."

Tom was a brave idiot. Garrett would give him that much. "Then she can listen, but Tom, I am going to speak with Beatrice. If it kills both of us to do it."

"Oh, for God's sake." Beatrice pushed between them. "I do not have time for this. I need to get to my father."

"Good." Garrett grabbed her firmly by the elbow. "I will talk as we move."

"You are not coming with me." Beatrice tried to pull her arm from him.

"Aye, Beatrice, I am." She had him until he knew she was safe. She might not like it, but he was taking her to safety. "I said I would see you safe to your father, and I will do so."

"Why do you care?" The words came in soft pants as he quickened their pace toward the docks.

Any moment, Godfrey could send another of his men to check on the prisoner. "I told you before, Beatrice, I love you. Somebody needs to take care of that huge heart of yours because you do not."

"I do not believe you." She sobbed softly.

It tore through him, and Garrett swung her toward him. "This is not time for declarations, sweeting."

"Do not listen to him, Beatrice." Tom stepped closer.

"Trust your heart. Just one more time, Beatrice, trust what your heart is telling you to be true."

Her eyes searched his. "I am not sure I can."

Garrett allowed her to see all of him. Everything. The man

he'd been, the man he was now, and the man he would dearly like to be.

"You hurt me," she whispered.

"I know." Garrett cupped her face between his palms. He wanted to weep with gratitude. He had his hands on her again. He'd believed his chance to touch her again was gone. "And I am terribly sorry. I love you, Beatrice," he said. "I love everything about you, and it does not matter if you cannot forgive me and love me back. It only matters you believe that much."

"I do not believe this," Tom muttered.

"I do not care what you believe." Garrett cared only about the beautiful girl in front of him. "It is what Beatrice believes that matters."

Tom thrust his chest forward. "If you love her as much as you say you do, you will keep your little confessions until we get her to her father. Beatrice neglected to tell you her uncle Godfrey is trying to kill her."

He'd known it. There was a grim sort of satisfaction in being right. Now was not the time to revel in it, however. "And you stopped to rescue me?"

Beatrice lifted her stubborn chin and nodded.

She'd done it again. Gone and tossed herself right into the middle of danger. God's bones, but she would be the death of him. Her uncle was trying to kill her, and what did Beatrice do? Did she run for her life? Did she hie herself off to her father's protection as fast as her pretty ass could sway? Nay. Beatrice took the time to rescue a sorry sod like him.

"We will speak of this." He grabbed her hand and set off at a trot. "After we have found your father."

# Chapter Twenty-Four

In the hours before dawn, London was a strange place, filled with sinister shadows. The taverns had fallen silent and many of the torches burned out. Newt led them through the lingering dark toward the river.

As she traveled, Beatrice was glad of her small party surrounding her. People loomed out of the gloom, the desperate, and the destitute.

Garrett moved by her side, alert and intent as they hurried onwards.

He loved her, and her stupid heart thrilled. She needed answers, but later, when the danger passed.

The boat Newt found looked none too safe. Newt spoke to the figure hunched in the boat before motioning her forward. "He says he will do it, but there is only room for two."

Garrett climbed aboard the boat and tugged her after him.

"Follow when you can," he called to Tom. Tom and Ivy stood beside the river. Tom so much taller, standing guard over the tiny Ivy. "And watch out for Godfrey. The moment he finds her missing, he will know where she has gone. He will, for certain, be watching the gates. Travel by river. It is quicker than the road."

The boat listed beneath her feet, and Beatrice sat quickly. The water glittered at her. The sky had grown lighter. King William's great tower, square and impregnable, its four turret's standing proud, was outlined to the east.

Urgency thrummed through her blood. It would be light before their boat reached Westminster.

"Get to the Black Friars, west of here," Garrett called as the boatman pushed away from the bank. "The friars have a barge that travels to Westminster."

Tom nodded and raised his hand. He touched Ivy on the arm, and she turned to follow him between the buildings.

Beatrice waved until he and Ivy were no longer visible. She sent a quick prayer of protection after them. Newt had already disappeared, his part of the bargain over. Beatrice prayed things would go well for him, too.

"Keep it down." The boatman's hood was drawn up over his features. He hunched like the harbinger of death in the bow. His voice emerged from the dark of his cloak as he poled the boat into the middle of the river. "Sodding water bailiffs are everywhere."

Beatrice huddled in the bottom of the boat. A chill wind whipped off the river, and she tucked her arms about herself.

Garrett squeezed in beside her. "Beatrice, I—"

"Shut it," the cloak snarled.

Garrett clamped his lips together. "We will speak later." His breath was warm on her ear. He lifted his arm and put it about her.

Beatrice snuggled against his warmth.

The boatman grunted as he turned the boat against the tide. "You, big 'un." A finger emerged from the cloak. "Grab the sodding spare oar and row. We work against this whore." He aimed a stream of spit over the side and heaved against his oar.

Garrett let go of her reluctantly. He grabbed the other oar and made his way precariously to the stern.

The boat hung motionless against the current. The men strained against the oars.

"Heave," the boatman grunted.

The boat inched forward, slowly at first, gathering speed as the oars caught the water.

Other than the swish of the water, the trip up the river was eerily quiet. Torches lined the riverbank but didn't illuminate them gliding over the dark water.

The silence chafed at her nerves. She kept her eyes fixed on the steeples of London, receding painfully slowly as the two men rowed. A haze hung over the city.

Sweat beaded on Garrett's brow and slithered down his cheek.

She prayed for speed. She prayed she wasn't too late to reach her father.

The sky blushed pink by the time the turrets of Westminster palace soared up ahead. Torches lost the battle against the day, flickering from the battlements, creating weak shadows against the walls. Her father was in there. As they drew closer, she heard the guards calling the hour.

Godfrey must have discovered she was gone by now.

The boatman drifted past the palace and pulled toward shore in its shadows. He raised his oars and motioned them to silence. They waited with the occasional drip of water from the locked oars the only sound.

She was ready to scream by the time the boatman dipped one oar and guided them to the shore. They barely made a ripple in the water.

The wet mud sucked at her slippers as Beatrice stepped out of the boat. She raised her skirts and tramped on, wrinkling her nose at the smell.

The boatman slipped back into the current like a ghost.

Westminster stood heavily guarded. Men at arms were everywhere, tense and alert, as they peered into the growing day.

Beatrice led the way.

Behind her, Garrett was a solid presence.

The time for stealth was passed, and she marched straight for the gatehouse.

A pair of pikes crashed in front of her, bringing her to an abrupt halt.

"I am the Lady Beatrice." The guard wore a lion, rampant on vert across his chest. The colors were unknown to her. "It is urgent I see my father, Sir Arthur of Anglesea."

The pikes stayed.

"Get away from here, girl." The guard's gaze flickered over her from either side of his metal nasal.

Beatrice knew how she must look to the guard, with her gown filthy from her night running through London and the stink of the river still on her.

"It is imperative you send a message to Sir Arthur." She straightened her shoulders, trying to maintain her dignity despite her disreputable appearance. "I am his daughter, and he needs to see me."

The guard snorted at her. "And who is he?" He motioned his head at Garrett. "The bloody king?"

"I am Lady Beatrice." She raised her chin and stared the man down.

The guard shoved his pike toward her.

Beatrice stepped back to avoid being jostled.

Garrett stiffened.

Beatrice put out her hand to stop him. She couldn't risk a fight at the gate. "Would you send him a message I am here?" They could at least agree to that. "I have to see my father. I will not leave until I do."

People moved in the yard beyond the portcullis. If only she could get past the gate. Her scream of frustration welled in her throat and she forced it down.

"No camp whores in the palace."

Camp whore? Had this man just called her a camp whore? Her mouth dropped open and she snapped it shut again.

Garrett gathered like a storm at her back.

Well, Garrett would just have to wait his turn.

"How dare you." She was Lady Beatrice, daughter of Sir

Arthur of Anglesea. How dare this churl call her vile names? When she got to her father she'd shove his head on that blasted pike of his. "My father will have your head for this."

The guard exchanged glances with his comrade. He shifted uneasily.

"You look nothing like a lady." His voice wavered.

"I am in this state because I need to see my father." *Not so sure now, are you, churl?* She glared down her nose at the man. Nobody called Lady Mary's daughter a whore.

The guard swallowed and slid a look at his fellow. "Sir Arthur will have my head if you are not who you say you are."

"He will have your head if I am." Beatrice was going to enjoy watching him squirm. "Send a message to one of my brothers, Sir Roger or Sir William. Let them come and tell you I am Lady Beatrice."

He thought it over for precious seconds. "Wait here." He stepped beneath the shadow of the gatehouse.

Whispering went on and on. Eventually, another soldier emerged from the gatehouse.

"We will send a message." The guard placed his pike across the path. "And if you are lying—"

"I am not lying." Beatrice turned her back, not prepared to waste one more moment on this ill-mannered oaf.

She was almost jumping out of her skin by the time the sound of approaching footsteps broke the silence. Beatrice leaped to her feet. A familiar figure strode across the bailey toward them, his long legs eating up the distance.

Her brothers were all tall, but Roger stood even a few inches taller than their father. He had Sir Arthur's dark hair, but his blue eyes and carved features were all Lady Mary. He was built like his father, powerful shoulders tapered into a slim waist. Beatrice's chest swelled with pride as her strong, handsome brother drew closer.

"Roger." Beatrice jumped up and down and waved her arms. Everything was going to be well again. She'd made it.

Roger stopped and his head jutted forward. "Beatrice?"

Beatrice sobbed with relief. "Roger." She beckoned her brother. *See there.* She tossed a haughty glance at the man at arms.

He went a little pale.

Roger jogged toward her. "It cannot be you." He shoved past the crossed pikes and came to stand right before her. "It is you. You look a sight."

"Oh, Roger." Beatrice flung herself at her oldest brother.

Strong arms folded around her. His surcoat was silky beneath her cheek, wearing her father's arms, a sable dragon rampant upon Argent.

Relief brought tears to her eyes. "I have to see father right away."

"What has happened?" Roger pulled her away from him. "Is it mother? Is she ill?"

"Nay." Beatrice waved him to silence. "Mother is fairing well." Beatrice desperately hoped she spoke true. "But I must speak with father. I have traveled such a long way to see him."

"But where is Henry?" Roger frowned and looked beyond her. "And your escort? And why do you look as if you have been dragged through a hedge backward? And what is that smell?"

"I will explain everything." Beatrice tugged on Roger's surcoat. "Only, tell these men to let us in."

"Who is that?" Roger narrowed his eyes on Garrett. He tensed and put his hand on his sword.

"I will explain everything, but I have to get to father. Now, Roger. We are all in peril."

"Peril?" Roger's face hardened. "You had best come along then."

She and Garrett followed behind Roger as he led them through the keep. The keep was bare of ornamentation. Only the various banners of the warring barons bedecked the hall in a glorious display of heraldry. There were knights and soldiers everywhere, busy but calm and well ordered.

They mounted the stairs to the upper level and entered a large, private chamber.

Sir Arthur stood poring over a map with William.

Joy rushed through her and brought tears to her eyes at the sight of them. Her father was so like Roger, only thicker around the waist and shoulders, and his dark hair was flecked with gray. William was as beautiful as ever with the aquiline perfection of his features, crowned by a pair of brilliant blue eyes, his hair so dark as to be almost black.

Her father snapped up straight. "Beatrice. Merciful God, what has happened to you?"

She ran toward him.

He hauled her into his arms for a huge hug.

Beatrice inhaled the familiar smell of horses and leather she associated with her father. With her father's strong arms about her, she was completely safe. She'd done it. She'd reached her father. Sir Arthur would fix everything. In her entire life, she'd never encountered a thing her powerful, gruff-voiced father couldn't put to rights. She was passed from her father to William.

Stiff and tense, hands clenched by his side, Garrett stood just within the door. His face appeared to be carved from rock.

Beatrice sent him a reassuring smile.

His face remained frozen.

"Now." Her father tugged her out of William's embrace. "You had best start telling."

Her father sat and listened. His face grew sterner as the story continued.

Roger paced the room, swearing quietly.

His gaze drifting to Garrett and back to her, William sipped his wine.

"Did you not speak with your mother before you left?" Her father rose to his feet.

She thought she had explained why her mother could not be worried. "I could not worry her." Sir Arthur, of all people, should understand that. "She is not well."

"For the love of God, girl!" Her father frowned mightily. "Why did you not take this to your mother?"

"I told you—"

"Beatrice, think." He punched his palm. "Why would I leave your mother unguarded?"

"Henry said he did not have enough men." Their conversation had veered from the way she thought it would go. "Should we not be leaving for Anglesea?"

"Calder had not reached Anglesea?" Sir Arthur paced the length of the table and back again.

"Nay, not before I left, but both Faye and Henry feared he could not be far behind."

"Jesu." Roger threw himself onto the bench. "I told you Henry would make a dog's ballocks of this."

Beatrice's head whirled. Nobody reacted as she expected. Secrets on top of secrets until she wanted to scream.

"Do not use that language in front of your sister," Sir Arthur said. "We can only hope Henry was sensible enough to go to your mother after Beatrice disappeared."

"What of Godfrey?" Roger slammed the table. "Jesu the lying whore...knave."

William caught his goblet before it fell and raised it to his lips. "Before I was banished from court, Godfrey was often in the company of the king and Calder. It is not a stretch to believe he has grown ambitious, and the king is always one to use such men to his advantage."

"We grew up with him." Roger stalked over to the casement. "Godfrey put me on my first horse."

William shrugged one elegant shoulder. Even wearing his hauberk, William managed to look like a courtier. "Mayhap, he grew tired of living in the shadow of the great Sir Arthur."

"What, in the name of hell, do you mean?" Roger bore down on his younger brother.

"It means simply"—William studied his wine—"Godfrey is a much younger brother. The only property he holds is through our father. With the three of us standing to inherit before him, there is no chance of ever increasing his holdings."

Roger loomed over William.

Raising a brow at him, William sipped his wine.

Beatrice grew tired of their posturing. Roger and William were constantly at each other's throats. She turned back to her father. "I think it is more important to ascertain what you are going to do now."

"Quite right, Sweet Bea." William grinned.

She'd seen him reduce ladies to a swoon with that smile of his. He needn't think it would work on her.

"Do?" Sir Arthur resumed his pacing. "I need to get to Anglesea and sort out this snarl. Roger, call up the men. We ride within the hour."

At last. Relief swept through Beatrice. Her knees weakened, and she caught the edge of the table.

Garrett's strong arms caught her.

"Do I know you?" William tilted his head and studied Garrett.

*Blast*! Beatrice froze.

"Nay." Garrett met William's gaze, his eyes blazing.

"I think I do." William swirled his wine.

"By the rood, Will," Roger snapped. "Get off your idle ass. We ride within the hour."

"In a moment." William waved a languid hand. "I know you from the village."

William had the sharpest eyes. Beatrice cursed, one of the new words she'd learned from Garrett.

Garrett thrust his shoulders back and raised his chin.

"What of it?" She made light of the moment. "There are plenty of people in the village."

Garrett's stance shrieked outright challenge.

Her brothers wouldn't hesitate to take him up on it. She rubbed her damp palms on her bliaut. "The danger is at Anglesea. I came all this way to warn you. You must act."

"And we will, Sweet Bea." William leaned his elbows on the table. "But I would like a few questions answered first."

"What is it, William?" Sir Arthur's eyes narrowed on Garrett.

"There is no time for this." Beatrice pulled at the shoulder of William's hauberk.

"You traveled from Anglesea without an escort?" William crossed his ankles as if he were settling in for the rest of the day. "With only him for company."

"And Tom," Beatrice said.

Roger and her father studied Garrett with the same intensity as William.

Bloody, blasted William. The damage was done. "I told you, Tom was with us. And we gathered some people along the way, but that is a tale for another day. The important thing is I am here now, and father must go home. He is sorely needed at Anglesea."

"Your brother raises a good question." Her father's chest swelled, and he balled his fists.

Beatrice stepped in front of Garrett. "I told you, his name is Garrett, and he helped me to get here."

"Why?" drawled William into his wine.

"I am also sure I know you." Sir Arthur firmly but gently pushed her to the side.

"Aye, you know me," Garrett said.

* * *

Garrett stared at the face he'd conjured in his mind for all these years. Sir Arthur had aged well. He looked craggier around the edges, and his hair was laced with white, but he still possessed the same strong features and stern eyes that stared back at him. He waited for the hate to thicken his blood.

* * *

"God be praised!" Godfrey charged through the door. "Thank God I found you before you left, brother."

Beatrice's heart leaped into her throat. She grabbed her father's arm.

"Godfrey?" Sir Arthur swung around.

"Get away from him." Godfrey pointed at Garrett. "He is here to kill you."

"It is not true." Fury surged through Beatrice.

"Look at him, brother. Do you not recognize Wulfric's bastard? He is here for vengeance." Godfrey's sword cleared his scabbard with a loud hiss. He sprang for Garrett.

"He is lying, Father." Beatrice blocked Godfrey's path.

Garrett pushed her. "Get her safe."

Beatrice stumbled toward her father, her head snapped back on her neck.

Sir Arthur shoved her behind him.

Godfrey advanced, and Garrett dropped to the floor and rolled clear.

She clawed the back of her father's hauberk. She had to save Garrett. Black spots danced in front of her eyes.

Unarmed, Garrett rolled to his feet, gaze locked on the blade.

Godfrey closed on him and swung.

Beatrice screamed.

Garrett staggered back. A red stain bloomed on his sleeve.

Dear Lord, he was hurt. Beatrice ducked under her father's arm and ran for Garrett.

Roger caught her waist and hauled her back.

"Nay." She flailed against her brother's hold. Godfrey would kill Garrett for sure. She had to stop it.

"Do not be stupid," Roger said. "Do you want to be killed?"

Roger's arm around her waist almost cut off her breathing as she thrashed to get free. She didn't care. She had to save Garrett. "You must stop it. Garrett is not armed, and Godfrey wants to kill him. You must stop it. Please."

Godfrey thrust.

Beatrice's heart stopped.

Dancing out of the way, Garrett ducked beneath the sword and rolled toward the table.

Godfrey's sword sheared through the wood and he tugged it free.

Garrett came up on the other side of the table.

Godfrey leaped onto the table.

"Stop him, Father, stop him. Garrett saved me. Godfrey tried to kill me." Didn't they see what was happening? Terror turned her blood to ice as Godfrey's sword arced toward Garrett.

"Enough." Sir Arthur's bellow shook the rafters.

Godfrey's sword stopped for a breath and then continued.

Her father sprang forward, his sword raised. Metal met metal in a ringing *clang*. Sparks flew as her father twisted his wrists, trapped Godfrey's blade with his, and pinned it to the table.

"What in hell is Beatrice shrieking about?" Her father's voice cut through the heavy air.

Godfrey licked his lip. His hand shook as he strained against Sir Arthur's lock on his sword. "She is bewitched by him." Godfrey panted, sweat streaming down his face. "He has seduced her into believing he cares for her, but he is only using her to get to you. I hurried here to save you, Arthur. He wants revenge for his father's death."

"It is not true." Beatrice clawed at Roger's hands.

"Stop it, Bea." He shook her hard enough to rattle her teeth. "Or I will be forced to hurt you."

"Beatrice." Godfrey shook his head at her and turned toward his brother. "She is enchanted by him and his smooth words. You know his face. He looks exactly like his sire."

"Drop your sword." Sir Arthur pressed on Godfrey's blade.

With a curse, Godfrey released his blade. "I was merely trying to save you, Arthur." He shook his wrist as if to ease it.

"She tells quite a tale, brother," Sir Arthur said.

"You know what she is like, Arthur." Godfrey jumped from the table. "Beatrice will believe anything anyone tells her. She is your daughter. You do not need me to tell you how trouble always finds a home with Beatrice."

Beatrice shook her head in horrified disbelief. The words dripped like honey from Godfrey's lips.

"Wulfric's bastard, after all these years." Her father's eyes were deadly intent as they fastened on Garrett.

"Arthur, you know your daughter," Godfrey said.

Beatrice sobbed her frustration. Godfrey, with his smooth words, twisted everything his way.

"I do," her father replied. "And she is impulsive, thoughtless, reckless, and inclined to believe any sad tale told her."

"Nay, Father." He didn't believe her. She had failed. The room wavered in front of her eyes as Beatrice swayed on her feet.

Roger took her weight.

"But she does not lie." Her father's sword blurred.

Godfrey's eyes widened at the sword against his neck. His gaze drifted up to his brother. "Arthur?" He swallowed convulsively.

"She does not lie."

Beatrice slumped against Roger. Her head seemed stuffed with wool, and she couldn't follow the rapidly changing currents in the room.

"Aye," Roger added. "Beatrice does not lie. As much as we would wish her to be less truthful at times."

"For the love of God, Arthur." Godfrey spread his hands wide.

Arthur's sword rested beside the vein pulsing in his neck.

"You cannot be seriously listening to the girl. Look at her. She is nigh beside herself. And him?" Godfrey sneered at Garrett. "The whoreson has been swiving his way through most of the village, and now he has turned his attentions to the keep. I saw them, Arthur, with my own eyes. He has had her, and she thinks like a woman bewitched."

"Why?" Arthur asked his brother.

"He is a comely knave, Arthur. He has a way—"

"Why?" Sir Arthur pressed his blade against Godfrey's throat.

"Arthur, I—"

Sir Arthur's voice grew hard. "Was it envy, brother? Did you want what I had?"

Godfrey's face tightened with anger. "You believe her?"

"Aye, Godfrey." Her father sounded terribly sad. "Now I want to know why my brother would try to kill my daughter, his niece, and jeopardize my family and our entire demesne."

"If I may?" William remained near Garrett, his sword drawn and within striking distance. "I think the answer lies in what he was promised to act thusly."

"Does he have the right of it?"

Godfrey stared long at his brother. His shoulders slumped, and he closed his eyes briefly before opening them. A glint of amusement shone in their hazel depths.

Beatrice stared at Godfrey in shock. His features were familiar and yet, so far removed from the man she had loved as an uncle. It was as if she had seen him for the first time. This cold, hard man had plotted her death with no remorse.

"King John wanted you gelded. You grew too powerful. Too many listened to your voice. And I—" Godfrey shrugged. "I merely wanted what is my due." He raised his hands. "Look at you, Arthur. You play war constantly and leave your lands in the hands of that boy, Henry. Your daughters run wild, and your other sons are like you. You are a great, savage brute, and this is a time for men of diplomacy and vision."

Godfrey cocked his head and smiled. "What now, brother?" He chuckled. "Now you have discovered you harbor a viper in your bosom, what will you do?"

"The thing about us savage brutes, brother—"

Beatrice's blood ran cold.

"—is we act first and think last." Sir Arthur's blade moved.

Eyes wide, Godfrey stared at Arthur and crumpled to the floor, blood pumping from the clean cut across his neck.

Beatrice hid her eyes against Roger's chest. She didn't want to see her uncle bleed to death.

"I will clean this up, and then we ride for home." Her father pulled her into his arms.

Beatrice collapsed into the embrace.

"Sweet Bea," he whispered against her hair. "Did you think I would not believe you?"

Tears welled behind her eyes and clogged up her throat. She nodded but couldn't look at her father.

"Of course I would believe you, Beatrice." Her father tilted her chin up with his finger. His face looked sad and drawn. "You are my daughter. I am aware of each of your faults, but also your great strengths. You were a very silly girl to come here like this, but also a brave one. Now, we must go home and sort out the mess my brother has left for us."

"Not quite yet," William called. "We seem to be forgetting something."

Her father turned and tugged Beatrice around with him.

William dropped his sword and drove his elbow into Garrett's face.

Beatrice yelled and tried to run for Garrett, but her father put her firmly aside.

Roger, not quite as quick as William, gave a roar and leaped for Garrett.

"Stop them, Father," Beatrice implored. "They will kill him."

"Nay." Sir Arthur looked quiet and grim. "But my boys will make him ache enough to know what happens to anyone who trifles with my daughter."

*Chapter Twenty-Five*

Garrett disappeared under a pile of flying fists. He defended himself, not valiantly, but effectively.

Her father stood firmly in front of her, preventing her from moving.

"Your mother will want to speak with you." Color climbed from his throat onto his cheeks. "There are women's matters. She will need...um...to discuss matters and the like with you."

Beatrice writhed inside. Her father knew of her amorous adventures. It was beyond mortifying. His embarrassment only made her want to crawl beneath the nearest rock.

"Beatrice." Tom hurtled through the door. "Your uncle came through—" He stopped. In a glance, he took in Godfrey's body. "I see you know already."

"Thomas," her father bellowed, loud enough to make her ears hurt. "I understand you were part of Beatrice's foolish notion."

"Aye, my lord." Thomas paled and dropped his head.

"You cannot blame Tom, Father." Beatrice dragged her eyes away from the mass of limbs in the corner. Her brothers wouldn't really hurt Garrett, would they? Or he, them.

Garrett seemed to be holding his own.

"He bit me." Roger's head popped up. He clasped bloody fingers to his ear.

Biting? Not exactly noble, but it was two against one. "Tom came with me because I asked him to."

"I do not blame Tom." Sir Arthur took her by the shoulders and turned her to Tom. "You have always talked him into trouble."

"Aye, sir." Tom straightened his shoulders. "But she has always talked me out of trouble shortly thereafter."

William stood up and glared at the tangle around him, bellowed, and leaped back into the fray.

Half-hidden by Tom, Ivy peered around as William yelled. "Should you not stop them, my lord?"

"And who are you?" Her father tilted his head to see around Tom.

Tom put himself in front of Ivy and raised his chin. "Her name is Ivy."

Sir Arthur barked a laugh. "Like that is it, young Tom?"

Tom flushed. "Ivy has had a rough go of it and is easily afeared."

"Aye, Father, stop glowering at her." Beatrice pinched him. She would not have her father frightening Ivy. "Will you not stop them?" All three of the combatants were bloodied.

"Let them settle it." He patted her shoulder. "And tell me about little Ivy."

Had her father gone daft? He wanted to chat about Ivy? "Father, Anglesea? Mother?"

"Don't fret so, Beatrice. What happened to Ivy?" Her father walked closer to Tom, tugging Beatrice with him.

"We rescued her from some vicious curs on the road," Tom said.

"You rescued her?" Sir Arthur raised his eyebrows. "You and Beatrice?"

"And Garrett," Beatrice added.

Near the fight in the corner, a bench went over and broke. The combatants appeared to be running out of vigor.

Sir Arthur grunted and motioned for Tom to continue.

Tom told the story.

Blood oozed from Garrett's mouth and nose, and one eye was already swollen shut.

Roger reared up from the fray, howling and holding his manhood. "The bloody whoreson—"

That was ungentlemanly. Beatrice winced.

"Language, son," Arthur yelled back at them. "There are ladies present. I am charmed to meet you, Mistress Ivy. You are a woman of uncommon courage." Her father bowed low over Ivy's hand.

Ivy's cheeks turned pink.

"Know that should you decide to make Anglesea your home, no further harm will come to you."

"Thank you, my lord."

Beatrice shook her head to try to clear it. Garrett was being beaten to a pulp, her family was in danger, and her father was laying on the charm for Ivy.

The tangle of fighters sent the table crashing over.

"My lord, should you not be addressing that?" Tom motioned the grappling men.

At last, someone showed some sense.

"They will run out of fight eventually." Sir Arthur smiled at Tom. "Now, tell me the rest of it." He fixed Beatrice with a stern eye. "You have had four days away from the keep. If I know my daughter, there has been no end of tricky situations."

"Not at all, my lord." Tom kept his face straight.

Beatrice wanted to kiss him.

"Nothing we could not remedy." She beamed at Tom.

He gave her a tiny wink.

"Arthur!"

Sir Arthur straightened, and his head jerked around to the door.

"Mother." Beatrice would know that voice anywhere.

Lady Mary stood in the doorway, her fists on her hips, her large belly protruding before her. Behind her stood Nurse.

Beatrice suppressed a groan.

Tom ducked behind Beatrice, pulling Ivy with him.

To Nurse's right, his blond head towering over their mother and Nurse, stood Henry.

Beatrice blinked to be sure she was seeing right. Henry was here? And not looking at her as if she needed a stern lecture.

Beatrice's heart gave a happy thump. Faye stood beside Henry. Beyond Faye's right shoulder loomed the stoic form of Sir Gregory, so tall, his head almost touched the lintel, his face as grave and stoic as ever.

"Mary?" Sir Arthur's stern features melted into the sweetest smile.

Beatrice's eyes filled. Sir Arthur and Lady Mary's story was the stuff of romantic legends. She wanted such a love for herself.

Lady Mary's gaze moved across the entire chamber. She paused when she got to Godfrey's body. "I see the morning has been eventful." She sighed and touched her hand to her belly. "Sir Gregory?"

"My lady?"

"Would you please?" She made an elegant gesture toward Godfrey's body.

Sir Gregory hefted Godfrey's lifeless corpse over his shoulder as if it weighed naught. He strode from the room, carefully skirting Faye and Lady Mary.

The corners of Lady Mary's mouth drooped. She shook her head slowly as she watched Gregory leave. She sighed as if resigned. "Such a great pity."

"And you." Lady Mary fixed Beatrice with a glare. "I will speak with you shortly."

She knew that look. Beatrice wanted to sneak away before her mother's "shortly" arrived.

"Mary." Sir Arthur stepped in front of his wife and held out his arms.

"In a moment, Arthur. I am terribly glad to see you, but first things first." She gently pushed aside his arms and stepped around her husband. "If you would, Nurse."

Lady Mary was lithe for a woman with such a distended belly. She stopped perilously close to the fight.

"Mother." Lady Mary could be swept into the tangle. Beatrice went to fetch her back.

Lady Mary struck like a viper, reached into the mess, and emerged with William. Keeping a firm grip on his ear, she dragged him out.

Nurse held Garrett by the seat of his chausses and sent him careening across the room.

The sudden silence fell like a pall.

Lady Mary brushed off her hands and turned to her husband. "Arthur." A huge smile lit her beautiful face as she embraced her husband. "It is lovely to see you." She turned her face up, and Sir Arthur kissed her cheek. "Although I cannot approve of what you allowed to take place here. We did not raise our children in a stable." She cupped Sir Arthur's face between her palms and studied him. She nodded, then turned and approached Beatrice.

"And you." She kissed Beatrice and held her face tenderly. Her beautiful blue eyes took in everything in minute detail.

Tears stung Beatrice's eyes. Her mother was here, and she wanted to take shelter in her arms and be told all would be well.

"My darling girl, I should beat you black and blue. I have been out of my mind with worry." Lady Mary hugged Beatrice around her enormous belly.

As Lady Mary released her, Henry got hold of her and squeezed her hard enough to crack a rib. "You are a wicked girl." He cleared his throat.

His eyes were damp as he held her at arm's length to look at her. "You should be lying dead in a ditch."

"But I am not."

"Nay, you are not." Henry pinched her cheek.

"You are a sad romp, Bea." Faye kissed her on the cheek. "But I am delighted to see you looking well." Faye looked lovely and composed; the tired lines had eased.

"What are you doing here? All of you?"

"We came to find you." Nurse frowned, and her wimple dipped over her brows. "Quite a turn you gave us, running off like that with my son."

Tom choked.

"I see you, Thomas." Nurse jabbed her finger at him. "And who is that you are hiding?" She bustled over to them. Immediately, her face softened. "Dear Lord, where did you find this sweet little thing? Goodness me, child, come out from behind my oaf of a son and let Nurse get a good look at you."

Ivy's shuffled into view.

"I have not forgotten about you, Thomas," Nurse said as she looked Ivy over. "I will get to you presently, but first, I must see to this poor mite."

"Who is at Anglesea?" Beatrice's mind raced. If her family was here, who was watching the keep?

"I think you are the one who should be explaining." Faye sniffed and went to greet their father. Faye seemed to float as she moved; her sister never did anything as ordinary as walk.

"I will get to that," her mother replied. "But let me greet my sons first. Good Lord, Arthur, what have you done to them? Have they not bathed?" Her lips pursed.

"Aye, Mary." Her father mumbled the rest of his reply as Lady Mary embraced William and then Roger.

Garrett stood to one side. He looked awful, with one eye almost completely swollen shut and his puffy lip oozing blood down his chin.

Beatrice rushed over to be with him. Her heart ached for his hurts. "I am very sorry." She dabbed at the blood on his chin with her sleeve. "I have no idea what came over them."

He tried to smile and winced.

His poor, battered face.

"Sweeting, you have nothing to be sorry for." He nudged her hand away. "Your brothers did no less than I deserve."

"Beatrice," her mother called, "perhaps you would introduce your family to your friend."

Beatrice straightened her spine. Fear fluttered in her belly as she turned to look at her family.

As one, their gazes turned to her.

"That is Wulfric's bastard." William wiped blood from his mouth with his sleeve.

"I did not ask you, William." Lady Mary raised her brows. "Would you please find me a place to sit? I think it is time we all had a talk."

Beatrice's family had all lost their minds, sitting and chatting while Anglesea stood poised on the edge of disaster. The entire half-hour seemed to be something out of a dream. Beatrice gave her thigh a pinch. Hard. Nay, it was real. "Mother, do we not have to return home?"

"Aye, and we will. After we have aired a few truths. William, are you still standing there?" Lady Mary rubbed her spine. "My back feels nigh breaking, being jostled in a carriage for three days."

William hastened to obey. He snatched up the one unbroken bench and brought it over.

"I told you not to go running the breadth of the kingdom." Nurse whipped out her kerchief and wiped the bench. "Fetch me some hot water," she snapped at Roger. "I need to brew your mother a tisane."

"I am Garrett, formerly of Alethorpe. Sir Wulfric was my father." Garrett stood beside her with his shoulders squared and a fierce look on her face.

Beatrice thrilled with pride.

"You have the look of your mother." Lady Mary eased her bulk onto the bench with a sigh. "Mistress Alyce, if memory serves, was the daughter of Sir William of Clarges. Do I have this right, Nurse?"

"You do, lamb." Nurse flanked Lady Mary. "He disowned her

when she went off with Sir Wulfric." Nurse snorted. "You can disown all you like, but blood does not change its color."

"Well said, Nurse." Lady Mary stretched her legs out in front of her. "And I believe you are responsible for bringing my daughter to London?"

"Aye." Garrett stiffened but kept his face blank.

Beatrice eyed her mother. What was Lady Mary about?

Roger arrived with her cup of hot water.

Nurse took out a small pouch of herbs and dropped it into the water. A sharp smell rose from the cup.

Lady Mary wrinkled her nose as she watched Nurse.

All other eyes watched Lady Mary.

"You always know exactly what I need, Nurse." Lady Mary and the other woman exchanged a secret smile. "I am assuming from the antics when I arrived that you did more than merely guide her to London?" Lady Mary blew on her cup.

Sweet Lord, her mother was as sharp as a blade. Beatrice took Garrett's hand. She drew strength from the warm pressure of his fingers entwined with hers.

"Aye, my lady," he said.

Her mother sipped at her tisane. "Then, I think the time for plain speaking has come. What do you intend to do about it?"

"We should string the bastard up by his balls." Roger cracked his fist into his palm.

Sir Arthur belted his oldest son about the head. "I will not tell you again about that mouth of yours."

"It is not like there are any virgins here." Roger shook his head. "Any more."

"Roger." Lady Mary pressed her lips together.

Roger averted his gaze, his face reddening. "Sorry, Mother."

"Now, back to the matter at hand. You were about to explain yourself, Master Garrett." Lady Mary handed her cup to Nurse.

"I will not give him up." Determination gave her courage. Beatrice stepped forward, her hand still held tightly in Garrett's,

"Beatrice." Garrett's tone was grave. "We spoke of this."

"Aye, Garrett, but I cannot give you up." His eyes were dark and somber, and she wanted to shake that look out of them. She had not come this far to meekly turn about and live her life without him.

"There is no future for us." He stroked her cheek. The skin of his hands was broken and bleeding, and she cradled one between hers. "I knew this, and I should not have taken what was not mine."

"Is my daughter no longer good enough for you, Garrett of Alethorpe?" Sir Arthur cracked his knuckles together.

"I think it is the other way around." Garrett's eyes lingered on her face, touching as sweetly as a caress. "I am not good enough for her."

"Damn right you are not."

"He is good enough." Beatrice whirled to face her family. Her blood surged hot through her veins. This was the greatest fight of her life. One she would win. "Garrett and I will be married."

Garrett jerked.

Beatrice gripped his hand hard as she turned to look at him. "You do want to marry me, Garrett, do you not?"

"With everything in me, if I thought I was worthy." He grimaced and dipped his chin. "I am little more than a beggar, sweeting. You are the Lady Beatrice, and I am the son of a whore and a traitor."

Beatrice flinched at his words. She hated when he demeaned himself thus. It didn't matter where he came from. What mattered was the man she saw now. And her Garrett was gentle, kind, courageous, loyal, and beautiful.

"No daughter of mine will marry Wulfric's get." Sir Arthur braced his legs apart. "The sire was a cruel, traitorous churl, little more than an animal. He could be just the same."

"I do not care." Beatrice glared at her father. Her heart leaped about in her chest. She had never spoken to her father thus. "I love him, and that is all that matters."

"What do you know of love?" Her father's face creased in a ferocious frown.

Lady Mary touched Sir Arthur on the arm.

He shut his mouth, but his face lost none of the fury.

Beatrice turned her back on her family. She took Garrett's face between her hands. His lip was torn, and she dabbed a speck of blood away. "I love you, Garrett. I do not want to be cut off from my family. It will tear me asunder. But it will kill me, for certain, if I no longer have you."

"Beatrice," he protested, but his arms moved to hold her against him. "I have nothing."

"You have me." Now and always. "I am not nothing."

"Nay, you are not nothing." A half-smile tilted the corner of his mouth not bloodied. "I do not deserve you, Beatrice."

"What nonsense." Certainty flooded her being. "If every one of us sat about waiting to be worthy of love, nobody would ever find a mate. You are deserving of my love, simply, by loving me back. And you do love me, do you not, Garrett?"

"Ridiculously so." Slowly, the graveness faded from his eyes.

A glimmer of hope took root. "I am strong." Beatrice increased the pressure around his waist until he gave a grunt of pain. "You are strong. Wc will build a life together."

"I could learn to farm?" He tugged on his ear.

Beatrice laughed. Garrett tilling the soil was a picture even she couldn't conjure. "Nay, Garret, you have not the temperament of a farmer. Mayhap an inn?"

Aye, that was a far better idea. "We could build a small inn along the road to London. God knows, there are not enough decent places for a body to rest along the way." An inn. It was the perfect thing. Beatrice would rule over her busy kitchen, her hair neatly bound by a kerchief, her arms covered with a dusting of flour, the smell of delicious pies heavy in the air. Garrett would come up behind her and put his arms around her. He would smile over her shoulder at their five, nay six—a good round number —children.

"Beatrice?" Garrett tipped her chin to face him. "We have not the coin to build an inn."

That could present a problem. Then again, had they not overcome one obstacle after another to get to this point. "We will get the coin. We will work as farm laborers until we have the coin. I can work in a bakery and—"

"Good God, Bea," Faye said. "Are you building castles in the air again?"

"Nay." Garrett kissed Beatrice on the forehead. "An inn. She is building an inn in the air."

"God's bones, would somebody end this torment." William looked ill.

"This is your plan, then?" Lady Mary spoke.

Beatrice turned within the circle of Garrett's arms to face her family. She loved each one of them. Beautiful Faye, stalwart Roger, and irreverent William. She even loved pious Henry. But her choice was made.

And she adored her mother and father. A piece of her heart broke away from the whole and embedded sharply behind her ribs. There could come a time when she was big with child like her mother was now, and Lady Mary wouldn't be there. When her father was no longer about to haul her into his huge arms and hug her.

Tears pricked the back of her eyelids. She would miss them.

"Look what such a choice would cost you, Beatrice." Garrett's arms tightened about her. "You talk of letting them go, but you would not know how much the cost until you lost them." He leaned his cheek against her head. "I have never had such a wondrous thing as this. Your people love you, Beatrice. For all you are and all you could be. Such a thing should not be thrown away."

"But what of our love?" Inside she felt torn asunder.

"Is our love more valuable than the love I see here?"

"Aye." Beatrice's throat clogged. Her family, her strength, and her roots. What would life be like without them? The years yawned before her without Roger's fire, William's nonsense, or Henry's moralizing. She mourned already, but she would give it all up if it meant she could be with Garrett.

"And so we are decided." Lady Mary's eyes filled with tears. "I could not live a day without my Sweet Bea."

A tiny flicker of hope burned through the sadness.

"You are not suggesting she marries him?" Roger gaped at his mother.

"Never." Sir Arthur's stance exactly mirrored his oldest son. Both of their legs braced apart and arms folded over their chests.

The hope died. Beatrice tightened her resolve. So be it.

"Do not make me angry, Arthur." Lady Mary placed her palm on her belly. "Of course Garrett and Beatrice must marry."

Beatrice's belly fluttered. Her mother's support was sweetly welcome but shocking.

Lady Mary raised her delicate chin, her eyes kindled.

"But he's—"

Garrett stiffened as her father pointed at him, spluttering for the right words.

"The son of Wulfric of Alethorpe and Mistress Alyce," Lady Mary continued. "Whatever their end, they were both of noble blood."

"Noble blood? You know what Wulfric was?" Arthur blinked at his wife. His color was high. "He was nothing more than a savage beast. He deserved to have his title stripped and his lands razed. You heard the stories; you know what he did."

"Really, Arthur?" Lady Mary sighed. "I think Garrett has already demonstrated his resemblance to his father is no more than skin deep."

"Not to me, he has not," Sir Arthur said.

Lady Mary grimaced and shifted on the bench. "This child lies heavy within me."

"I told you, the trip was not good for the child." Nurse dug around in her apron and produced another sachet.

"Aye, Nurse." Lady Mary smiled at Beatrice. "But does the child in my belly take precedence over all my other children?"

Beatrice's chest glowed. Her mother's love was like a balm that took away the heartache.

"Mary." Sir Arthur gentled his tone. "He was going to use Beatrice to exact revenge against me. To callously seduce her and toss her aside."

"But he did not." Beatrice drew strength from her mother.

"Exactly so." Lady Mary gave her beautiful smile. "Instead, he stands here, before her entire family, having taken a beating from her brothers. Does he urge her to leave with him? Nay, he reminds her of her love for her family. I have heard all I need to hear. He loves her, Arthur, and that is good enough for me."

"He did manage to keep her in one piece, more or less, all the way to London." Faye crossed the room to her mother's side.

Sir Gregory followed on her heels.

"And does he not have reason to be wroth?" Lady Mary asked.

* * *

Everything within Garrett stilled. He tightened his grip around Beatrice, ignoring the pain to his damaged ribs. She was his hold on reality.

Sir Arthur swung angry eyes in his direction.

Garrett met his stare.

"Aye." Sir Arthur dropped his gaze.

Garrett's chest tightened. Sir Arthur acknowledging his right to anger made his head spin.

Lady Mary took her husband's hand. "I know you are not proud of what happened that day. I was there, Arthur. I remember your remorse once the bloodlust had cooled."

And the blows kept coming. In all his wild imaginings, this had not formed part of it.

"I do not regret the death of your father." Sir Arthur squared his shoulders. "Wulfric was naught more than a beast, raising his fist to anyone weaker." Sir Arthur's face was still fierce, but doubt flickered in the depths of his eyes. "I tried to find you once it was over."

"You could not have tried very hard." Garrett's anger was old and constant, and it snarled from within him. It was bad enough he must walk away from his long-fermented vengeance. There was no forgiveness for an action that had cost him and his mother everything.

As if she sensed his thoughts, Beatrice took his hand. The warmth of her touch flowed upward and soothed his pain. His anger retreated grudgingly.

"Aye, I have regrets." Arthur flung the words at him like a challenge. "But it does not mean I will let him have my daughter as an act of atonement. I was acting under the command of the king."

"Nobody is suggesting you toss Beatrice on the pyre as the sacrificial lamb." Lady Mary gave a soft tinkle of laughter.

The hair on the back of Garrett's neck stood on end. He wasn't a fanciful sort, and he didn't believe in witchcraft, but these women...

Sir Arthur shifted.

Lady Mary lay her hand on his arm. "Beatrice will marry Garrett for the simple reason she loves him." Lady Mary's smile was beatific. She let it caress every face in the room in turn. "And he loves her enough to drag her out of any number of scrapes, which he gladly lets her lead him into."

Sir Arthur opened his mouth to argue. He frowned and snapped it shut again.

Garrett thanked God the woman in his arms had not inherited this trait for witchery. Had she? He peeked down at Beatrice. He wasn't a bit reassured by the smile resting on her lips. It looked alarmingly like the one her mother and sister wore.

"I cannot like it." Sir Arthur ran rough fingers through his hair. "She could look as high as she likes for a bridegroom."

"Indeed she can. And we are all well aware of how those

searches went. Really, Arthur, you cannot say that you have chosen well for your daughter thus far. That last betrothal." Lady Mary shuddered.

Sir Arthur's shoulders slumped.

"I think she has chosen well." Lady Mary turned her lovely smile on him.

The hope Garrett had dared not entertain sprung forth like sunlight through the clouds and infused the cracks of his being until he feared he would burst with it. He did not deserve any of this, but he would take it.

Beatrice turned and laid her head against his chest. "I think I have chosen perfectly."

"Sweet mother of God." William shuddered. "If the cur is going to be part of the family, we, at least, need to teach him to fight like a knight. This biting and ball kicking is shameful.

# Chapter Twenty-Six

Sir Arthur clenched his jaw and nodded. "So be it; we leave for Anglesea."

The joy hit Beatrice in a rush. Her knees collapsed, and she leaned into Garrett. Tucked in his arms, she was precisely where she most needed to be.

"Beatrice," her mother said. "Let that young man go. We have more to say, you and I."

She wasn't quite ready to do that.

"You had best come with us." Roger jerked his head at Garrett. "Make yourself useful."

Beatrice tightened her hold on him. She would not let her brothers and her father have another go at Garrett.

"Do not fret, Bea." William strode over to them. "We will bring him safely back to you. For the most part."

"I will go." Garrett kissed her temple.

Garrett followed her father out. Beatrice's heart stuck in her throat.

* * *

Garrett trailed the four men as they crossed a small antechamber and descended to the lower level.

Sir Arthur stopped suddenly.

Garrett tensed.

"Go on. We will join you shortly," he told his sons.

Roger stepped forward. "We will stay."

Sir Arthur thrust back his shoulders. "Do you imagine I require your protection, whelp?"

"The bastard is handy with his fists," Roger replied.

"I could take him and you with one hand."

"You could try, old man." Roger grinned. He turned and nudged William to follow him.

"That boy." Sir Arthur sighed. "I should kick his ass to teach him a lesson."

Garrett waited. His body still ached from the mauling the brothers had given him. He did not want to fight Sir Arthur. For Beatrice, he would try to keep the peace. But the old man was big and in fine form. And Garrett wouldn't allow himself to be bullied.

"That day." Sir Arthur cleared his throat. "At Alethorpe."

Old anger simmered in Garrett's gut.

"King John wanted Wulfric removed. He was a traitor, consorting with the French. We had proof," Sir Arthur said.

"I may be a churl, but I know my history. My sire was more than a traitor. He was a bloody tyrant."

"Aye." Sir Arthur nodded. "I knew that. I could not abide the tales we heard of what was happening in his demesne. I acted out of good conscience."

That was too far. "You threw us out with nothing. Was that your lofty conscience?"

"Jesu." Sir Arthur's face flushed. "Settle down and let me speak. This is not easy to say. I believed in John."

Garrett made a rude noise. King John. The miserable whoreson.

"That was before he put aside his wife and married that

infant, Isabella, and got her with child." Sir Arthur seemed to be struggling with words. "It was before we discovered he had starved the wife and children of de Braose to death."

"I have no interest in a recitation of King John's perfidy."

"Nay, indeed." Sir Arthur cleared his throat. "What I am attempting to say is that I am sorry for my actions that day. Toward you and your mother. I discovered later that she had not returned to her father, and I made some attempt to find her."

"So you said." Garrett had his doubts as to how much effort Sir Arthur had made.

"You are a hard one, young Garrett."

"Life has shaped me that way."

"Verily." Sir Arthur drew in a deep breath. "I am sorry for what happened to you and Mistress Alyce. I was young, and my belly was full of fire. I did not consider how my actions would punish the innocent along with the guilty."

Garrett rocked back on his heels. Sir Arthur's words hit him with the weight of an anvil. Had he not said the very same about Beatrice?

"I know better now." Sir Arthur clenched his fists. "It does not mean I will not be watching you. I do not like you or trust you."

"Old man." Fire sparked in Garrett's belly. "If I had the slightest bit of affection for you, that would wound me."

"Old man?" Sir Arthur narrowed his eyes. "Try me, bastard?"

"Another day."

"Just say when." Sir Arthur turned to descend the stairs, the slightest trace of a smile hovering about his mouth.

* * *

The door shut behind Garrett.

"Now," said her mother. "You can explain yourself."

"I love him." Beatrice's cheeks heated. This was the conversation she'd been dreading.

"We all know that." Faye rolled her eyes. "I believe mother was talking of your decision to go running off to London."

"Oh." If her face got any hotter, it might burst into flame. "I did what I had to, to save my family."

"Sit down, Beatrice." Nurse lowered her bulk beside Lady Mary. "You will give yourself a neck ache if you keep tossing your chin about like that."

Beatrice perched on the edge of the table. She felt a bit foolish with all the women in her family looking at her as if she greatly amused them.

Tom met her eye and shrugged.

Ivy gave her a tiny smile of encouragement.

"You should have come to me," Lady Mary said.

"You were ill. I did not want to worry you." Beatrice kept her eyes on the dirty slippers beneath her hem.

"I appreciate that, dear, but I am with child, not infirm. A bit of bad news is not going to carry me off."

"Henry said you should not be worried about this."

Lady Mary snorted. "Is Henry now the expert on childbirth? Henry who cannot look at a woman without blushing."

It sounded ridiculous when her mother put it thus. Beatrice risked a peek. "Faye said the same."

"I came to my senses." Faye pursed her lips smugly.

Which brought up another unanswered question. "What of Calder?"

"Faye will remain at Anglesea," Lady Mary said.

"Will he not take the boys?"

Nurse gave a loud bray of laughter. "I would like to see him try."

"That point is not debatable." Lady Mary's jaw firmed.

"I cannot return to Calder." Faye clasped her mother's hand. Faye's knuckles turned white. "You do not know what he has become."

Sir Gregory stirred behind Faye. How much did the silent Sir Gregory know?

"Would you tell me?" There were more secrets in the air. It was like fighting through a sticky spider's web, tendrils of things felt and not seen, sensed and not known.

"I will tell you, Bea." Faye gave her a sad smile. "But do you think it could wait until we return to Anglesea?"

The tension disappeared, and Beatrice glowed within. She loved her sister. And her sister loved her. "I think that would be best." The boys were her immediate concern. "Mayhap Calder will agree to have Simon fostered in our household? Simon will remain his heir."

Faye nodded. "It is what we were thinking."

"And if he does not agree, will he make war over this?" Beatrice shuddered at the thought of more fighting threatening the men she loved most.

Faye grinned.

Again, she was missing something.

"Tell Beatrice what you told me, Mother." She winked at Beatrice. "I warn you, it will make you feel somewhat foolish. It did me."

Beatrice was growing, unfortunately, accustomed to feeling foolish.

"How many brothers do I have, Nurse?" Lady Mary asked.

"You have five brothers, lamb." Nurse poured hot water into Lady Mary's cup. She dropped a sack of herbs into it. "And a great favorite you are of all of them."

"Aye." Beatrice was still not clear of where this was heading. "I am well aware of how many uncles I have. But they are wroth with father over this war."

"Where did you hear that?" Nurse demanded.

"I can guess," Tom said.

Beatrice glared at him. He looked exactly like his mother when he pulled that disapproving face.

"They may not agree with Arthur," her mother replied. "But tell us, Nurse. What would my brothers do if, say, someone were to have the sheer idiocy to try to attack a keep I was in? What would happen, Nurse?"

"Why, lamb," Nurse chuckled. "Not one of them would stand idly by. They would rush to aid you."

A picture formed in Beatrice's mind. Forget foolish and rush straight to idiotic. She wriggled in her seat.

"You did not tell me any of this, Beatrice." Tom rubbed at the back of his neck, which had gone as red as his cheeks.

"I did not think of it." And she really, really should have.

Sir Gregory grunted.

Faye swung around to glare at him.

He met her look impassively.

"Neither did I." Faye grimaced.

That eased the sting marginally.

"Now, Nurse." Lady Mary sat back with a smile and folded her arms over her belly. "How many vassals does Sir Arthur have?"

"Why, lamb, I could not say exactly, but—"

"Enough, Mother." Beatrice raised her hand in surrender. "I think I get the point."

"Do you now?" Lady Mary gave her a tight smile. "And you can see how foolish the two of you have been. You," she pointed to Faye, "for not coming to me before the situation with Calder became unbearable. And you," Beatrice faltered under the icy wave of disapproval, "for hatching some elaborate scheme and going off on some wild chase for naught."

"Not entirely." Beatrice writhed inside. "Someone still had to get to Sir Arthur, and Henry was not going to do it."

"My husband would never have left me unprotected." Her mother gaped at her. "Nor any of his children or his property. Do you think he was not aware of how precarious our situation was? He does not like my brothers, but he loves us. He made arrangements before he left."

It was Beatrice's turn to gape. Of course, it was all so simple now she understood everything. "I did not know." She clung to her tattered bit of outrage. "Because nobody ever tells me anything."

"I think we have all learned not to keep matters from you." Faye rolled her eyes.

"And I have learned never to listen at doorways." Beatrice was painfully clear on this point. "I never hear anything good."

Tom gave a great bark of laughter, which set them all of.

"We have treated you like a child," her mother added. "It was not entirely fair of us. But you have always been our Sweet Bea. We never wanted anything to make you sad."

Beatrice had to blink away the tears. She had lived sheltered in her family's love. And reveled there. In truth, she'd made no real effort to be anything other than a happy child. "I have not always been as responsible as I could be."

Nurse snorted.

"I know nothing of your life before." Ivy's quiet voice cut through the room. "But you were woman enough to fight those men off me. And you have taken care of Newt and myself and even Tom."

"Tom got stabbed." Beatrice winced at the memory.

"What!" Nurse whirled in her seat. "Stabbed?"

"It is all right." Tom reddened.

Nurse gripped his tunic as she lumbered to her feet. "Where were you stabbed?"

"Leave off, Mother." Tom attempted to wrestle his tunic free.

Beatrice almost told him not to bother. Nurse had a grip of steel.

"Across the side and back." Ivy stepped beside Nurse. "It was a deep cut, but I stitched it."

Nurse tugged Tom's shirt over his head. Tom grunted, the sound muffled by the shirt covering his face. When he emerged, he was so red his ears seemed to throb.

"Lord have mercy." Nurse clapped her hands to her bosom. "You are gutted like a pike."

Tom had the body of a man. They had grown up together,

and Beatrice had never, not once, noticed how nicely put together he was. He'd always been Tom, her best friend, and confidant. She suddenly found herself looking at him as another woman would, a woman such as Ivy.

Except Ivy was intent on Tom's wound. "The knife glanced off his ribs." She indicated along the angry gash. "I soaked the wound in vinegar before I stitched him."

"Did you clean all about the wound?" Nurse peered closer.

"Aye." Tom grimaced.

"You are a good girl." Nurse patted Ivy on the cheek, her face softened. "There are some wounds that take a bit longer to heal."

"And as for the rest. I think that Godfrey is to blame for the biggest part. It was him bending Henry's ears and feeding Faye's fear," Lady Mary said. "When I heard the truth from Henry and Faye, I had this terrible feeling my brother-in-law was in this up to his neck."

"I never liked him." Nurse straightened and folded her arms over her chest. "It is those eyes." She jabbed two fingers at her eyes. "Do you remember, lamb? When we first came to Anglesea, I said he had those eyes." Nurse squinted. "Like a fox."

"Aye, Nurse." Lady Mary winked at Beatrice.

"And I went racing to London when all I needed to do was come to you." Beatrice was no fonder of confession now than she had been with Garrett in the wood.

"Indeed." Her mother gave her a tight smile. "But then, I think there was more driving your decision than merely your family."

Beatrice blushed.

"Not that I can blame her," Faye added. "A girl can do worse than arrange a little trip around the back roads with a big strong man."

Beatrice choked. This from Faye? Virtuous, perfect, fairest Faye?

"I am not blind, Beatrice." Faye pursed her lips. "Your man is comely enough to get under anyone's skirts."

"Do not be vulgar, Faye." Lady Mary gave Faye a haughty look, then ruined it by laughing.

Nurse wheezed a chuckle from beside them.

All the tension rushed out of Beatrice, and she laughed.

Even Ivy smiled and nudged a glowering Tom.

Behind Faye, Sir Gregory went so red Beatrice thought his face would burst into flame. She threw back her head and laughed harder.

*Epilogue*

It was the perfect day for love. Beatrice lifted her face to enjoy the morning sun on her skin. Already the breeze carried the coming cold. Leaves twirled and dipped in their dance with the wind. An arrow of birds winged their way to warmer climes in the clear arc of blue above. The summer blooms had disappeared. There were not many fine days left before the autumn would draw in.

However, this year, she looked forward to a long winter confined to the keep with very little to do.

Such a picture to make a girl burn. Logs roaring in the great hearths, warming where they touched naked skin. A woman lay amongst the furs, her hair spread over the pillows like a wanton. A man lay beside her, his strong hands caressing the limbs gilded by firelight.

Aye, it would be a good winter. She hoped her father would return before the cold set in.

Sir Arthur had been called to London to swear fealty to the boy King Henry. Many whispered John's passing was not entirely natural, but Sir Arthur waved those rumors aside. There was a new king to protect and one barely old enough to be let out of leading strings.

Sir Arthur predicted more difficult times to come. But here at Anglesea, they had a brief respite.

Lady Mary had been safely delivered of a boy. There was some sadness as it became clear young Mathew was not as quick as the other children had been. He'd recently passed his first year, and the difference between Mathew and the other children of the keep became more marked. Still, he was a loving child and a particular favorite of Nurse's.

Simon, Faye's oldest, was much taken with Mathew and hovered over the boy like a guardian angel.

Tom had been granted his land and was much less to be seen.

Beatrice rode over to visit when she could. She missed her friend, but she had Garrett now. And Tom was busy turning his allotment into a farm good enough to support a family.

And Ivy.

Nurse had taken to Ivy. Beatrice didn't know how much Ivy told Nurse, but Nurse treated Ivy as the daughter she'd never had. The two were often found with their heads together over a basket of herbs. As the months passed, Ivy blossomed. The men of the keep swarmed about her, but she showed no interest in any of her suitors. William had tried his best and failed to raise so much as a smile out of Ivy.

A soft whistle cut the air.

Beatrice grinned.

There he stood, by the thicket.

One shoulder propped against the trunk of a tree, arms folded across his broad chest. The breeze ruffled his dark hair.

He jerked his head.

She really must work harder to rid him of that habit.

"I thought you were at arms training," she said.

"I am in training." He grinned as he tugged her into his arms. He walked her backward.

Heat unfurled in Beatrice's middle. She knew that look in his eye. Her spine hit the hard bark of a tree.

He kept coming until he was pressed fully against her. "I

thought of something better to do with my day." He nipped at her ear before trailing hot kisses down her neck. His good idea pushed at the apex of her thighs.

She needed the tree for support as her knees melted beneath her. "And what idea was that?"

"I am rescuing Parsley," he murmured against her mouth. "He has disgraced himself."

Parsley calmly cropped the grass at the edge of the wood. He appeared rather sanguine about his fall from grace.

It was difficult to care about aught but the wicked play of Garrett's mouth over hers. "What did he do?" Her mouth opened beneath his, inviting his kiss.

He toyed with her a moment, letting his mouth hang a hairbreadth away from hers.

Beatrice slipped her arms around his neck and tugged him closer.

"He bit William." Garrett grinned against her mouth.

"You should get a proper destrier."

"Parsley and I understand each other." He moved his lips over hers.

"Kiss me," Beatrice whispered.

"You know where that leads, my lady wife." He nipped at her bottom lip.

"Aye, Garrett, I most certainly do. You will be in trouble if William or my father catch you."

He pulled her deeper within the concealment of the trees. "It will be worth it."

* * *

If you enjoyed **Sweet Bea**, don't miss the next book in the Sir Arthur's Legacy series, **My Lady Faye**.

* * *

### *A love too long denied...*

She is known as Fairest Faye. A flawless beauty. The perfect lady. Yet her lovely exterior hides an ugly past filled with tyranny and abuse. Now, Faye is finally free, and able to rebuild her life, but the memory of the man she once loved—and could never have— still haunts her.

Released from servitude as a warrior, Gregory is ready to pursue his dream of entering the church. But a war wages within. How can he serve God when his heart belongs to his Lady Faye?

When Faye's son is kidnapped, Gregory rushes to her aid. The danger escalates, and the hunt for her son turns into a deadly game. With each passing day, Faye and Gregory struggle against a desire that burns brighter than ever. Even if they find Faye's beloved son, can these two wounded hearts ever find lasting happiness together?

* * *

Read My Lady Faye

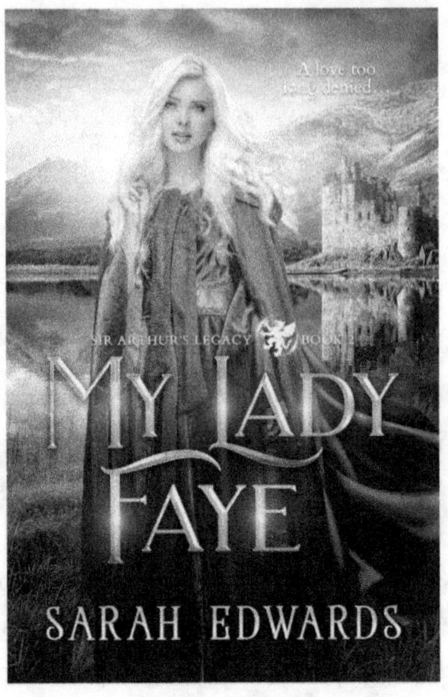

***

## Chapter 1

Faye was an unnatural wife. She stood beside her father, Sir Arthur of Anglesea, and received the news of her husband's death. Behind her polite facade, she felt nothing.

Not a wife anymore, but now a widow.

"How did he die?" Her father spoke the question she had not even thought to ask.

The young squire, fresh-faced and pretty, colored to his hairline. "He...um..." His gaze flit to her and away again. "He choked. On a chicken bone."

Faye understood the boy's discomfort well. She almost took pity on him and told him to spare his blushes on her behalf. Calder had been with another woman at the time of his death.

Sir Arthur sat forward on his large, carved wooden chair

before the great hearth of Anglesea. "He choked on a chicken bone."

"Aye, my lord." The boy nodded. "It was a terrible accident."

*Was it?* Faye had been wrong to think she felt nothing. Nay, she felt relief. Calder was dead, she and her boys were safe. A year ago, she had run from him with her boys. Gregory had aided her and brought her here.

The thought of Gregory sent a shaft of agonizing pain through her middle, and she gasped. Tears sprung to her eyes and spilled over her cheeks.

"There now." Her father rose and tugged her into his embrace. "My lovely girl, I am so very sorry."

Faye pressed her face to her father's tunic and let him believe she wept for Calder. The truth would be so much harder to explain, and Father would blame himself for giving her to Calder.

"My lord?" The squire cleared his throat. "There is more to my message."

"God's bones, boy!" Sir Arthur thundered, his voice reverberating through her ear. "Can you not see the Lady Faye is overcome?"

Pushing herself from her father's comforting embrace, Faye drew a deep breath. Tears for Gregory were a waste of time. He was as lost to her as Calder. "It's all right, Father." She took the kerchief he offered and tidied her face. "He is only doing what he was told to do."

Sir Arthur growled and turned to the quaking squire. "Well, spit it out!"

"Sir Hugo...the earl's brother...um, he demands the return of the boy earl and his brother, with the Lady Faye to Calder Castle." The boy went paler than a goose feather. "He insists that as guardian to the young earl, he must be returned to his demesne."

"Never." Faye hadn't realized she had spoken aloud until bother her father and the squire's gazes locked on her. She didn't care. She would never go back there. Never put her boys or herself in that miserable place again. It had taken her seven years to escape, and she would never return. "We stay here."

The squire gaped at her. "But—"

"You heard my daughter." Sir Arthur put his hand around her shoulder. "She and her boys remain here. If Sir Hugo wishes to take issue, explain to him that he takes issue with Sir Arthur of Anglesea."

* * *

**For first dibs on news, deals, and giveaways, and so much more, join the @Home Collective**

**Or if Facebook is more your thing, join the Sarah Hegger Collective**

**Anything and everything you need to know is on my website
http://sarahhegger.com**

# About the Author

Sarah Edwards is also published under the name
Sarah Hegger


Born British and raised in South Africa, Sarah Hegger suffers from an incurable case of wanderlust. Her match? A hot Canadian engineer, whose marriage proposal she accepted six short weeks after they first met. Together they've made homes in seven different cities across three different continents (and back again once or twice). If only it made her multilingual, but the best she can manage is idiosyncratic English, fluent Afrikaans, conversant Russian, pigeon Portuguese, even worse Zulu and enough French to get herself into trouble.
Mimicking her globe trotting adventures, Sarah's career path began as a gainfully employed actress, drifted into public relations, settled a moment in advertising, and eventually took root in the fertile soil of her first love, writing. She also moonlights as a wife and mother. She currently lives in Ottawa, Canada, filling her empty nest with fur babies. Part footloose buccaneer, part quixotic observer of life, Sarah's restless heart is most content when reading or writing books.

# Praise for Sarah Hegger

**Drove All Night**
"The classic romance plot is elevated to a modern-day,
wholly accessible real-life fairy tale with an excellent mix of
romantic elements and spicy sensuality."
Booklife Prize, Critic's Report

**Positively Pippa**
"This is the type of romance that makes readers fall in love not
just with characters, but with authors as well."
Kirkus Review (Starred Review)

"What begins as a simple second-chance romance quickly
transforms into a beautiful, frank examination of love, family
dynamics, and following one's dreams. Hegger's unflinching,
candid portrayal of interpersonal and generational
communication elevates the story to the sublime. Shunning
clichés and contrived circumstances, she uses realistic, relatable
situations to create a world that readers will want to visit time and
again."
Publisher's Weekly, Starred Review

Hegger's utterly delightful first Ghost Falls contemporary is what other romance novels want to grow up to be." – Publisher's Weekly, Best Books of 2017

"The very talented Hegger kicks off an enjoyable new series set in the small Utah town of Ghost Falls. This charming and fun-filled book has everything from passion and humor to betrayal and revenge." –
Jill M Smith, RT Books Reviews 2017 – Contemporary Love and Laughter Nominee

### Becoming Bella
"Hegger excels at depicting familial relationships and friendships of all kinds, including purely platonic friendships between women and men. Tears, laughter, and a dollop of suspense make a memorable story that readers will want to revisit time and again."
Publisher's Weekly, Starred Review

"...you have a terrific new romance that Hegger fans are going to love. Don't miss out!"
Jill M. Smith – RT Book Reviews

### Blatantly Blythe
"Ms. Hegger has delivered another captivating read for this series in this book that was packed with emotion..." Bec, Bookmagic Review, Harlequin Junkie, HJ Recommends.

### Nobody's Fool
"Hegger offers a breath of fresh air in the romance genre." – Terri Dukes, RT Book Reviews

### Nobody's Princess
"Hegger continues to live up to her rapidly growing reputation for breathing fresh air into the romance genre." – Terri Dukes, RT Book Reviews

"I have read the entire Willow Park Series. I have loved each of the books ... Nobody's Princess is my favorite of all time." Harlequin Junkie, Top Pick

# Also by Sarah Edwards

Sports Romance

*Ottawa Titans Series*

Roughing

Contemporary Romance

*Passing Through Series*

Drove All Night

Ticket To Ride

Walk On By

*Ghost Falls Series*

Positively Pippa

Becoming Bella

Blatantly Blythe

Loving Laura

*Willow Park Romances*

Nobody's Angel

Nobody's Fool

Nobody's Princess

Medieval Romance

*Sir Arthur's Legacy Series*

Sweet Bea

My Lady Faye

Conquering William

Roger's Bride

Releasing Henry


*Love & War Series*

The Marriage Parley

The Betrothal Melee


Western Historical Romance

*The Soiled Dove Series*

Sugar Ellie


*Standalone*

The Bride Gift

Bad Wolfe On The Rise

Wild Honey